ANGELA GREEN grew
up in Kent, Scotland and
Hampshire and read
French at King's College,
London. In the late
nineties she gave up a
business career in order to
write full-time. She lives
in Surrey and Brittany.
Cassandra's Disk is her
first novel.

CASSANDRA'S
DISK

Angela Green

CASSANDRA'S DISK

PETER OWEN
London & Chester Springs

PETER OWEN LTD
73 Kenway Road, London SW5 0RE

First published in Great Britain 2002
by Peter Owen Publishers

A catalogue record for this book is available from
the British Library

ISBN 0 7206 1144 X

Printed and bound in Great Britain by
MPG Books Ltd, Bodmin, Cornwall

For Graham

Aghios Georghios, Ithaca
21 September 1999, 11 a.m.

They are coming down the corridor with tea. Earl Grey. A cup of smoky bergamot every two hours. Dr Mike approves of this surviving pleasure and so do I: perfumed steam wafts warm against my forehead. When it is drained to the leaves, I settle the laptop back upon the starched linen and watch the cursor blink. My fingers are ringless, knuckled and brown; oddly, where they rest on the keyboard they spell the word that describes their new appearance: T-H-I-N.

Begin.

Yes, but where? And how?

After years of looking at the world through a viewfinder, at first I see pictures, an album. It opens on a large baby, glowering in sepia arms. Beyond are the deckle-edged black-and-white snapshots of childhood, then teenage years in sunbleached pastel. At the end, digital images sparkle like frost . . .

But no. Pictures are not enough. Memory is too trackless and vast to fit through the eye of a single lens; it cries out for a wider horizon: the infinite longitude and latitude of words.

My fingers stir on the keyboard, ready to cast the first tentative line down into the past . . .

I remember
Deeper . . .
I remember
Deeper . . .
I remember
Yes.

I remember a thunderstorm rolled over Hampstead on the night we were born, like a rattle from an announcing drum.

Ha! You see . . . the first lie!

Hey. Though at thirty-nine my memories are still as richly coloured and detailed as a book of hours, I can't claim to have my namesake's clairvoyance. (Though I *was* born with an ability to scale the walls of other minds and peer in at their thoughts – which has proved itself useful on occasion.) But to go back to the moment of my *birth*? Tricky, even for me.

'Do you think talking to someone would help?' asks Sister Andrew kindly. 'Perhaps not a priest, though Father Gregorio on Cephalonia is an excellent listener.'

Oh, please.

There are other ways around the problem. My way is this: instead of limiting myself to what can be remembered, whenever my memory blurs I shall gently turn the focus of my imagination. Unknown events and conversations will sharpen into obedient clarity, and I shall look back with prescience to the past.

See?

In other words, I give fair warning: I shall lie a little.

Sometimes a lot.

So.

Begin again.

Where was I?

Where am I?

BIRTH

It is thirty-nine years ago and high over London I plane with lazy hawks on a dark May morning and watch the gathering of clouds.

Listen. Is that the thunder? Look down on the mosaic of streets and find the hospital. It was still there last time I was in Hampstead. Clarify now. There it is. See?

*

At six a.m. the sky behind the heath darkens to damson and Denise Byrd screams as lightning crackles down into the hospital gardens. Outside the labour ward window the burnt air smells of danger. My mother runs her hands back through her dripping blonde hair and screams again as the contractions come, heavy as a blind hydraulic press.

'Here's the first babe,' says Senior Midwife (her name is lost in time – what shall we call her? Atkins, I think: a reassuring, homely name and therefore one my mother would instinctively have disliked). 'Right. Push now. Push now, Mrs Byrd, love, come on.' The midwife glances at her watch; another hour and she'll be home at her flat in Swiss Cottage, sweeping the rainwater off the balcony and feeding the cats. 'Come on, my dear, make an effort now, we're nearly there.' These stuck-up women are the worst, in her experience, with all their indignant whimpering. Sister Atkins glances over at the pair of conferring doctors and then taps my mother on her stirruped foot.

'Come on, dear, bear down, do.'

Clenching her teeth Denise strains forward. A broad dark head advances steadily, pushing and stretching.

It is me!

Denise feels her tenderest flesh tear strand by strand. She grabs the metal handrail and outscreams the thunder, willing, *ordering* me to stop, but I drive on downwards, as I must do, stretching her further and further still. Make way there! We all hold our breath. Airless minutes, years, aeons pass, and at their end a wet red mass slithers out of my mother's body and lies between her legs.

I am here!

The midwife scoops me up and shows my mother her firstborn.

'A girl, Mrs Byrd, a fine big girl, look.'

My mother looks at my blood-smeared black hair, my greasy torso, the hanging, purplish cord that disappears inside her. She shudders in distaste and turns her head away. Mrs Atkins, who has seen it all before, cuts our cord and passes me to the young assistant nurse, who carries me to the far side of the delivery room to begin the ritual acknowledgement of my arrival: I am weighed (nearly nine pounds, not bad for a twin) and measured (twenty-three inches, well done!), and the worst of my mess is wiped from me.

Lying on the narrow bed, my mother suddenly feels her pelvis fill again and arches her tired body up in protest. But this time she need not worry: the rapidly emerging head is fair and small; a slender baby girl comes smoothly through the passage I have hewn for her. Denise breathes gratefully and round blue eyes blink up into her face.

'Chalk and cheese, these two,' says Mrs Atkins brightly. 'Cheer up, my dear; just look at this pretty little miss.'

I cannot see my sister, but I know she's here. Years later I find that we are not only twins but twins to the power of three, astrologically speaking. Every sign we have is in the house of Gemini.

FEARGAL

My father, Feargal Byrd, was too nervous to stay at the hospital while Denise was in labour and so spent the evening at home correcting fifth-form translations of Virgil. At seven, and again at ten, he walked down to the phone box at the end of the road to call the hospital and asked how his wife was doing.

Things were progressing quite *normally*, the sister said.

Feargal returned home, stared in the bathroom mirror and wondered what horrors lay beneath the brisk word. (Dadda was never good with pain. He shrank from the sight of blood and regularly ignored the splinters picked up from worn school desks, even though he knew that they would fester and that my mother would fondly scold him and probe his finger with a sterilized needle.) So in front of his bathroom mirror Feargal Byrd, agonized father in waiting, screwed his face up into the sort of scream that would bring the contents of Denise's vastly swollen belly into the world. Poor Dadda. Aged nine, he had heard his own mother howl like an animal through the night of little Patrick's birth and felt the weight of man's original sin fall about his boyish shoulders.

At two o'clock, still unable to sleep, Dadda padded downstairs on thin bare feet. He emptied the overflowing ashtray into the bin, opened a second packet of Embassy and poured himself a large whiskey. (When that failed to work, he probably poured another one.) At six thirty he awoke thirsty and stiff-necked in the armchair. He rinsed his face over the kitchen sink and hurried down the road to call the hospital again.

Ah yes, Mr Byrd, good news for you, they said proudly, as if he had won a competition in the newspaper; you're the father of twin girls, born just after six.

Joy.

My father often used to tell us how he ran, dazed and happy, to catch a bus to the hospital. He arrived at seven fifteen, his smoker's lungs wheezing like an old harmonium, only to be told that his wife and the babies (us) were asleep, as was everyone else in the ward and that he should return at the proper visiting time at four in the afternoon.

Feargal telephoned his parents-in-law, but they had already had a call from their daughter shortly after she returned to the ward. Brian Forrester's voice boomed out of the receiver.

'So, Feargal my boy. Twins, eh? Marvellous. Never thought you had it in you.' He laughed hollowly. 'We'll be popping along to the hospital tomorrow; of course Christine's desperate to see Denise, as you can imagine.'

Dadda nodded helplessly. Most of his conversations with Denise's father were like this: a cuff of patronizing humour followed by announcements. Eager to share his momentous news with some-

13

one he vaguely liked, he went off to school as usual and spent a pleasant ten minutes in the staff room basking in the congratulations of his fellow teachers. One of them tucked a foul-smelling cigar into his breast pocket. After lunch his favourite colleagues, Miss Hackett and Miss Farlow, sidled up and proffered a bunch of roses from their garden.

'For your wife, Mr Byrd,' said Amelia Hackett, blushing. Father was the youngest Classics teacher the Academy had ever had.

He left school promptly at four and caught a bus to Hampstead. The hospital was, as hospitals always are, oppressively hot; Feargal eased an inky finger around his collar and wished he had gone home first to change out of the patched tweed jacket he wore winter and summer. The polished corridors squeaked beneath his crêpe-soled shoes as he toiled along, following sign after sign after sign, to Heathside Maternity Ward.

At last he reached double swing doors and a noise of babies crying. Timidly, my father pushed his way inside. In two rows of identical beds mothers sat waiting for visitors, and beside each bed there was a crib containing a neat mound of blue or pink blanket.

Where was she? Lord, where were they?

There we were.

Five beds down on the right. Denise, pale and drawn, but otherwise disarmingly normal, was wearing the cap-sleeved nylon nightdress she had bought specially for her hospital stay. She was holding a tiny blonde baby close to her face.

Sweet Jesus, thought Feargal, trembling, I am a father.

Denise saw him approaching and held out her hand in a gesture of impulsive tenderness. Feargal laid the roses on the blanket, perched his slight frame on the edge of the bedside chair and bent forward awkwardly to embrace his wife. Then he brushed the top of my sister's head with his lips, smelling his own tobacco breath mixed with the sweet scent of her hair.

'Helen, that's your daddy,' whispered Denise. And then, in an awestruck sigh, 'She's perfect, Feargal, look.'

Denise and baby were staring at each other as if their eyes were four blue beads threaded together.

Feargal nodded dumbly.

Denise patted the side of the metal frame bed. 'Feargal,' she said, her voice so pleased and gentle. 'Here, hold her.'

So.

Gingerly Feargal wipes his ink-stained hands down his jacket and holds them out.

But wait, he has forgotten something.

Just as he bends forward to take my sister, a loud wail rises from a plastic crib on the far side of the bed. Above a hump of pink blanket a red fist waves desperately.

It is me!

Feeling guilty at having forgotten my existence, Feargal turns and walks over to peer at me.

Solid, with a cap of thick black hair and a round, creased face, scarlet with the exertion of crying, I fill the crib.

My daughter. My other daughter, thinks Feargal emotionally. *That's better.*

'Shush you,' he tells me, in the same voice his pop once used to quieten jittery horses in Donegal, 'Quiet the girl now.' I stop crying and stare up at him, my dark eyes wide and watchful. Feargal waggles a black-tipped forefinger just beyond my grasp.

'Hello there. Well, you're a loud one, Miss Byrd, that's for sure. So what'll be your name, then?'

I return his gaze steadily.

Though the doctors warned my parents to expect twins, for some reason it had never occurred to them to choose two names of the same sex. Over the winter, as Denise grew larger, they had always imagined 'the twins' as a boy and a girl, a perfect instant family.

15

'Helen and Alexander,' said my father with calm certainty, imagining Denise's classical profile and blonde hair replicated in masculine and feminine miniatures. Denise hadn't objected, but now she ignores his question: she is holding Helen close, so that the pale round head fills all her vision.

'Helen Byrd, you are the most beautiful baby in all the world,' she whispers against my sister's seashell ear.

Well!

Feargal stares down at me and asks again.

'Nisa, if your little blonde one is Helen, who's this then?'

I cannot tell him, so I wail instead, causing a passing nurse to sniff irritatedly.

Dadda peers into my face, 'What's up, kidda, eh?' He is searching for resemblances to his Donegal family. His father, paternal grandmother and two sisters had the same chocolate irises and gypsy brown skin. But I am very different in scale from those small boned and whip-thin Byrds. Briefly, he wonders whether he will one day take me to meet them, to see if a mutual flash of recognition will arc between us. But is doubtful if a grandchild or even twin grand-daughters will ever be able to make things right with Grannie Byrd.

Mary Byrd had been distraught when her son announced he was leaving for England, and Feargal stole away the following morning before the rest of the household was up. When he wrote to tell her about his appointment to the Academy, she did not reply. Nor when he wrote to her about Denise. When, a year after that, he sent her the long hopeful letter and a flock of pasteboard wedding invitations, she tore hers up in front of everyone. Feargal never told Denise that his mother had refused to come to the wedding on principle. 'She's far from well, the poor old girl,' he said cheerfully. After the honeymoon Denise sent her unknown mother-in-law a piece of wedding cake in a small white box. There was no reply.

The week after our birth Denise will send pictures of Helen and me, with a dry note, and neither expect nor receive an answer.

So, my father stares out over the city, thinking of names. Through the window comes the faint hum of early evening traffic; grey clouds sail towards the distant dockland cranes, propelled by a stiff north-westerly breeze. Curious, searching for clues to me, he reaches into the crib, loosens the tight blanket and stares down at my solid, nappy-clad body, the Buddha bands of fat around my bolster torso. Braceleted with flesh, my flailing fists look almost tanned. I quieten and stare up at him. My gaze is unblinking and full of foreboding, as if with a clear vision of what is to come.

Then Dadda hears himself answering his own question.

'It's Cassandra,' he says with finality. 'This one's Cassandra, sure enough.'

And the big, black-haired baby (*I, me, Cassandra*) takes a breath and crows with delight.

DENISE

As they had told Feargal they would, my maternal grandparents visited their daughter in hospital on the day after the birth, though Grannie Christine Forrester gagged at the overheated medicinal atmosphere which evoked memories of her own painful confinements. Grandpa Brian urged her down the ward to their daughter's bed, his chest half hidden behind an enormous pot of pink hydrangeas tied about with a satin bow. Briskly, Grannie pushed cards and fruit to the far ends of the bedside table and told Brian to set the pot down; it looked opulent, impressive. Satisfied with the effect, she turned to Denise and beamed.

'When you go home, you can take it with you, darling.'

Denise nodded and then unexpectedly burst into tears as first her mother and then her father bent to give her a quick peck on her cheek.

'Buck up now, brave soldier, the worst is over,' said Brian, patting her hard on the back, 'Get out of here, get your hair done, lose a bit of weight and you'll be back to normal in no time at all.'

'Brian, be quiet, dear. How can you possibly understand how she feels?' Christine dabbed at her daughter's eyes with a lace-edged hankie. 'I was thinking of you all night, sweetie. Was it *too* dreadful? And anyway, where *are* the little lambs?'

Denise was still sniffing pathetically against her mother's Jaeger jacket but raised her head long enough to point to the two cribs side by side under the window. Christine stood, leaned forward and squealed joyously at the sight of a pale blonde head.

'Ooh, she's *beautiful*, darling. Look at her pretty hair, Brian. Just like ours.'

As you can tell, this blonde is beautiful business started long before I was born. Brian and Christine had openly admired each other's pale hair when they met thirty years before, thinking it an aristocratic emblem that had somehow drawn them together. They had been delighted to see it reproduced in their own children and now in their children's children: a fine blond halo gilding a third generation.

'You clever, clever girl,' said Christine gleefully, squeezing Denise's toe through the blanket. 'And where's her sister?'

She leaned over the second crib and stared down in open astonishment at the big, black-haired baby (*me again*) with its cabochon ruby cheeks, looking for all the world like one of those Russian dolls which must surely conceal a finer, smaller version inside its rounded shape.

'Oh,' said Christine, disappointed. 'So they're not identical, darling?' My grandmother had been looking forward to spotting differences between us, like two near-identical drawings in a magazine puzzle, until she could provoke admiration among her friends by knowing at any time which of us was which. Such expert attention to detail was clearly unnecessary now.

'No, Mummie,' said Denise, blowing her nose into the hankie. 'And Feargal says her name is Cassandra.'

'Sounds like trouble,' Brian joined his wife at the crib side and peered down. I stared back into his haughty, raddled face.

'Dark Irish eyes, I see,' he said briefly, wondering why some babies never seemed to blink.

We all came home a week later (no rush for empty ward beds in those days!). In hospital Denise had made a half-hearted attempt to feed us both herself. Her breasts, which I suppose must once have rested like small apples in the palm of Feargal's hands, were now grotesquely swollen and painful, yet from the outset they failed to produce enough milk for the two of us. And so it had been decided by the probationers in the nursery that I, large and hungry from the start, should be bottle-fed. Encouraged by the cheery midwives, Denise gamely persevered with Helen. But after a couple of weeks back home in the tall house in Kilburn she glimpsed herself in the mirror and was appalled by the sight of the open maternity brassière with its cumbersome flaps and hooks and Helen's mouth suckered on to her veined breast like a tiny carp.

Denise informed the health visitor that from now on Helen, too, would be bottle-fed. The woman made a face, but Denise would not budge.

'Please don't look at me like that, because I simply *will not do it*. OK?'

The health visitor sniffed disapprovingly, but it was clear that this strange, deceptively fragile woman was not the type to respond to a lecture on the advantages of breastfeeding. Shrugging, she wrote down adjusted quantities of feed for my smaller sister.

So there you have it. At least Helen's miniature beauty had

earned her two precious weeks of mother's milk. Things had started the way they would go on.

THE TWINS AT HOME

In the freshly painted nursery Dadda struggled atop a ladder to fix a mobile above our cots: dolphins for Helen and puppies for me.

'They can't focus, you know,' called Denise, laying piles of neatly folded nappies in the airing cupboard. 'Not for weeks yet.'

Feargal glanced down at the cots: he always found babies' eyes remarkably knowing. And, of course, he was right; for once he had hung the mobiles Helen lay on her back for hours, her eyes peacefully following the blue-green fish as they dipped and swam in the breeze, while I grunted and beat my fists on the quilt, challenging the brown revolving dogs to come closer so I could show them a fight.

At first, despite the differences in our physical appearance, our mother was intent on dressing us alike. We were twins after all. Thus, at two months Helen looked edible in a wardrobe of sprigged smocked cotton dresses, fluffy matinée jackets and gossamer bootees knitted by her grandmother, while I with my stocky one-year-old's build looked like a frilled weeble, my flounced rompers so tight that they left cruel garter marks around my thighs. Even Denise had to acknowledge that she was merely drawing attention to our differences. Reluctantly, she abandoned her plan and bought six baggy cotton sundresses in toddler's size; I wore them over a vest on cooler days. My feet had never been small enough for Grannie Christine's little bootees anyway; in the pram I kicked sturdy brown legs and wriggled shameless bare toes in the air.

Over the next few months our household settled into its new rhythms: feeding, afternoon sleeps, nappy changing. Bathtime was at six. Denise splashed and soaped Helen, lapping gentle wavelets over her tiny limbs. Lifted sweetly dripping from the bath, my sister lay curled on a towel, beautiful as a miniature Venus and smiling with pleasure as Denise brushed her damp hair with the finest of baby hairbrushes.

My own bath was always a shorter, noisier affair. At the first touch of water I screamed, wriggled and squirmed, my body a slippery red-brown sausage in my mother's grip. Denise wielded my sponge like a scrubbing brush. Minutes later she swaddled me in a fiercely tight bath towel, dumped me on my changing mat, fixed a large nappy around my hips, pulled a vest over my head and, as soon as she decently could, thrust me screaming and damply thrashing into my cot. Then, exhausted, she stood looking down at me, her blue eyes cool on mine, sometimes for minutes on end.

In those long silent moments, what was she thinking? I wish I knew, but at such times her mind was firmly closed against me. Did she ever wish she liked me? Did she ever rehearse a faint smile, just to see how it would feel? Or did she simply look down and savour her power over me?

I don't know. All I remember is that eventually she turned away, picked up Helen from her cot and carried her carefully downstairs. Sometimes Cassandra's cries (*my cries*) followed her, but Denise knew that if she only closed enough doors they would eventually be inaudible. Then she would settle herself against the cushions on the sofa, cradling little Helen, who lay wrapped in a double layer of maternal love, hers and mine. And as Helen's eyelids drooped and closed and her weight settled lightly against Denise's neck, my mother bent and kissed the fragile golden head, and the two of them, Madonna and child, communed wordlessly in perfect peace.

Don't let's disturb them.

It's late, and so, as therapists say, 'We must leave it there for now', and tiptoe away up the stairs to the present, back to this white-walled room, where it is suddenly evening and the air is plangent with goat bells and the first rasping of crickets. The sisters will be here soon, bringing a tray of wholesome food which I will pretend to eat. Then they will close the shutters, and when the lights are turned out at ten o'clock the moon will rise and lay bars of shadow across the sheets.

I press the three keys that are like the rhythmic pat of a hand on a baby's back. End. Save. Close.

24 September 1999, 7.01 a.m.

Since I woke I have been scrolling back through these earliest childhood memories. (The fact that they are re-created rather than authentic imbues them with special meaning, I believe. Yet if I were to show them to the excellent Father Gregorio on Cephalonia I expect he would lean forward on his chair and say, as so many of my New York analysts did back in the eighties, 'Yes, yes, that is all very well, Cassandra, but how did you *feel* . . .?') And he and they would mean, what was it like to be from the outset my mother's unloved child, her cuckoo's egg, the Beast to Helen's Beauty?

Well.

Back then, lying on their comfortable couches, I stared into their mild, intelligent faces and replied, 'But beauty attracts its own unhappiness, don't you think?' And they would nod and tap a pencil against perfect teeth and ask the next question which was inevitably, 'Is that what *you* feel, Cassandra?'

Occasionally, feeling waspish, I would tell them that psychiatrists love to over-dramatize such things; that it really wasn't so bad; that I coped, as children usually do, and, what's more, on many an occasion in later life I turned the whole situation to my advantage.

And if Father Gregorio were suddenly here in the white room and laid a compassionate hand on my arm and asked me the same question? Well, if he caught me unprepared, I might just blurt out a different reply: 'Oh, Father, Father, it cut me to the living core. It left me deformed and damaged and not wholly responsible for my actions in later life.'

Which is a true answer, as the other two answers were also true.

Because long before I could articulate the idea, I had formulated my idiosyncratic (some would say bizarre) strategy for coping with life as a child who was not beautiful and so could not rely on attracting love. And I have to say that for someone so young it was a remarkably spirited approach.

I would be myself, only more so.

I was a large ugly child. In order to command respect, if not love, I had only to fulfil my potential. If I could control the way people felt about me, however negative that feeling was, then I put them in my power. For now, my task was to become a larger-than-life caricature of a Big Bad Baby.

I began, tentatively at first I grant you, to experiment.

THE BIG BAD BABY

Spring came. In the mornings when Feargal was in school, Denise took us for walks in the park. The twin pram was a present from Brian and Christine. A triumph of deep-bellied coachwork, it had leather shock-absorbing straps, cream lining and a dark green folded gabardine hood at either end. Denise pushed it down the tree-lined avenues with both hoods in full sail, feeling the insane pride of *une mère éprouvée*.

She put Helen at the front end, where she could see her, and so that Helen would be the one that passers-by looked at first. Old people and young mothers cooed over my sister, at nine months such a beautiful baby: such pretty blue eyes, such fine white hair, such delicate fingers. When at last good manners dictated that they turn to the twin at the other end of the pram, there was a comic, barely suppressed recoil. I stared boldly out at them, a ruddy, cheerful toad. Their peering faces retreated rapidly, fumbling compliments.

My sister was still small and delicate. For some time Denise had been concerned about her lack of appetite: Helen rarely managed to finish a bottle and could not be coaxed into feeding between meals. By contrast, I was an enthusiastic eater. When I gustily sucked air from the bottom of a bottle, I cried for more. (*Well, what else is a baby to do?*) But Denise found my enthusiasm repellent. 'God, Cassandra, don't be so *greedy*,' she drawled every mealtime, rolling her pale eyes to the kitchen ceiling. But I ignored her and pursed my lips, desperately searching for a fresh teat.

One morning, partly out of spite and partly just to see what would happen, Denise gave me a second bottle, and then when that was finished offered a third. I drained them all, like a bridegroom on a stag night. The mottled skin over my belly was shiny and ominously stretched, like a fruit about to rupture.

'Cassandra, for God's sake, look at yourself,' said my mother.

The unlovely expanse of my padded bottom filled the crook of her arm, my lolling head thumped against her collarbone. Always loath to touch me, she patted at my back with feeble distaste. 'You're *obese*.' She hefted me higher and my stomach pressed against her shoulder.

Obese. *Oh, please*.

Deep within my trunk I released an answering tremor. There was a soft parting sound, and a river of curdled milk erupted from my mouth and poured down the back of my mother's cherished navy cashmere jumper.

Denise held me out at arm's length, but I belched up a second, bigger gout of milk and sent it splattering over the parquet. A third gargling wave spewed over her nylons and filled her best navy court shoes. Denise retched in disgust caused by *me*. But my triumph was short-lived. That afternoon I doubled up with colic: my nappy flooded, foul-smelling diarrhoea puddled around my back and stained my thighs a curious shade of yellow. Denise rolled my soiled bedding into a ball and threw it in the dustbin. The following morning she sent the navy jumper to be dry-cleaned, but when it returned she complained there was still a lingering scent of sour milk. Eventually she wrapped it up with some old shirts of Feargal's and gave it away to the church jumble sale.

See what I mean about power?

Anyway, my father calmed Denise down and cleaned her court shoes himself, lovingly wiping every seam. Afterwards he polished them with a soft cloth, until they gleamed and smelled once more of musky leather and the lily of the valley talcum powder which she sprinkled inside in summer to keep her feet cool and dry.

FEARGAL AND NISA

Some nights, when she eventually carried her darling up to bed, Denise found, to her distaste, that I was still crying. As she climbed into the screeching, she cupped a protective hand around Helen's ears to deaden the noise, but my twin never woke, even when Denise laid her down alongside my rattling cot. That didn't stop Mother worrying, though, and sometimes she crouched by Helen's bed, watching the tiny lift and fall of the blanket, the sweet pouting curl of her lips. She stayed there until it grew dark and Dadda's supper could not be put off any longer. Then she blew Helen a last goodnight kiss, stood stiffly and went downstairs.

In the kitchen at the bottom of the tall house, my father sat until late on weekday evenings, finishing his marking. Unlike many of his colleagues, he was a fastidious teacher and made long, helpful annotations in the margins of even the most lamentable homework. But when he heard my mother come downstairs he pushed away the pile of books and tilted back his chair. Denise went straight over to the cooker, a tense figure stirring soup. Feargal rose and stood behind her, folding his arms around her waist and drawing her to him. He always said that these moments in a warm kitchen, with good food cooking, his wife in his arms and their children asleep upstairs (not that I was!), were the most precious to him. He snuffed deep in Denise's hair, breathing the resinous scent of her dandruff shampoo.

'Nisa, you smell gorgeous. Like a cedar wood in Attica.'

He put his hand on her neck, felt the unruffled beat of her blood; with deliberate slowness he approached her nape with his lips.

Denise bent forward, lifted the wooden spoon to her nose.

'Really? This'll be ready in a few minutes.'

She turned in the confined space between Feargal and the stove. 'Did I tell you Helen put on half a pound last week?'

My father suppressed a sigh and moved away to put the glasses on the table. Our birth had put a distance between them. Their quirky coupledom, which had overcome the resistance of both families and somehow thrived, was cooler now. Feargal inserted the point of the corkscrew, driving it gently down into the cork. On his small salary they couldn't afford to drink wine every night, but once a month he liked to splash out on a bottle of Bull's Blood from the off-licence at the end of the road. After a couple of glasses Denise grew flushed and sparkling-eyed.

Now he took the bread knife and cut the loaf into doorstep slices, ignoring my mother's exasperated tutting. But Dadda always enjoyed dipping hunks of fresh bread into his soup, feeling the hot savoury liquid cool and thicken. He liked to wipe the crust around the bowl from top to bottom when it was drained, until the last drop of soup was blotted into the receiving bread. He said it made him feel like a figure from an ancient wood carving, *The Peasant at Supper*, though Denise, who always dipped her spoon silently into the far side of the soup dish and lifted it, undripping, to her mouth, never liked the implication that she was the peasant's wife.

My mother had lovely manners, a complete set, like a canteen of complicated cutlery. So she knew and taught Feargal how to peel a pear without touching it, how to eat peas, how to use a butter knife and a jam spoon, how to crumble a roll in one's hand and butter each tiny individual piece ready for eating. Dadda sensed these things were important to her and tried to avoid embarrassing her with his lack of refinement when they ate in public. But here in his own kitchen, at his own hearth, he believed that a man should be able to wipe a soup bowl with a crust once in a while. He posted the sopping bread into his mouth and sat back with a comfortable sigh.

'Denise Byrd, did I ever tell you your vegetable broth is pure ambrosia?' Denise's spoon paused, steady, an inch in front of her lips. She smiled.

'Yes, Feargal, many times. Does that mean you'd like some more?'

Feargal shook his head: he was full. His appetite was a shadow of its former hearty self. It was probably something to do with smoking, he thought, as he picked up his cigarettes and stepped out into the back garden. Smoking reduced his appetite, that was for sure. He was thinner now than he had been when he had met Denise three years before. She had been such a slender thing then – a blonde, coaxing elf, he told us later, 'my very own Star of the County Down'. (Except that Denise's hair was yellow instead of nut brown, and they met in Donegal – but, then, Feargal had always adored the song.) And he had loved her from the first . . .

*

But I'm drifting too far back now. And it's getting late.

Quickly now, find the garden again.

See Dadda?

There he is.

The late August evening smells of blackberries and woodsmoke. Out in the garden my father strikes a match and watches the end of the cigarette glow brightly. After a few minutes the light goes on in my parents' bedroom window, making the dusk outside even darker. My mother has escaped upstairs to read her magazines in bed, leaving Dadda to finish his marking.

As I said, things hadn't been easy between my mother and father after our birth. It took weeks for the stitched flesh to heal (my fault, of course), but for months after that Denise continued to find reasons to slide away from Feargal's seeking touch. Often she brought my sister Helen into their bed, to make intimacy unthinkable. On these occasions she also banished Dadda to the spare room so that he would not roll over and squash the bird-boned baby lying between them.

On meek, sleepy feet my father shambled across the landing. Sometimes, if he heard me crying in the nursery, he crept down to the kitchen and made me an extra feed, tiptoeing back up the stairs with the warm glass bottle hidden in his dressing-gown pocket. He leaned over my cot.

'How's about a little of what you fancy, Cassie, eh, my darling? Come to Dadda, hush now, that's my good girl.' He lifted me up and settled himself into the low nursing chair between our cots and tilted the bottle. From far away outside came the mournful rumble of trains heading away from the city into the surrounding darkness. But it was peaceful, in the soft orange glow of the night-light, as I took long hungry draughts of milk and gripped my father's finger tightly in my chubby fist. When the food was finished, Dadda talked to me. I listened in his arms, quiet as I never was for Mother, and for an hour or two we were comfortable together and happy.

So it's sad to see Dadda standing lonely in the garden at dusk, looking up at the square of yellow light and hoping that Denise's silhouette will move across it to call him inside.

It doesn't.

When the midges begin to bite he stubs his cigarette out against the rockery, sighs and goes back inside.

Say goodnight, now, Cassandra.

Goodnight, Dadda.

28 September 1999, 5.22 a.m.

These days I wake early, often before dawn. If I stood at the window now I could watch the sun strike the topmost crest of the mountain and the pink-gilt light move slowly down over the slopes of the far valley side.

How many more mornings are there, I wonder?

Thirty?

Sixty?

A thousand?

How will I know when this one is the last? Will there be a sign? An ominous cloud on the horizon, a black bird on the bell tower, a swirl of grey, portentous mist? Or will it be just an ordinary sunlit morning like this: an everyday backcloth to that most ordinary of human events, when the cave mouth of Hades opens and we slip away from life?

MYTHS

I've always found comfort in legends. Dadda had a treasure-house of myths and told me them before I could even speak. Once Denise discovered him leaning over my bed, murmuring a rapid foreign babble into my ear. She frowned, sniffing popery.

'Nisa, it's the *Odyssey*, for goodness' sake,' laughed Dadda, blushing happily. 'Anyway, she seems to like it right enough.'

I beat my fists on the sheet and giggled, and Feargal reached out and stroked my thick black hair. 'I've just been telling her about the Sirens, haven't I, Cassandra? Half-bird, half-woman, with a cry that could charm a hero ashore. She's going to practise, so she says.'

I drummed a tattoo on the quilt.

Denise laid a drowsy Helen in the neighbouring cot. Then she stood at the door, her hands on her hips, 'Well, don't keep her up, Feargal. It's me who has to cope in the middle of the night when she wakes Helen with her bad dreams and caterwauling.'

Feargal winked at her and turned back to us. 'Ah yes, Cassie, your mother's right now, we mustn't be too long. And, Helen, hello there. Are you listening, too? Well, quiet yourselves, and I'll tell you both a story.' He settled himself on the low chair between the beds, his elbows resting on his knees, looking from Helen's small pale face to my big red one and back again and smiling at us both so even-handedly that my heart swelled with joy and pride.

'So then, what shall it be? The beautiful Helen of Troy or the clever Cassandra who could see the future? Shall I choose? Right, I will. In English this time, so you'll know? Now, let's think. "One blue day, high on a mountain in Illyria . . ."'

So, through our infancy and then our early childhood we lay quiet and listened to that mild Ulster voice reciting the ancient tales. He told us about the great heroes, and Odysseus, Aeneas, Hercules and Alexander strode through the room, their eyes on the far horizon. Later, he told us about the Fates, the Muses, the Graces and the melodious Sirens and we heard the baleful howl of three-headed Cerberus in the skies above Hampstead Heath. On schooldays the hot breath of the Minotaur pursued us down High-gate Hill, the Gorgon turned its head to stare at us across Kilburn High Road, and our small bodies stiffened. Later, Dadda recounted the darker stories of pain and desire, violence and hatred. Helen wept for her beautiful namesake and for Danae in her tower and sobbed at the fate of Niobe, Psyche and Eurydice.

And when we were ten – and so in the last year of his stories, though neither he nor we knew it to be so – Dadda told us the most terrible tales of all, the eternal cycles of blood and suffering and death. As Oedipus, Orestes and Clytemnestra advanced from the shadows Helen shrank back against his side. But I sat still and straight and hollow-eyed beside him and recognized the dark places in my own budding soul. I understood completely: in life, violent, unpredictable forces seek out their victims and destroy them, no matter where they hide. Nevertheless, it took me a while to recognize my own good fortune and to understand that physical unattractiveness and wilful eccentricity could provide safe haven from the high seas of emotional experience whenever I needed it.

But back then, at the beginning, I lay in my little bed and listened, and the hypnotic rhythm of Dadda's voice encoded itself in me like endless wavefall in a shell. Much later, when I needed it, my talisman would be there – like a genie lamp charged and ready or a madeleine dipped in tea – the phrase that promised there was a pattern if not a purpose in a life: 'One blue day, high on a mountain in Illyria . . .'

28 September 1999, 7.52 a.m.

It's still early. The square of sunlight is high and egg-yellow on the white wall of my room. In its centre a butterfly sits, its red-brown wings spread seductively as if posing for my camera. Before, I would have captured it on film in less time than it takes to describe it in words.

They won't let me put photographs up in here, but it doesn't matter – I have them galleried in my memory anyway, thousands of images: faces, landscapes, bodies, objects, rooms. Yet I'm still glad I brought my portfolio. It's here in the bedside cupboard; the soft black leather case, custom-made to my design in Milan, holds a book of photographs interleaved with finest tissue. Twenty original Byrds. Worth, my agent Marco Bertone tells me sternly, 'a rich kid's ransom, so for God's sake don't leave it on an aeroplane somewhere, Cassandra'.

I unzip the case and the folder falls open, as it always does now, at the picture that made my name. (Not my face, though, as you will see. No, not my face.)

Ha!

The Birds.

The Byrds.

THE BYRDS

Under the veil of pearly paper our plumage still gleams as lustrous as the long-ago day I took it. We were in my loft in Manhattan; I remember the November light, the iron smell of imminent blizzard that seeped in from the skyline and rose in the stairwell from the street.

We were twenty-three, already half-known in fashionable New York circles. English sisters, the gossip went, apparently non-identical twins: an actress and a giantess/photographer. Oh yes, the Byrds were odd creatures: fabulous, bizarre, eccentric or original, depending on the journalist and which of us he or she had interviewed. We had reached the outer edges of fame or notoriety. But this single picture of mine changed everything; this one photograph went around the world and captured the imagination of audiences in Tokyo, Paris, San Francisco and Rio. It made us a memorable, enduring icon.

I prop the leather case against my knees and gently peel back the tissue.

We stand staring out at the viewer: like Homer's Sirens, half-bird, half-woman, our heads feathered and our bodies of naked flesh. Helen's face and shoulders are concealed beneath a mask of pure white feathers, a smooth Godiva fall that turns her slim arms into folded wings, separates her small high breasts and descends down over her belly to cup her sex in soft white down. Even her pale eyes are dove-like, both inviting and acquiescent, resting their gaze lightly on the beholder's. It is impossible to see such beauty without desiring to cherish or possess it.

I stand to Helen's left, dwarfing her. My eagle's head is magnificent: each feather caresses the next in a gauzy brushstroke of grey and black; my eyes are glints of jet in amber disks, my wings are powerful and pinioned; my beak, breasts, hips and sex are carved and curved in readiness for prey.

We stand side by side: Sirens, desirable and deadly, victim and predator, archetypal and individual. *The Byrds* demanded a choice from everyone who saw it: Which are you? Which do you dream of? Which do you desire? Students have written theses on *The Byrds*. Last year alone there were a million downloads of the image from its website. It has been etched into marble in corporate atria, projected briefly and blasphemously on to the twin towers of Nôtre-Dame and sent out into the emptiness of deepest space. (Marco has a genius for promotion.)

Yes, the image belongs to the world now. So much so that a few years ago a young photographer, Tom Pfeiffer, brought out a digitally reworked version called 'Twins', with Helen's slim body beneath both masks. Marco set our Manhattan lawyers on to the boy, but also I wrote to him myself and told him, rather brutally now I come to think of it, that he had utterly missed the point.

So, *The Byrds* is still the Byrds. Still a photograph of Helen and me. I stare into my long-ago eyes and wonder.

People have always asked me, were our identities already formed, or did we become the iconic Byrds, developing over time into the image, in the same way as the print emerged in my dark-room?

Back then I'd draw on a cigarette, fix a narrowed stare upon the interviewer and say, 'Surely, what you recognize here is simply reality transmuted by art so that it reveals a essential, eternal, genetic truth: that constant nature underlies all fickle, irrelevant nurture.'

But I was wrong. If I took the picture again today it wouldn't be the same. Not just because time has eroded my skin and hair and bones, but because experience – a lifetime of actions, reactions, choices and abdications – has been working away on what I thought was *me* until I'm changed almost beyond recognition. All those past selves are lost, isolated and forgotten in their individual pockets of time. To see a pattern, to understand, I must connect them; and to connect I must remember.

Ah.

DR MIKE

The door opens, and Dr Michaelides comes in. I call him Dr Mike. Short, wiry and grey-haired, he nods over the top of his gold half-moon spectacles and, reaching down, gently prods my abdomen. I am visibly swollen now – a return to my old bolster shape as an apparent birth announces itself.

'How is our little one coming on, eh, Cassandra?'

Our black doctor–patient humour still amuses me, but, of course, we both know this swelling of ours will not emerge: its role is to consume.

Dr Mike smiles, but his fingers are busy, passing over the surface of my body as if it is incised with secret messages, a fleshy Rosetta stone. His Greek shorthand on my chart is indecipherable, but so far, at least, I believe he answers my questions honestly enough. He draws up the sheet again and writes his mysterious notes.

I pick up my Pentax and wait until his pen makes the perfect angle with the clipboard and a starpoint of afternoon sunlight glints from the nib. Click. Dr Mike screws the top on his pen and slips it into the pocket of his white coat.

'Good, excellent, Cassandra. Pain?'

I shake my head, my eyes still hidden behind the lens.

'How's the writing coming?' He clips the metal chart to the end of the bed.

'Slowly.' I focus again on his lined face, kind eyes, wait for his smile and then take the second picture quickly so that we can say goodbye face to face. 'Words take longer than pictures.'

Click.

Dr Mike glances down at the album on the bedside table, open at *The Byrds*.

'Extraordinary,' he murmurs. 'My favourite photograph of all time.'

'Really?' I say, and close the folder.

Comforted by Dr Mike's matter-of-factness, sitting almost upright against the pillows, I sip the third Earl Grey of the day and steady my mind to go back once more into the past. The butterfly shifts in the hot sun.

TWINHOOD

I often fantasized that Helen and I were originally Siamese twins, unequally divided at birth. Sometimes I told myself I felt a phantom connection, a bereaved pain at shoulder, rib and hip. At such times I told myself sternly that it was good we were now separate, different and not identical grotesques joined in one stretched envelope of skin. (Imagine trying to strangle your unwanted Siamese twin if your other arm was shared with her!)

Ha!

So no, we were not identical. We were emotionally and physically as disparate as Mrs Atkins's predicted 'chalk and cheese'. There were glaring unfairnesses too: Helen had absorbed a larger share of calcium in the womb and grew strong white teeth that never needed filling, while her hapless sister (guess who?) was condemned to squirm under the dentist's drill every six months for the rest of her days.

But as I grew I discovered compensating virtues: I inherited a double share of courage. Thus, while timid Helen trembled on the brink of every new experience, I launched myself fearlessly, no, recklessly, into life. And whereas Helen could not abide conflict and would go to great lengths to avoid confrontation or unpleasantness, I thrived on it and gloried in each test of my growing strength.

Yet despite all our physical and psychological differences and the uneven share of motherly love we received (Helen – all; Cassandra – none. *Ha!*) we were still twins, and so were, whether we liked it or not, indissolubly bound to each other. When one of us drew danger down upon herself, the other found, often reluctantly, that she could not stand idly by. This solidarity began early.

An example?

At three o'clock one sunlit September afternoon in 1961, my mother and her sister-in-law, my Aunt Pauline, are standing in our bedroom. Outside the open window late bees drone through the overgrown buddleia and a lawnmower whirrs in the neighbouring garden. Helen and I are fifteen months old. My sister lies smiling up at her mother and aunt, her eyelids drooping into afternoon sleep, while I, my cot banished to the far corner of the room, give out my best rattling war cry.

'Should we pick her up, do you think?' says Aunt Pauline timidly. My sobbing unnerves her: it touches her in some deep maternal place where refusal is inhuman. My mother, not having such a place as far as I am concerned, shakes her head. After all, how can Pauline possibly know how to deal with a difficult child? Her blond sons are polite, well-mannered to the point of blandness and utterly adored by Denise's parents. 'Those two lads are Forresters to the core,' Brian says, reciting the chant that sounded throughout Denise's own childhood like a blazon on a shield.

Helen's hair and fine-boned beauty have already qualified her as a member of that proud, exclusive band, thinks Denise with satisfaction. But, God, this one?

'Doesn't Cassie look like her daddy,' Grannie Christine always says, in her gayest grandmother voice, which cleverly implies and so never needs to add the words 'poor child'.

A fat bee drifts in through the window, its buzzing instantly overridden by the sound of my wailing. Brightly, my mother says, 'Pauline, would you be a darling and go and put the kettle on? I'll settle Cassie for her nap and join you outside in a minute.' Her smile is kind but dismissive, and Aunt Pauline turns obediently and heads for the stairs.

Denise waits for the kitchen door to close, then grips my cot rail and shakes it savagely.

'You can stop that fucking noise right now.'

What?! Though astonished, I don't let my bellow miss a beat, I promise you.

'Stop it, do you hear me, you little beast?'

I thrash my head from side to side in a way I know she particularly loathes.

My mother bites her lip, glances behind her, then leans over and pinches me harder than hard on my bare leg.

I fall into a sudden, hiccuping silence, while my face darkens. When the trapped noise finally emerges, even I am scared at the sound: a terrible animal howl.

In the neighbouring cot Helen's eyes snap open. She looks up fearfully at the dolphins which circle above her cot like sharks cleaving a sea of sunlit dust motes. Briefly her face crumples as if in pain. Then my sister blinks, fills her lungs and joins me in a high, looping harmony of screams.

Mother swivels around in astonishment. It is always Cassandra who cries, never Helen. This is my fault: I have somehow managed to infect her darling. She shakes my cot again, 'Now look what you've done.' Her voice rises. 'Shut up! Shut up! Shut up!' She shoves my cot savagely against the wall, and my head pitches sideways and bangs against the bars. Helen's scream becomes a weird, frantic screech. I hear it through my pain, and half hate her for being free to cry by choice. I do not want her snivelling sympathy.

But I need it.

'Denise? Is everything OK up there?' Aunt Pauline's voice rises from the hall, full of syrupy concern.

'Of course it is,' shouts Denise over the cacophony, her teeth clenched. She lets go of my cot and leans over Helen. 'Hush, darling. Baby. Please.' But for once Helen's eyes are squeezed shut against her; tears lie in the peach dimples of her cheeks. Under her breath Denise mutters, so low I can hardly hear it. 'All right. I'm sorry. Sorry.'

With perfect synchronization, Helen and I stop crying.

My mother turns back to me. It is my turn to savour the moment. I open my eyes, stretch my mouth into an unfamiliar shape and favour my mother with a slack, victorious grin.

Denise runs out of the room. As the door slams behind her, I turn to look at my sister. Our thoughts, smooth and unformed, swim together through the two sets of bars, unhampered by words, as Helen and I exchange rare, wary smiles.

Like the Sirens, when our voices combine, we are powerful.

29 September 1999, 8.55 p.m.

Looking back, perhaps that story seems unfair to my mother, since naturally I can have no real memory of that day or Denise's swearing or the pain. But on my right leg, high inside my once-broad thigh, I do have a double brown birthmark which looks for all the world like two opposing fingerprints. Once, when I was eight and getting ready for my bath, I asked my mother about the mark: had anyone ever pinched me there when I was little?

She grabbed my thigh and turned it like a gammon to the light, then sighed wearily. Not that she could remember, she said, then shrugged and slapped it lightly: look at the size of you – always far too much meat there for anyone to get a grip, girl.

Yes, I can assure you that my mother's dislike of me was far more real, far more enduring and far more painful than any pinch, so does it really matter whether a specific incident happened or not?

After all, it may have. May well have! Who knows? No one can tell me now.

I yawn.

A little computer housekeeping is necessary. Save document to drive A:/. End. Close down.

(The black disk will slide out into my palm, and I shall hold the only truth that matters.)

30 September 1999, 5.45 a.m.

Resume.

THE KNOT GARDEN

Just after our fourth birthday our landlord, a colleague of my father's at the Academy, returned from an extended lectureship in America and reclaimed his tall house in Hampstead. We Byrds moved downmarket and downhill to a tiny rented terraced cottage on a slanting road in Kilburn. The front door opened directly on to the pavement and at the back was a small walled garden overgrown with brambles and weeds and spiked with rubbish.

As she mopped listlessly at greasy plates, my mother scowled out of the kitchen window at heaps of broken brick and remembered the broad green lawns of her childhood and the view of distant Thames-side willows from her bedroom window. Perhaps she felt she had been cheated in some way, robbed of ease and youth and promise or, more specifically, denied her parents' opulent vision of her future: a soft-focus photo in *Country Life*, a string of good pearls and a house in Wiltshire with a labrador dozing by the range. Yet surely she knew she could not honestly blame my father for that. After all, in the beginning, she had, as Christine darkly described it, 'set her cap at him'.

My mother and father met during a summer vacation in 1957, three years before we were born. Feargal was working as a guide in the ruined abbey outside Donegal Town, his fluent Latin making elegant work of the inscriptions and tombstones. And one afternoon, as he leaned like a young Byron against a slab of worn granite, a blonde English girl lingered behind the others in her party and, squinting at him in the sunshine, asked him a host of shy, sly questions. By the end of the tour, he had somehow, surprisingly for such a timid young man, arranged to meet her by the river after supper.

As the twilight fell and mist rose damp and scented from the water, he held her hand and told her how beautiful she was with her cool swatch of ash-blonde hair. Denise stared back into his eyes, saw her silhouette mysteriously reflected against the pearl grey of the river and moved closer. Instinctively, Feargal put his thin arms around her and held her carefully, as though she were fine-blown glass. Then, after the first moments of mutual shock had passed, he held her tighter, nuzzled her neck and breathed marvellous words into her ear until she clung to him, dazzled and flattered.

When she returned home at the end of August Denise told her parents that she intended to marry a man she had just met: a young poet and Classics teacher whose name was Feargal Byrd. Brian and Christine waged a long and unsuccessful campaign against the match.

'Let her do it,' said Brian resignedly six months later. 'One day, she'll be back.' So Denise was married from the lawns of the tall house beyond the Thames-side willows and began the voyage that would deposit her three years later in a drab terraced cottage in Kilburn.

However much Denise hankered for striped grass and espaliered peach trees, Dadda still wasn't interested in clearing the garden.

'We're only renting,' he said. 'What's the point? And surely you can get good cheap peaches in the Co-op.'

Mother clicked her tongue in irritation. Even if she could never hope to transform this small house into anything like the bright, spacious home she had known as a girl; even if there would never be enough money for carpets, curtains and table lamps, for polished floors and rugs, surely they could afford to do this one small thing? Denise realized she had never thought seriously about money before; it had simply existed, buoyant and reliable. Money had bought her the view of the distant willows. It had bought her dancing lessons, a pony, a kidney-shaped dressing-table and her first cocktail dress. Its lack now brought builders' rubble and damp brickwork. She stared out of the window and let her imagination wander.

Over those first months I think she began to see the garden as her small fiefdom, her private estate. Only out there could she shape reality to her own design. Finally, some three months after we moved in, Mother pulled on a pair of heavy leather gloves and marched outside carrying secateurs, a weeding fork and a stainless steel spade given to her by a sympathetic Grannie Christine. We girls watched her from the kitchen window.

First she hunkered down and began cutting back the brambles and stabbing at the roots of couch grass and horsetail with her little fork. It took her a week to work her way to the far side of the plot. Then she threw the heap of drying weeds on a bonfire and stood, wiping her forehead on the back of her hand, watching the flames lick and crackle and the smoke pour up into the grey sky.

Both of us brightened at the sight of the cleared space and asked Dadda if we might have a garden swing, but Mother had other ideas, culled from the women's house and garden magazine she now consumed every week. She got books on gardening from the library, and in the evenings she cut pictures from her magazines and traced intricate patterns on to squared paper. Since our plot was so tiny, she had decided to make a witty feature of its size and fill it, wall to wall, with a miniature knot garden. There would be no room at all for a swing, she informed us briskly. Feargal saw our disappointed faces and promised frequent compensatory trips to the park. He didn't want to dampen Denise's new-found enthusiasm: she had grown tetchy and withdrawn since moving to the little house. At least with the garden she had found something to interest her. Sometimes when she showed him the pictures in magazines she was so excited she leaned across the bed and hugged him, and he blushed and stared down at the glossy page, wondering if now was the right time to slide a hand down across her narrow shoulder-blades.

AFTERNOON IN THE PARK

By the following spring Mother had got the soil as fine as sieved flour. In March she marked out the ground with pegs and string, drawing tight curves, ogives and rigidly straight lines. When everything was prepared, she planted tiny box bushes (another present from Grannie Christine) at precise distances apart and watered them with tender attention every morning and evening as the days lengthened.

Feargal, coming home from the Academy at four thirty on a June afternoon, found Helen and me sitting alone on the living-room floor, listlessly turning the pages of our picture books. We were not allowed to interrupt when Mother was gardening. When Dadda stood at the back door and called to her, Mother looked up, held a gloved hand up to shade her eyes, waved briefly and returned to her weeding. Dadda loosened his tie and slipped off his jacket and made us a glass of lemon barley water. Then he took us by the hand and walked us down to the park.

In the playground mothers dressed in brightly coloured summer dresses sat and chatted while their children whirled around on carousels or flew back and forth on the swings. With a surreptitious glance at Dadda, I slipped out of my sandals: I have always loved the feeling of cool dust between my toes. I pounded over to the slide on big bare feet, climbed the worn metal steps with great concentration and plonked myself down at the top of the chute. From this vantage point Dadda was a small, telescoped figure and I was a giant, powerful and strong, high as the branches of the trees, staring roosting pigeons straight in the eye. I sat motionless in the sunlight, absorbing the sounds, smells and sights of the playground, wilfully oblivious of the queue of impatient, jostling children forming behind me.

Helen was on her favourite swing. Feargal lowered her into the safe confines of the box; she stuck her tiny sandalled feet forward through the wooden bars and gripped the worn chains tightly.

'Push me. Push me, please, Dadda.'

Feargal placed his hands against her narrow back and pushed her gently forwards.

'Not too high, Dadda. Not too high.'

She always said that. All because of the afternoon when, for once exhilarated by sunshine and freedom, she had let him swing her as high as the chains would allow, only to feel the treacherous seat drop away beneath her as she reached the very highest point. Delighted and appalled, I'd watched her plummet until the chains jangled taut and jerked her arms savagely in the process. Nowadays she would only swing within a timid, controlled arc, where she could watch her skirt gently fill and empty with summer air.

'Not too high, Dadda. Not too high,' she bleated. Dadda smiled and patted her shoulders gently on each backswing. It made me sick inside see how gently he pushed her.

Helen looked up and saw me staring at her from the top of the slide, my wide brown face following her like a sunflower. Behind me was the queue of children shouting at me to go down the slide, but I just sat there, watching.

Helen was embarrassed. 'Cassie,' she called. 'Slide, Cassie. Now.'

I grinned over the park and shook my head. *No.*

The topmost child on the ladder, a burly, ginger-headed boy, began to prise my fingers from the slide one by one, as if peeling a suckered starfish from a rock, until he had my hand imprisoned in his. He squeezed my bent knuckles for luck.

No.

Helen shouted again, making her tiny voice reach over the sandpit and the see-saws and the carousel, right over to the tree tops and the tall slide.

'Let go, Cassie. *Now.*'

No.

A grate of teeth on bone was followed by a taste of iron flooding through my mouth.

Suddenly the ginger-haired boy was yelling and sucking his hand and there was red on it and I was feeling better and smiling and nodding at him as if we had just had a nice conversation. All the children in the queue behind me had fallen silent. I shuffled forward, and the warm smooth metal squeaked under my thighs. Helen watched in appalled admiration as I slid slowly and majestically down to the ground, where a gaggle of indignant mothers was gathering to scold me.

Happy days.

2 October 1999, 8.15 a.m.
Straight to work today.
Mustn't be late, not this morning!
See me here, in my first school photograph?

SCHOOLDAYS

Aged five, but tall and solid as a ten-year-old, I stand four-square on my pine-trunk legs, my big face round-eyed and serious. For it is early September 1965 and Helen and I begin our formal education today. Our Alma Mater is Kilburn Mixed Infants in the High Street. (Denise took us to the school outfitters to get our uniforms. When we got home she made us try them on, stood us in front of the knot garden and took our photos, separately.) Now, on our first morning, the identical grey skirts, white shirts and ties lie folded in readiness over the backs of our bedroom chairs.

But across the landing, in our parents' bedroom, Mother is complaining loudly. About me. On this landmark day it is not the reassuring start I had hoped for.

'She's bad-natured, Feargal. She's rude, she's greedy, she's fat and slow.'

Oh dear.

'She can't, or most likely won't, control her temper. And she's as messy as an animal when she eats. She *smells*, for goodness' sake.'

Well, don't we all?

Apparently not. I swear my mother has superhuman hearing for anything that is slightly scatological. She must linger outside doors, listening, for my every enjoyable tuba fart is overheard and commented upon later at table amid nose-pinched grimaces of distaste. As mother always points out, *Helen* never feels the need to break wind like that (of course, fart and guff were not words she ever stooped to). I say I'm sure Helen would feel better if she did, and I certainly encourage her to try, particularly when we have guests. She repays me by denouncing me every time I release the smallest effluvium. The Big Bad girl in me takes this as a personal challenge.

Now comes Dadda's voice. 'Nisa, hush, the girls will hear. Sure, Cassandra's just different, that's all there is in it. She can't help her size, poor kid – mentally she's all there and halfway back, if you just give her a chance.'

Thank you, Dadda.

Feargal reaches across to the bedside table and lights his first cigarette of the day, 'She'll be fine at the school, Nisa, wait and see.'

Denise clenches her fists. 'You just won't accept it, will you? Mummie's right, we should have Cassie checked by a doctor. She may need . . . help.' She shoots an angry glance at Dadda. 'For God's sake Feargal, will you listen to me for once? We should have put her into care from the start.'

My father winces and sits up at that, his thin chest with its sparse hairs rising and falling in passionate indignation. Watching him blaze, Denise suddenly sees a trace of her once-flamboyant young poet; but now he is merely cross.

'Will you be quiet now please, Denise,' he says sharply. 'Your mother's a mean-spirited snob sometimes, you even say so yourself. The girls love us and each other and that's the end of it.'

Denise snorts derisively, 'Helen still has to put up with her. We shouldn't ask that of a child, it's too much.'

'They understand each other well enough, Nisa.'

'You're soft,' says Denise rudely. She swings her thin legs over the side of the bed: if she lingers, Feargal may reach out for her, forcing her to refuse him and watch that sad expression flit across his face. She stalks down the landing to the bathroom and sets about brushing her teeth with exaggerated vigour.

Feargal shuffles downstairs in his shabby towelling dressing-gown. He lays the table, lights his second cigarette and blows a blue-grey smoke ring over the kitchen table, as he leafs absent-mindedly through the top sheets of a typescript. The new translation is going slowly, in fact it is virtually at a standstill. And now the holidays are over there won't be much time to write. Of course, he is lucky to have the Academy job in the first place: hardly any schools choose to teach Latin and Greek nowadays. Dead languages are a dead-end job, as his father-in-law loves to joke.

Denise came into the kitchen, her pale hair scraped back into a smart french pleat, her eyebrows pencilled and lashes mascaraed, ready to meet other mothers. She was wearing her best grey tweed dress, which fitted smooth and narrow over her hips. Getting her figure back after our birth had been a struggle, but she had done it by remorseless exercise, starvation and willpower.

All credit to her really, thought Feargal wistfully, who had secretly adored her new roundnesses, the pleats and folds of skin that had softened her angularity.

Denise saw him staring at her breasts. 'What is it?' she said warily.

'My slender elf.' Feargal grinned and widened his dark eyes at her.

Blushing but mollified, Denise tied a pinafore tightly around her waist. 'Enough blarney from you, Feargal Byrd. Call the girls, or we're going to be late.'

Upstairs, sweating, I bent my chin to my chest in a sullen struggle to fasten the buttons on my new white shirt. Helen was dressed and ready. She sat on the bed, neat and pressed, swinging crossed, white-socked ankles and smiling at my efforts in her calm, superior way.

Feargal's voice came echoing up three storeys, 'Girls, will you get down here now, please, the both of you.' Helen stood, moved towards the door, but on the threshold she turned, questioning. Which I have to admit was always one of the nice things about her.

Go, I told her.

She pattered lightly down the flights of stairs.

I forced handfuls of crumpled shirt inside the waistband of my grey school skirt and lowered myself on to the floor to buckle my expensive new school shoes.

I was afraid.

'Cassandra Byrd, get down here *right this minute*,' Denise screamed from the kitchen.

I adjusted the last buckle, got to my feet and trundled down the landing.

In the kitchen, sunlight poured through the bay window, lighting the blue and white china, the red and yellow packet of cornflakes.

'Will you look at the two young students, Mummie.' Feargal stood proud in the doorway, his arm high around my shoulders, low on Helen's neck. 'Brains and beauty combined; you've a great future before you, girls.'

Denise sniffed, banging a spoon down beside my bowl. *This one hasn't.*

I tilted my head up at her.

'Don't just sit there staring at me, my girl. It's school for you today if you hadn't noticed. Get your breakfast.' And in a different voice, 'Helen, sweetheart, what would you like?'

'Frosties, *please*, Mummie.' My sister always put on this silvery fairy voice when Mother was angry with me. It made my temper boil.

'Me too. Me first, Mum. I'm hungry. I'll have them, too,' I shouted.

'*Please,* Cassandra. How many times do I have to tell you, say *please?*' Denise sighed in exasperation, pouring a sheaf of flakes into Helen's bowl. 'And I'm *not* your mum.'

What?

The truth at last. It was awful, but it explained everything. I was not my mother's child. I gaped, looking from Mother to Dadda, round-eyed. Helen sat eating her cereals, oblivious to my bewilderment. Like a schoolgirl from a Persil advert, her white-cuffed hands guided her spoon steadily up and down, up and down, between mouth and bowl.

Denise hid a smile and turned away to tend the toaster. Over her shoulder she said airily, 'I've told you enough times, Cassandra. Stop calling me "Mum" or you'll feel my hand on the back of your legs, young woman.'

Oh. I see. A joke, that's all.

I slouched forward, disconsolate, spilling milk and cornflakes from the tip of my drooping spoon.

With a quick glance at Mother's back, Feargal took the spoon and placed it securely back inside my fist. 'Come on now, Cassandra, that's the girl. Get a good breakfast inside of you today, yes?'

I shook my head.

Not fair.

Dadda guided the spoon towards my tightly shut mouth, but I turned my head away sharply, spilling milk and cereal down my new school skirt.

Keeping his body between Denise and me, Feargal scooped up fallen Frosties from between the grey pleats and put them back in the bowl.

Dadda.

I smiled my special secret smile.

Dadda smiled back, put his finger to his lips.

But Denise had seen.

'For Christ's *sake*, Cassandra Byrd, don't you know where your mouth is by *now*?' She strode up to the table, waving a sour dish-cloth in my face. 'Wipe yourself clean, you dirty child, go on.'

I took the cloth and dabbed clumsily at the dark stain. The rag left a larger smear of pearly fat on the skirt, and Denise grabbed it from my hand.

'Now look what you've done. See what I mean, Feargal? Give it here, you idiot girl.' Denise picked a clean corner of the dishrag and yanked at my skirt. I looked across her bent head into Dadda's eyes.

Poor Cassie. He leaned forward and patted his wife's shoulder, 'Let it rest, now, Nisa heart. Let it rest,' he smiled. 'They've got a big enough day ahead of them as it is.'

When breakfast was finished, Helen and I took their bowls and placed them side by side on the draining board. Then we toiled back upstairs to brush our teeth. Denise put her cardigan on over her dress and checked the time on the gold Swiss wristwatch with the black leather strap which Brian and Christine had given her for her twenty-first. Twenty-one jewels ticked away the precise time for our departure.

'Will you get down here *now*, girls, *please*. It's late.'

Feargal stood at the bottom of the stairs and swung each of us down the last few steps to the hall. Our skirts swirled out around our hips.

'*Valete, puellae*,' said Feargal. It was his standard farewell. 'Off you go now. Good luck and . . .'

'Be home soon,' we chorused, Helen's voice high and fluted, mine husky and low.

'Oh, for God's sake, get a *move* on,' yelled Denise and grabbed us by the hand.

From his writing-room on the first floor Feargal watched us go. At the gate, as we always did whenever Mother took us out, we twins turned to wave up at him, before allowing Denise to pull us away down the hill. As usual, Helen's thin little legs kept perfect double time with Denise's while I lumbered awkwardly along beside them at a half-run, my sturdy calves bowing out from my knees. The three of us turned the corner and were gone.

And what did Dadda do then?

Well, I'm sure he shook his head, clearing it of Denise and us, then he walked over to his desk, clamped his cigarette between his lips, found his place in the text and inserted a sheet of paper in his typewriter. When he next looked out of the window, he saw not the flaking brickwork of the house next door but a sunlit plain in the Peloponnese three thousand years ago.

Save. Close.

4 October 1999, 7.02 a.m.

My window crops a view of the far valley side. To the left, just in frame, the ridge rises to a hilltop, a mountain really, with dark green chestnut and cypress groves on the lower slopes, terraces of ancient olives further up and at the top a hazy jagged peak. In the morning the topmost crag is rimmed with rising gold. In the afternoon it is shadowed charcoal and white, and in the evening it flushes pink, before darkening down through lavender to indigo and black. Odysseus must have known this hill. Perhaps flashing-eyed Athene and Iris, fleet of foot, looked down from there and saw him looking up.

I wish Dadda had could have seen it.

I've often wondered if he did.

Did he hear the Siren's call and sail to Ithaca?
I wonder.

DADDA'S VIEW

Dadda's writing was his retreat and his only freedom. Taking ancient Greek verse and working it into timelessly transparent English, so that every image shone, accessible yet faithfully restored, was his all-enveloping, pure delight. His first published translation of *Antigone*, just before we were born, had caused a minor sensation. 'At last, a shimmering blend of poetry and erudition,' said one critic. 'A new classic,' said another. At the hurriedly organized launch party, his publisher Timothy Harris had introduced him to a slim, bearded man in black corduroy whom he had vaguely recognized.

To great acclaim, Caspar Mycroft had directed the film star Ariadne Vassos in a landmark stage production of the *Oresteia* the previous year. Afterwards he had publicly voiced his hope that he might be able to lure her back to London for another season sometime in the near future. Now he clasped Feargal's hand, 'I hope you don't mind, Mr Byrd, but I've sent Ariadne your translation. I know she'll be thrilled.'

Quietly ecstatic, Feargal had floated home to Hampstead on a cloud of champagne and compliments. Denise hadn't known who Ariadne Vassos was but was oddly relieved to hear that she was older than Dadda and that she lived in Greece. 'Well done, darling,' she said proudly, trying to avoid his vinous breath. 'Mother and Father will be thrilled.'

Three months later Caspar Mycroft telephoned Feargal one lunchtime at the Academy to say that Ariadne was in town and would like to meet him. And so Dadda polished his shoes and brushed his faithful tweed jacket and went along to the Savoy Hotel. Caspar was in his trademark corduroy, and sitting beside him was a striking beak-nosed woman of about thirty, with waving black curls and a wry, passionate mouth. As Feargal approached, escorted by a doubtful waiter, she rose and took both his hands in hers and in her deep, astounding voice said, 'Oh, Mr Byrd. I am *so* delighted to meet you. You have written a pure *marvel*.'

Within minutes, they were talking about Greek tragedy with such laughter and enthusiasm that Caspar Mycroft eventually had to give a little peevish cough and remind Ariadne it was time to leave. She sighed and stood. She would return, she told Feargal, as soon as her filming schedule permitted, and she would be delighted to appear in *Antigone*. Watching heads turn to follow her as she walked through the hotel and out on to the Strand, Feargal found that he badly wanted to have the next play ready for her; for her to read, for her to read with him.

The kitchen clock struck nine: the girls would be starting school. Feargal glanced at his watch. The 6th of September, already. The Academy went back in two days: there was so little time. He lifted up his *Odyssey* and the postcard of Ithaca fell from the page where he had hidden it. The Greek was warm, melodic.

My dearest Feargal,

This is the place I told you of, my house called Peloros. Do you find it intriguing, my fantasy that the abode of the Sirens might have been Ithaca itself? Since you are a scholar you will disagree, I know, but I have always believed that the Sisters truly loved Odysseus and never meant him harm. How foolish he was to bind himself to the mast, when he could have escaped so many dangers and disappointments by following the Sirens' call to home! Lest you are bound, too, I shall speak plainly: here is someone who understands; join me if you are brave enough to hear. Your Ariadne.

When Dadda next stared out of the window in search of the Peloponnese plain, he saw instead a far island, high-peaked and green in a turquoise sea, and coming across the water towards him was the most beautiful song in the world.

He bent to type.

SCHOOLDAYS

Outside, the north London streets smelled of traffic and late summer rain. 'Mummie, wait, wait a minute. I've got a stitch. Wait, Mummie. *Please*,' I yelled.

Denise tightened her grip on my pudgy fingers. 'Keep up, Cassandra. You haven't got a stitch and you're not going to make us late on our first day.'

Peevish and anxious, Helen glanced back me. 'Hurry up, Cassie. We mustn't be late, they'll be cross.'

I dragged my mother to a standstill. Denise let go of my hand. Her face looked hot and her eyes were narrowed to slits. 'Cassandra, if you don't come now you can stay right there. I don't give a damn. It's up to you.'

She turned her back on me and walked Helen on down the hill. I sat down with a thump on the dusty pavement, my chubby legs apart. 'Ow. Hurts, hurts.'

Helen missed a step and stopped to look back at me. 'She can't, Mummie. She can't. Wait.'

Denise, suddenly dragging Helen's dead weight, jerked to a halt. She let go of her hand and stalked back up the hill towards me. 'Get up, idiot,' she hissed, glancing around to see if anyone was watching. 'Get up. Get up, damn you.' She grabbed my hand, digging in her nails.

'No,' I said. Above me my mother's thoughts pulsed red and murderous.

'Mummie, Cassandra *has* got a pain,' said Helen, frightened now. 'Really she has, Mummie.'

'I don't care. She's a vicious, naughty girl.' Denise yanked my arm high in the air and held my soft, heavy body swaying there, my toes barely touching the ground. I'm allowed, I have every right to do this, she thought briskly. Then she brought her free hand down in a series of stinging front- and back-handed slaps across my bare calves.

Smack. Smack. Smack.

'*That's*-for-being-a-*rude-spoiled-wilful-wicked*-child.' Red handprints blossomed over the white flesh of my leg. I flushed and glared at her. We both knew that my refusal to cry was sheer provocation. Mother raised her arm again.

Smack. Smack. Smack.

'And-*that's*-for-making-us-*late*, so you'll never do it *again*.' She let go of my upraised arm. I stood mute, my red face set firm, my thick legs square-braced in their new conker-brown Start-Rite sandals. 'Now then, say you're sorry. Go on.'

I shook my head.

Denise lifted her hand a final time.

My eyes widened and I felt my body shudder with release.

Denise looked down and saw a stream of pee running down my legs, filling and spilling over the big shiny shoes.

Ha, ha, ha.

'You dirty little bitch. You filthy creature,' screeched Denise, hopping out of the path of the rivulet that was running across the pavement towards the kerb. 'Take off those wet knickers right now. Go on. Right here in the street. You'll go to school for your first day in your bare bottom, and I shall tell your teacher why. *Take them off.*'

Obediently I lifted my skirt, hooked my thumbs in the waistband of my knickers and tugged. The saturated crotch hung down and then fell soggily around my feet. Mother bent down, retching dramatically, picked up the wet cotton between two disgusted fingertips, ran over to a waste bin and dropped it in from a height.

A small noise by my side.

'Ha, ha, ha,' I pointed at Helen. 'Ha, ha, ha.'

At my sister's feet, a thin trickle of water edged into the dust and ran zigzagging down the hill beside mine. Helen smiled shyly up at me from under her pale fringe.

Ha, ha, ha.

Mother screamed.

Helen and I stood side by side in our puddles and waited for whatever came next.

'Helen Byrd, why are you crying *now?*'

Four years had passed since that first day. Miss Lloyd looked towards the back rows of her crowded junior school classroom. Beneath the steamed-up windows and the crudely drawn maps of Britain in dry green poster-paint, heads lifted and turned in unison. Except one. At least with Helen and me you could always tell which twin was which, since we were as unalike as two sisters could possibly be. So, yes, Deirdre Lloyd was sure it was *Helen* Byrd who sat with her blonde head resting on the desk, her delicate shoulders heaving uncontrollably.

'Helen! Speak to me, dear, and tell me what's the matter.' Recently, in fact since she came back from the Christmas holidays, Helen Byrd had started crying in class like this: two or three mornings a week she would just sit there, her face wet with tears. She would never say what was wrong. In desperation Miss Lloyd now turned to me, Helen's tubby black-haired twin.

'Cassandra Byrd, what on earth is wrong with your sister now?'

I looked up solemnly. I had no hesitation in shopping the Lennox brothers, even though they were probably not the cause of Helen's tears this morning. (Helen wept over anything: a ladybird, a beggar in the street, a poor mark in English; but sometimes, of course, she cried because she was remembering something unspeakably terrible, which was almost certainly the case today.)

To Miss Lloyd, with her hairy mole and wire-wool hair, I simply said, 'It was Lenny Lennox, Miss.'

'Oh, *what?*' Lenny Murray wheeled around in his chair to face his accuser. 'Oh, Miss, don't listen to Cassie Byrd, Miss, she's barmy.'

'Be quiet, Lenny,' said Miss Lloyd, mechanically. 'What did you do? Helen, Helen, I'm talking to you, dear. What did he do to you?'

Helen lifted her pretty, tear-stained face and whispered piteously, 'He touched my legs, Miss.'

'Touched your legs, where?'

'Up here, Miss.' Helen slid her skirt to the top of her hollow thighs.

Lenny bridled. 'Oh, Miss, I never. I'd never touch her, Miss, honest.'

Miss Lloyd pursed her lips. 'Lenny, come and sit at the front of the class and get on with your work. Helen Byrd, stop crying and see me after school.'

Helen dried her eyes on the back of her hands, while Lenny Lennox packed up his schoolbag, venting his indignation with huge sighs. Aware of sympathetic murmuring from his classmates, he swaggered past Helen's hunched shape, pulling a sour face. He came level with me just as Miss Lloyd turned back to the board. Suddenly Lenny screamed and fell heavily forward on to the parquet floor. Orange and blue marbles spilled from his pockets and rolled like glass eyes across the worn wood floor.

'*Now what?*' yelled Deirdre Lloyd. '*Get up*, Lenny, for good-ness' sake. Stop showing off.'

But Lenny Lennox was sitting rocking backwards and forwards, his hands cupped over his bulbous thigh, from which protruded the brass nib of a fountain pen. Miss Lloyd rushed down the aisle yelling at us all to be quiet and half-carried a limping Lenny off to the office. A barrage of noise broke out as she left the room.

I kept my eyes decorously lowered.

Helen still sat with her head on her arms, but at least she had stopped her pathetic crying.

5 October 1999, 8.35 a.m.

The sky is low and grey this morning, turning the hillside into a cliff of dirty rock. Though the opioids (I love the word, my little alien friends) have taken away the pain, I'm cold, and even though I rub my hands together furiously my nails are purplish blue, fingertips chilly white. In this light, the room is a nun's cell and I suddenly find myself nostalgic for company, wood fires and warmth.

Yet better to be here, far better to be here, than back in Marlow at Christmas-time, nearly thirty years ago . . .

THE BEECHES, CHRISTMAS 1970

Every year following our birth Mother and Dadda spent Christmas with Denise's parents at The Beeches. A large Edwardian Gothic house on the outskirts of Marlow, it had four vast bedrooms around a galleried landing and two chilly attic rooms above and was thus large enough to accommodate what Grandpa Brian, or GB as he liked us to call him, always referred to as the 'Full Gathering of the Forrester Clan'.

At first my father had tried to refuse the annual invitation, but gradually he realized that in marrying him Denise had not surrendered her family name but rather enrolled him, whether he liked it or not, as an associate member of her father's tribe. How he must have dreaded the Christmas gatherings at The Beeches. Denise responded to the irresistible pull of Forrester gravity and spent hours in the kitchen with her mother preparing unfeasible amounts of food. That left him marooned in the stultifying company of GB and Uncle Derek. Only with Derek's mouse-like wife Pauline was there an unspoken alliance of outsiders.

Nevertheless, on Christmas Eve 1970, as on so many Christmas Eves before, our ancient black Morris crawled up the drive for another week of Forrester ritual celebration. It always rained at The Beeches. I remember the sound of water dripping and dripping all day long from the branches of smooth grey trees. The terrace sprouted green ferns and its stone balustrades were mossy prison bars.

Grandpa Brian watched our approach, only moving back from the window as we rattled to a halt in front of the house. He had long ago abandoned any idea of 'having a word' with his son-in-law about his choice of car. Feargal was a pleasant enough chap, but it was clear he would never achieve the comfortable standard of living Brian had provided for his own family. Surely it could only be a matter of time before Denise came to her senses, admitted her mistake, 'upped sticks' and left her disappointing schoolmaster husband to return to The Beeches.

Brian checked his appearance in the hall mirror, smoothed back his long grey hair and straightened his golf-club tie. There was only one flaw in their dream. If Denise came back home now, she would not be alone. With her would come gallant little Helen, honorary Forrester of course, who would be no trouble at all; but there would also be me. Cassandra. *Good God*. GB's reflection blanched: Christmas was bad enough, but having The Throwback as a permanent inhabitant of The Beeches was unthinkable.

The doorbell rang and Grandpa Brian flung open the studded oak door. The porch was empty: playing our familiar game, we girls were hiding. 'Happy Christmas! Come out, come out wherever you are,' bellowed GB, enjoying, despite himself, the role of genial grandfather this ritual always conferred upon him.

'Here we are, Grandpa Brian,' laughed Helen, darting out like a blonde elf from behind a pillar. Brian grabbed her slight form under the arms of her red wool coat and swung her into the air. He was still fit for his age, despite the incipient paunch. The golf kept him active, of course. He lowered her gently to the ground. 'Ah, la belle Hélène.' He stroked her silk-white hair, lifted her chin. 'Where's your sister?'

Helen sucked her thumb. Even at ten she enjoyed childish gestures.

'She's hiding, GB.'

Grandpa Brian sighed. 'Cassandra?'

My excited, throaty gurgle rang out from behind the far pillar.

'Come out now. It's cold.' Brian shivered in his cashmere sweater.

I peeped around the pillar. 'No, Grandpa, come and find me. I'm hiding.'

Brian remembered how much he disliked my deep, husky voice. In his most commanding tone, he said, 'Cassandra, you're letting all the hot air out of the hall. Come in *now*. Come on, jump to it, girlie.' He strode toward my pillar. As he came level with it I bounded out of hiding and landed with both feet on his instep.

'Grandpa. Swing *me*!'

Grandpa Brian staggered back, clutching his bruised foot.

'Hell's bells, Cassandra. What d'you think you're doing, you great carthorse? You've broken my bloody ankle.'

I held out my bulky blue arms. 'Swing *me*, Grandpa Brian, *please*.'

Brian pointed sternly to the open door. 'You're too old and far too heavy. Inside, Cassandra. Now.'

My face fell. 'That's not fair. We're *twins*, Grandpa,' I muttered as I shambled off after Helen into the gloom of the oak-panelled hall.

Brian limped out on to the porch, swearing under his breath. Yet again I had confirmed his darkest suspicions. How could his nymph-like Denise possibly have produced this black-browed creature?

'Daddy? Where are you?' Denise was at the back of the car watching Feargal struggle with their heavy suitcase.

'Right here, my love,' called Brian. 'Happy Christmas.' Composing his face into a beam of paternal welcome, he forgot his limp and strode out to the drive, throwing his arms wide to receive his daughter's fragrant, dutiful hug.

In the hall there was a thud of feet descending the staircase at speed: our cousins, David and Desmond, had seen the car. Uncle Derek stepped out in front of them as they reached the bottom step. At thirty-one he already sported a small pot belly and his thin face was prematurely lined, but his blond Forrester hair was still plentiful, giving him an air of faded youth. Uncle Derek had deliberately cultivated his father's booming voice; he found it gave him a useful aura of authority at the office. Now he held out two restraining arms.

'Boys, boys, boys. Manners, please. Shake hands properly with your cousins.'

The boys had inherited the narrow Forrester head and the thick gilt thatch. Of their mother, the sad, mouse-haired Pauline, there was hardly a trace. Stifling giggles, David stuck out his paw towards me and I promptly hid mine behind my back. Meanwhile, Helen's tiny hand was being pumped furiously up and down by the wolfish young Desmond. The brothers changed places, but I just shook my head at Desmond and kept my hands firmly out of reach. David shook Helen's hand even harder than his brother. When he had finished I saw her wipe her palm down the side of her coat.

'Girls, take your coats off and go upstairs.' Denise's voice always sounded much louder when she was at The Beeches. I fought my way out of the blue coat and let it fall to the floor.

'Pick it up right now, Cassandra. Grannie bought that for you in John Lewis. Don't you dare throw it about like that.'

I picked up the coat and took it into the cloakroom. Out of sight of Mother I crumpled it into a bundle and stuffed it underneath a pile of damp raincoats. Helen came in and hung her red coat from its tab, straightening and brushing the velvet collar as she did so. As she went out, I slipped it from its peg and kicked it into a corner by the dog baskets.

Ha!

Dadda had taken our suitcases up to the smaller of the two attic rooms; our cousins had, as usual, commandeered the larger south-facing once.

'Cassandra, Helen, when you've finished up here will you come down and play with the boys?' Dreading the adult company downstairs himself, Feargal understood our vehement head-shaking only too well. 'Well, why don't you just unpack and then read a book until tea.'

We nodded. Dadda shrugged sympathetically and disappeared downstairs.

Her patent shoes tapping on the bare boards, Helen walked across to the big mahogany wardrobe and unlocked the door. It swung open with a long protesting creak, filling the room with the chilly scent of old clothes and mothballs. Holding her breath, she hung her two dresses and cardigans from the lower rail and arranged her underwear in neat piles on three of the six shelves that ran down the left-hand side of the cupboard. When she'd finished, she slid her shoes under the bed and turned to me. I was sitting on the bed, staring at the floor.

'Cassie, are you going to hang your clothes up?'

'No.'

'Mummie'll be cross with you.'

'I don't care.' I took a book from my case and flung myself stomach down on the mattress, which sagged under my weight. I leafed through the pages to find my place. It was my favourite story, about the adventures of a family of gruesome skeletons who lived in a haunted house. Helen said it was frightening, but it made me laugh aloud. I sprawled on the worn pink candlewick and propped my head on my hands. After a moment, as I knew she would, Helen picked up my suitcase and unpacked it. She smoothed out the creases from the crumpled blouses and cardigans and hung the wide-waisted frocks beside her own. Then she closed the little cardboard case and stood it side by side with hers. Straight lines always gave her a feeling of calm.

Her own book was *Heidi*. It was lying ready on the bedside table in its brightly covered dustjacket. She perched on the bed and opened it. Dadda had given her a beautiful green leather book-mark, stamped in gold with a complicated Celtic cross. I watched her trace the design with her fingertip, while her thoughts went with Heidi up the ladder to the Alp Uncle's hayloft. Once, years later, she told me that the sweet scent of that hayloft even over-powered the attic smells of mothballs and the damp candlewick.

It was quiet up there at the top of The Beeches. As darkness fell, I was aware of Helen's melodious thoughts drifting across the space between the two beds: *mountains, cowbells, evening*. My own tramped noisily around my mind, shouting as loudly as they pleased: *bones, rattle, night*.

As I say, adversity always brought us closer together.

Downstairs Denise and her mother were in the kitchen listening to the *Festival of Carols* on the radio and preparing the traditional supper of gammon, pork pies, Stilton, beetroot, tomatoes and let-tuce. Christine gave Pauline, who was at a bit of a loose end on these occasions, the thankless job of spearing pickled onions from a vast glass jar.

Feargal, imprisoned in the study with Brian and Uncle Derek, watched his father-in-law shut out the December night with a swish of heavy green baize.

'This your poison, Feargal?' said Derek, holding up a bottle of Amontillado.

'Oh no, Derek, thank you. I'll take a Jamieson, please, if you have one,' said Feargal, who took wry pleasure in contrariness.

'Oh. On the hard stuff already, are we?' Brian winked at Derek and sat down in his tapestry wing chair, his hand ready cupped for the sherry glass.

'Just a finger,' said Feargal mildly. He saw Derek wink back at his father as he poured a huge slug of whiskey into the tumbler.

'Soda?'

'Just water. A splash only.'

'Cheers, m'dears, and welcome.' Brian raised a crystal glass, beamed jovially. He enjoyed playing host.

Welcome. Feargal's vision swam. He raised his glass and silently toasted not Brian's hollow bonhomie but the sudden memory of Ithaca his word provoked. Five months ago, almost to the day, he had sat on the terrace at Peloros and Ariadne Vassos had raised her thimbleful of raki to him, and the word and the liquor had set his heart and mouth aglow. And after a day spent studiously in the library at Vathi, assuaging his helpless guilt in scholarly research, he returned each evening to the terrace and watched the sun set over the Ionian sea and talked to a woman whose dark voice was rich with the scent of flowers . . .

'*Slainté.*' Feargal took a mouthful of stale malt and let it run down his throat, wondering if its pale, flickering warmth would see him through the next five days.

*

In the kitchen Denise was leaning against the breakfast bar watching her mother make mayonnaise with an electric hand whisk.

'There, that's done. Perfect. Never had a failure yet.' Christine dipped a beringed finger into the oily yellow mixture. 'Ever since Saint Raphael last summer Daddy simply can't get enough of it, you know.'

Denise shuddered, for some reason reminded of Feargal's face in the mornings.

Christine untied her apron and hung it behind the pantry door. 'I'm thinking of doing a Cordon Bleu course next year; there's one on Friday mornings at the adult education centre in Henley.'

'Are you, Mother?' Pauline looked up from the vinegary fumes of the pickle jar, 'I didn't think you liked foreign food.' Christine and Brian had exchanged open moues of distaste over Pauline's ambitious paella at Easter, bemoaning the absence of what she considered the traditional turkey and trimmings. Derek had been mortified.

Christine unplugged the whisk, 'I don't like *foreign* food, Pauline, but I do like *French* cuisine. Look, not like that, Pauline dear, it will take all night.' She took over the fork and jabbed it viciously into the jar.

'Feargal likes garlic,' put in Denise, feeling that this news, which had in fact been obvious to her parents since they met him, might now be well received.

'Really? Hmm. Do you think he's got Spanish blood in him?' asked Christine, brandishing a large brown onion. 'I mean, the Armada and the Irish coast, one never knows. Or Romany, perhaps. And there's Cassie, of course.'

Denise blushed. Her mother's references to my and Dadda's colouring were always hurtful, even more so because the thought had crossed her own mind many times.

'Mummie, don't be horrible.' She opened a dresser drawer. 'Do you want the Bruges lace cloth for tonight?'

Christine smiled, 'Oh, yes, sweetheart, as it's the Clan Gathering. I think so, don't you?'

Clan and outsiders struggled together through the Christmas Eve supper.

I dropped beetroot on the Bruges lace, ate almost the entire bowl of pickles by myself, fed half-chewed scotch eggs to the labrador and belched loudly to confirm that I was full. Dadda, who was still drinking to forget, shook his head and giggled quietly to himself while a flustered Denise apologized and Helen blushed and kept her head bent to her plate. I was not alone in disgrace though: nervous Aunt Pauline had drained three large goblets of Chianti and her ravaged face was wet when she kissed us an early good-night and swayed off upstairs on the arm of her grim-faced husband. And after GB had made a last futile attempt to send our letters up the chimney to Father Christmas, we children were also packed off to bed.

It was cold up in the attic rooms, and not even Helen lingered in the glacial landing bathroom. Predictably, the rule was 'Ladies First' at The Beeches, and so I managed to leave a lingering post-pickle smell in the lavatory for the boys to enjoy. Or not.

In our room Helen and I burrowed between icy sheets and pulled them up over our ears. At first we were too shivery and excited to think of sleep, but by the time the clock in the hall chimed eleven the sheer weight of dampish bedding was gradually making us drowsy.

Which I am now, for here in Aghios Georghios it is late, too, and my eyes are gritty and dry from staring at a little screen all day. Perhaps the laptop and I will amuse ourselves by playing solitaire, or perhaps I'll press the buzzer and see if anyone is still there in the long polished corridors outside.

6 October 1999, 8.57 a.m.

It's here again, that faint chill in the air, unusually marked and early, too, this year. I fell asleep playing cards last night and forgot to close down the laptop. Now it's warm under my hands, like a heated stone in a Victorian muff. Perhaps I should switch off for a while, allow it some remission. It's been so docile these last weeks, obediently recording every word without a flicker of complaint, even during the frequent power cuts we get up here in the mountains.

In the short darkness last night, before the emergency generator cut in, it sat beside me, patiently waiting, as I am now, for the power to begin again.

GRANDPA BRIAN

Yes.

It was almost midnight, almost Christmas day, and I was still awake. My stomach was protesting at its load of undigested pickle vinegar, but above the gurgles I distinctly heard the staircase squeak. The third tread was cracked and the seventh, remembered from Christmas last year, groaned under heavy weights. There it was again.

Helen and I lay still in the darkness as someone tripped and swore outside on the landing.

'Blasted rug.' Grandpa Brian's voice, a thick, curdled whisper.

The latch clicked up, the door swung opened and a rectangle of light fell between the beds, a forked shadow in the middle of it.

'Girls?'

I willed Helen to be quiet, though she did not need to be told. We held our breath.

Grandpa Brian tiptoed in, carrying two bulging red woollen stockings. He hung one on the end of my bed and crossed to Helen's side of the room. There was a long silence and the sound of sheets rustling. Then a low, low murmur, 'Hush, my dear, it's only GB. I said I'd give you a Christmas Eve tuck-in, like last year.

Remember?' A pause. 'Is this you?' There was a light gasp.

After a long while, the door shut with exaggerated care and the feet creaked back downstairs to a bedroom on the galleried landing. The springs of Helen's bed were creaking rhythmically: she was sobbing. I jammed my fingers into my ears so hard that they drew blood.

I could have stopped it, you see. I knew it was wrong. I could have pretended I was having a nightmare and screamed for Dadda or Grannie Christine. I was big and strong, I could have launched myself at Grandpa Brian's back and pummelled him with my fists until he stopped. But these were things I thought of when I was older and more resourceful and had acquired a wide sexual confidence and experience of my own. By then it was too late for GB to be brought to justice by me or Helen or anyone else.

But, *why* didn't I call out?

I can't remember.

That's not true, of course. I can. I've always known which maggotty thought kept me lying there like a statue.

I was jealous.

Jealous. Oh yes, I was. I lay there while the frantic mantra of delight thudded through Grandpa Brian's brain: *Oh, God, you beautiful, beautiful child. My little blonde Helen. Oh, God, my little Denise. I love you, I love you. Oh.*

And so I lay there and despised and pitied and envied Helen and did . . . nothing.

I didn't even pretend to wake up when he'd gone. I kept my fingers tight-wedged and hunched my knees into my self-inflicted stomach ache.

After a while, I guess we both slept.

Early on Christmas morning the boys clacked open the wooden latch and pelted us with tangerine peel and silver paper from their stockings. Helen lay still, turned to the wall. But, belatedly heroic, I hitched up my pyjamas, charged across the room and beat the intruders back on to the landing with my pillow.

'Get out, you fucking bastards.'

That stopped them in their tracks, and they ran bulging-eyed downstairs, almost stumbling in their eagerness to tell on me. I leaned over the banisters and dropped two well-aimed gobs of spittle at their pyjamaed shoulders: with any luck the stains would be produced as evidence of my disgusting behaviour and keen eye.

And they were.

After a show trial at the breakfast table Grandpa Brian decreed that I should be beaten with a slipper by Feargal, who was under orders to lay it on severely or GB would see to the black-haired hooligan himself. How Dadda managed to make a joke of the whole thing and still spank me (lightly and with such an affectionate conspiratorial air) was and remains a mystery. Anyway, the drama served to distract everyone's attention from Helen, who spent most of the morning silently hunched over a jigsaw puzzle on the drawing-room side-table, complaining of stomach ache.

I was sympathetic, much to my mother's surprise.

'That's what happens when you eat too many pickles, isn't it, Mummie? Shall I bring her a hot water bottle?'

All day long I watched Grandpa Brian being Grandpa Brian. He took Grannie Christine's arm when we walked through the village to church. Fascinated, I watched his narrow grey-blond head as he sang the hymns, staring at the altar over the heads of other worshippers. At home he poured gin and tonics, stood for the National Anthem, carved turkey into reddish joints and doily slices of white, put on a funny hat and poured a flood of burning brandy over the pudding. When he had eaten and drunk his fill, he settled into a deep armchair in the drawing-room and snored while his women-folk did the washing up and the sky grew dark outside.

I saw Helen glance across at him then. He lay with his legs spread wide, his trousered belly resting on his thighs like a small suet in a cloth. Occasional coughs and snores emerged from his congested windpipe. Helen bent once more over her jigsaw and, when the pieces wouldn't fit, I saw that she was forcing them hard together with the heel of her hand.

At six Grannie Christine called me to the kitchen and told me to take GB a cup of tea. She handed me Grandpa's big half-pint cup with the golfing cartoon on it. Hot tea was already slopping in the saucer as I waddled along the passageway, and I was concentrating so hard on holding it steady that it was hardly surprising that just as I reached the hearthrug I caught my foot and pitched forward.

I cried out in pain. Luckily I had suffered only a small (but visible) burn on my wrist as the tea flew skywards. But Grandpa Brian screamed much, much louder when the scalding liquid flooded across his lap. Christine and Denise came running.

Dadda had seen what happened. He rushed over and scooped me up and carried me out to the kitchen, 'You *are* in the wars, Cassie love,' he said as he held my blistering wrist under the cold tap. It hurt a good deal, so I didn't even laugh when I heard Grandpa Brian in the cloakroom next door bellowing at Christine to be careful, Goddamn it, as she unbuttoned his steaming trousers.

My small scald soothed with butter, and sucking on a consoling toffee I sat by the fire in a wing chair, certain that Dadda wouldn't let me be punished twice in one day.

'Brian, sure she was only trying to be helpful,' he said cheerfully, dabbing at the stained rug with a tea towel. Grandpa Brian scowled at me and went bandy-legged upstairs to change.

I gave Dadda a big, grateful kiss at bedtime.

Helen was already asleep or pretending to be.

I could have said something then, too, I suppose, but I didn't.

*

Ouf, it's past seven. My hands are cramped from hours on the keyboard, and the computer is buzzing with strain. Our batteries need recharging, though it must be done quickly. There is, as John Lennon once remarked, 'a certain amount of hurry-up involved' now.

See how phlegmatic I am?

Silence.

I can't deny I sometimes miss the uncritical sympathy of friends.

6 October 1999, 10.23 p.m.

I must have slept, I think, for suddenly, outside, the corridors are empty.

The walls and floors of the old stone building are so thick that they won't hear me move slowly across the room. I unplug the computer and carry it back to bed with me. Switching on, I swim once more in its battery-fed aquarium glow. My shadow on the wall is a huddled blur – a blanket around my shoulders gives me the shape of a fortune-teller hunched over a crystal ball.

I like the silence here. Yet when I first arrived the lack of noise kept me awake into the early hours of the morning, until a thin drift of incense came through the shutters and the open window, followed by the first faint chant of the day echoing up from the chapel. Women's voices sound deeper and warmer than boys', I think. The rise and fall of Greek Orthodox plainsong sounds oddly modern, like Ella Fitzgerald singing torch hymns into the curve of the high vaulted ceiling:

> One day he'll come to me, my saviour strong,
> And take me in his arms
> Where I belong.

Sister Immaculata says they pray every day for everyone here and, though I find the idea more than a little odd, I'm still touched by their kindness and say nothing sceptical or smart. Sometimes she sits on the edge of my bed and eats a grape and asks me why I don't have visitors, and I tell her it's because I have asked people not to come. Which is almost true.

So. Another day ends. Bone weary, but still methodical, I shall back everything up to disk before I clear the screen and shut down for the night. A dipped finger tells me that my bed-time glass of warm milk cooled hours ago, and I must fish off the skin with a spoon before I can swallow the little plastic cupful of hoarded pills which will be more than enough to float me through the rest of the night.

7 October 1999, 8.15 a.m.

This morning I feel poorly: thick-tongued, gummy-eyed, dry-mouthed. There's pain in the usual places, though nothing too bad as yet. Busy white-robed sisters, bright-eyed from dawn devotions, are gliding in and out noting temperature, blood pressure, timing of micturition and bowel movements; they consult charts and administer precise dosages of medication.

Pain Management – it sounds like something one could make a useful career in. 'Yes, I'm a junior Pain Manager, with a diploma in Slight Discomfort. And you?' But I know better than to make fun of them. (I've read *Sons and Lovers*; I know what agony I should be feeling. And I'm not.) So, grateful and meek this morning, I've been lying still, letting them do what they want with me, while in my mind I'm travelling back to Kilburn, to the little terraced house in the sloping street, in the fateful winter of 1971.

ANSWERED PRAYERS

January and February are bitter. Denise is missing what she fondly remembers as the centrally heated Christmas splendour of The

Beeches' reception rooms, though for our own reasons Helen and I are still shivering from our nights in the attic. We are glad to be back in Kilburn, even if our frost-breath rimes the draughty windows and we have to wear extra protective layers of jumpers and thick socks over our pyjamas at night.

Helen is very quiet. Perhaps she feels I have let her down. My small scald cannot compare with her shameful, secret martyrdom. She cries at school a lot now: every playtime I find her hidden between pegloads of damp gaberdine in the cloakroom. Even my stabbing of the innocent Lenny Lennox fails to cheer her for long. When we get home Helen goes straight up to our room and lies on the bed until tea-time, rocking like a wound-up doll, her knees drawn up to her chin. She cries on in the dark at night, with her hand over her mouth to muffle the sound.

She is growing thinner than thin. Dadda keeps gently asking her what's wrong, but Helen shakes her head and won't say. Once Denise even calls *me* in to ask if *I* know, which just goes to shows how worried she is.

'Don't know,' I say, looking at her accusingly from under my thick black brows. I know she knows, because I can hear her thinking.

Don't say it. Don't you dare say a word. I'll ask, but don't ever, ever tell me, do you hear?

I say nothing.

March isn't far away now and after that it will be April, and in April it will be Easter and the holidays again. We are bound once more for the attic rooms, damp candlewick, mothballs and the squeaky stair. Every morning I stare at a picture of Jesus in my school Bible book and tell – order – him, silently scream at Him or God or anyone to hurry up and send a miracle to save Helen and me from The Beeches.

And d'you know what? They do.

The miracle announces its imminent arrival in the form of a mysterious moan in the night, so faint that at first I think it is a dream. Except it wakes me, and I can hear a terrified thought whimpering behind it: *Jesus, Mary and Joseph*.

Two weeks before Easter, the miracle becomes manifest.

Over breakfast Mother announces there has been a change of plan and we're not going to The Beeches after all.

Yes!

I feel a surge of proud gratitude. Yes! Thank you, Jesus, God, someone, thank you.

This feeling curdles later that morning when I realize that the reason why we cannot go is that Dadda is suddenly very, very ill. He went to see the doctor a month ago, but now he is suddenly too thin and weak and yellow to go to school for the end of term and the doctor comes out to see him twice in a week. Dr McKenzie and Denise hold whispered talks in the hall, but though I listen hard, lying flat on my stomach right up against the landing banisters, I can't understand what he is saying. But as she closes the door and leans her head against it, I know that the only thing running through my mother's mind is panic.

It's a bad miracle that's happened, and it's all my fault.

In the park I pick guilty handfuls of daffodils and stuff them into jam jars for Dadda's bedside table. When Helen and I creep in to his room he is lying propped on pillows in the middle of the bed, not on his usual side. His face is yellow as old newspaper and his cheeks are sucked right in, as if he is trying to swallow something very sour, and his eyes are different, bigger and darker in his face. How have I not noticed these changes before? I'm suddenly frightened.

He likes the flowers though.

'Lovely, Cassie, perfect. Now, girls,' he says, in a funny wheezy whisper, almost managing to turn his head to both of us, 'each of you, tell me a story. Take it in turns to choose.'

So Helen and I sit on his bed most afternoons that Easter fort-night and tell him back the stories he has told us across the years. We do a good job, too, because sometimes he cheers up completely and laughs and laughs until he can't catch his breath and we get frightened and shout for Mother to come. And sometimes his eyes fill with tears and he clasps our hands in his, which feel strangely dry.

But at night I have bad, Cassandra-like dreams. I dream that I am trying to wake Dadda up, only I can't find him anywhere, so I run through the streets on my big flapping bare feet asking every-one if they've seen my father and no one has. Though I don't want to, in the end I force myself to ask Mother when Dadda is going to be well again. She begins to say 'soon', but then her eyes fill up and her face goes red and shiny and she says, 'I just don't know.'

And I wish she hadn't said anything, because now I am really afraid. Perhaps I am dreaming all this trouble into the house. The moaning at night is so loud now I have to wrap the pillow tight around my ears to stop it. I don't think Helen understands how serious things are. I try to explain, but she just sighs and tells me to go to sleep, and her voice sounds so much like Mother's I want to laugh out loud, but I can't because I am too sad to laugh my Big Bad laugh.

The end was my fault, too.

It was a Saturday morning in May, just before our eleventh birthday. Mother took Helen into town to buy her a new pair of shoes.

'You're in charge, Cassandra,' she told me. 'Take Dadda in his tea and biscuit at ten thirty. Let him be till then, because he's had a bad night.' I remember Mother looked tired, too, probably because of Dadda's non-stop coughing.

The house was quiet when they'd gone. I was curled up on

a chair downstairs, reading *Jane Eyre* and enjoying it because her troubles were even worse than mine. The pages turned and turned, and it was almost twelve when I remembered and eventually trundled along to Dadda's room carrying a cup of tea with a digestive biscuit balanced on the saucer. I stood outside for a moment, trying to swallow a big mouthful of dry crumb from the McVitie's I'd pinched from the packet in the pantry. When my mouth was almost empty I edged the door open with my foot and went in.

Dadda's room was cold and smelled like a disinfected toilet. I crossed the room, concentrating on keeping the cup steady, because Mother had had a pale blue carpet laid in the bedroom and she always said it showed the smallest stain. The bedside table was covered in bottles of pills, and it took me a while to squeeze the cup and saucer in between them.

Dadda was still fast asleep. Softly I called him, 'Dadda, Dadda, sorry it's late. I've brought you your tea.' But he must have had a very bad night indeed, because he didn't move, and I didn't want to wake him on account of all those broken nights, so I left the tea to cool, though it wasn't very hot by then anyway, and went back downstairs to see how Jane and Mr Rochester were going to get out of the fix they were in.

When Mother came back she hung up her coat and went straight upstairs to see Dadda. Helen danced around in front of me like a soppy ballerina, holding out her skirts and showing off her new shoes which were shiny black patent as usual, this time with ribbon bows. I was just telling her how unfair it was that I only had my big brown lace-ups, when I heard Mother make a strange loud, yelping noise.

I jumped up: I must have spilled the tea on the pale carpet after all.

But it wasn't that, of course.

Mother's face when we ran upstairs was frightening, as if someone had sat on it and squashed it out of shape. She was sitting on the bed, holding Dadda's bluish purple hand and saying, 'Ohnoohnoohnoohnoohno.' She turned her funny face to me and said, 'Where *were* you, Cassandra? Where *were* you? Why weren't you *here*?'

'I was reading,' I said and sat down with a bump on the pale blue carpet as if someone had cut my strings.

I knew what had happened. I wasn't stupid.

9 October 1999, 6.15 a.m.

It's raining again today. I can hear it falling in the soft earth of the courtyard outside and dripping from the dusty trees. There is a smell of damp earth and a first curl of autumn bonfire smoke.

It was raining that day, too.

Though it was not in autumn but in late spring that we buried Dadda.

A FUNERAL

Despite the heavy showers, and the conspicuous absence of most of the Ulster Byrds, there was quite a crowd at the cemetery that May morning. Squeezed around the open graveside (no cremation for Dadda; his mother would have been pleased, if she'd troubled to come), we huddled together like black sheep in the shelter of a dripping yew tree. Denise scowled from under the veiled brim of her hat and gripped Grannie Christine's arm. 'Who *are* they all, Mummie? Where on earth did Feargal *meet* them?' It was incongruous that people she didn't know should insist on saying goodbye to her husband. Couldn't they understand that she wanted to be alone with him, this one last time? Surrounded by curious black-clad strangers, it was impossible to summon up the feel of his fingers or the weight of his warm body or to recall the cool evening mist over a riverbank in Donegal.

The priest swung the censer about and Grannie Christine flapped a hand and coughed pointedly. Another squally burst of rain passed over us as Denise obeyed the priest's urging and drew Helen and me forward to the graveside.

'We have to put our flowers in, now, darlings.'

'In the hole, Mummie? They'll get dirty.' Helen is reluctant. I am, too.

'It doesn't matter. Look, throw them on to the . . . box down there, where Dadda is,' says Denise and I hear a retching sound in her throat. 'Like this.' And she holds out her rose and lets it drop. I look at her face. Mummie is crying now as I have never seen her cry. *Oh, Feargie, Feargie. Where are you?* Big retching sobs have her doubled up as if someone invisible is punching her in her middle. *Now I'm all on my own.* I put my arm around her black-coated waist, and, astonishingly, she lets me keep it there.

Helen is very brave. She steps forward, ignoring the mud on her new black patent-leather shoes, and lets fall the arum lily she has carried all morning. It floats down into the hole like a green boat with a white curved sail. Still holding Mummie's waist I lift up my own bruised flower. Perhaps I can throw it from here, without letting go of her. And if I throw it hard enough Dadda will hear me. I grunt as I hurl the lily into the grave. It skitters down over the polished wood, dislodging trowelfuls of earth.

Dadda? Bye-bye?

Nothing.

Nothing?

Nothing at all.

Back at the house in Kilburn it is hot and crowded and noisy. There is a crush of people trying to talk to Denise. One by one they introduce themselves. There's a man called Timothy from the publishers', who has a smooth voice and speaks without stopping and promises to be in touch about Dadda's last translation. There are two old women, weeping uncontrollably, who have to be introduced by a colleague and turn out to be a Miss Hackett and a Miss Farlow from the Academy. Then there is a beery man called Dermott from The Spaniard, bluff and already inappropriately cheerful.

As Denise sends Dermott over to the buffet, a tall thin man in black corduroy shakes his head in mute sympathy and turns to a woman standing just behind him. His hand at her elbow, he draws her forward.

'Mrs Byrd, I'm sure you know . . . ?' His face is turned aside, and Denise does not hear the name he is murmuring.

A short but imposing woman, smartly dressed, lifts back her veil slips a gloved hand around Denise's. Her eyes are ringed in black, like those on an Egyptian sarcophagus.

'So sorry, my dear.' The voice is foreign, low and resonant. 'And this must be Helen?' she stoops to kiss the shiny blonde head. 'And Cassandra.' To my surprise, she buries her nose in my nest of curls. 'Poor lamb.'

Her skin smells of rich dark flowers.

Denise pulls me gently back to her side.

'I'm sorry, I don't think we've met.'

'No. We haven't. I am . . . Ariadne Vassos.'

The pause for recognition is out of habit, and she moves smoothly on, 'I am appearing in your husband's play this autumn.'

'Oh.' Denise's voice is flat. Suddenly she is jealous now of all these people who took up Feargal's time. '*Antigone*.'

Ariadne Vassos. Denise tries not to stare at the dark eyes and strong, hooked nose. The woman is talking.

'I had great respect for Feargal, Mrs Byrd. A talent, a spirit, a good man.'

Denise nods emptily. The gathering is thinning now, Dermott leading a less than discreet move back to The Spaniard, where, as a long-time friend of Feargal Byrd, he has organized a bit of an Irish wake.

The foreign woman watches them go and smiles. 'Pouf. I hate funerals.' Then she collects herself and says firmly, 'Denise, if I may call you that, I feel I almost know you through Feargal. Denise, when my first husband died, years ago, everybody said to me, "If there is anything I can do . . ." It was meaningless and I refused, as one does. I was too sad, too proud. But now I know that one should never lightly refuse an offer of help. So let me say something specific. Denise,' she takes my mother's hand, peering with frank interest into her puzzled, swollen face, 'I have a house called Peloros, on the island of Ithaca. If you and the girls would like to come and stay, if you can spare the time, you would be most welcome.' She sees my mother begin a polite refusal. 'Ah, but don't answer now. Call me, whenever you have had time to think it over properly.' She hands Denise a card. 'Goodbye. I shall hope to see you in the summer.'

She stands in front of Helen and me and touches us on the shoulder, 'Bye-bye, little ones. Perhaps you'll come and see me in the Ionian sunshine, on Ithaca where the Sirens lived. Yes?'

I clear my throat. 'The Sirens didn't live on Ithaca. Odysseus did, Dadda told me.'

Ariadne laughs and all around the room, people fall silent and stare at us.

'You may be right, Cassandra. But perhaps they lived there all the time and were only trying to call him home. What do you think?'

She gives Denise one last impulsive hug and is gone. I stare after her retreating figure. Further down the street a long black car is purring blue-grey fumes and a man gets out to hold an umbrella over the foreign lady. She turns and looks back up at us. Especially at me.

Come. Don't be afraid.

I lift up my free hand and wave back.

That night Helen crept into my bed. We lay curled like spoons, first me on the outside, protecting her, and then later, when we half woke and turned over, she lay against my broad back, though it would have been hard for anyone to tell whether she was actually a shield or a burden. Before morning I woke and found myself alone, rocking, rocking, like a crazy chair that cannot stop. On the other side of the room, in her own bed, I could hear Helen rocking, too.

11 October 1999, 8.00 a.m.

BARRING THE DOOR

We didn't go to Ithaca that summer. Or the next.

Though everyone advised Mother against taking major decisions in the months after Dadda's death, I think she probably couldn't bear to stay in the tiny terraced house without him.

It was understandable. Dadda's books were still on the shelves of his writing-room, his clothes were in the wardrobe, his jacket hung on a peg by the door and his shoes were dusty and curled in the storm porch, but *he* wasn't anywhere. That summer there were no stories, no giggles, no jokes; his typewriter didn't clatter and when Helen and I looked out of the window there was no red cigarette pinpoint glowing and dimming in the knot garden at night. At school the other pupils avoided talking to us, as if your father dying could be catching.

Though I wasn't always sure he was dead. Sometimes I heard his voice saying my name. Not calling me exactly but saying my name, quietly and sadly, over and over again, just behind my head. One Saturday morning his voice was so near I thought I'd go and look for him. I walked through the streets, asking everyone I met if they'd seen my dadda, Mr Feargal Byrd, who wasn't dead because he talked to me.

Later Mother came and found me in the park sitting at the top of the slide. 'Come down, Cassandra,' she said in her tired voice. 'Look. I've brought your shoes.' I slid down slowly and took them, slipping them on to my dusty old feet. Then she took me by the hand, and without saying a word we trudged back up the hill together in silence. At home, wearily, she sent me upstairs to wash. I sat in the bath, glancing every few minutes over my shoulder at the half-glazed door in case she thought better of it and came raging through in a fit of uncontrollable temper. But she didn't. I think she'd already forgotten I was there.

Though it was sometimes useful, in other ways Mother's new vagueness was worrying. Helen and I watched the piles of envelopes mount up unopened on Dadda's desk. The house seemed to fill with grey clutter and within a few months her beloved knot garden had disappeared under a tangle of unkempt weeds. She didn't seem to notice. Every night she went down to the phone box and spent an hour on a reverse charge call to Grandpa Brian and Grannie Christine and came back just before our bedtime, tear-stained and full of headache from weeping. While she was out Helen and I did our homework (badly) and when she returned we crept around like sweet considerate mice (quite an achievement for *me*, I felt), making her mugs of warm milk, which she never drank. But it was no use. By July Mother had given up her brief career as a plucky, independent widow and we had all three moved back to The Beeches.

In what had been the boys' room on the attic landing Mother unpacked our books and filled the painted pine bookcase. All the old familiar titles were all there: the *Iliad*, *The Hardy Boys*, the *Odyssey*,

Swallows and Amazons, The Golden Bough, King Solomon's Mines.
We began to cheer up. But then it appeared that this was to be my room and that Helen was to sleep on her own in the room we'd once shared, across the landing.

'Oh no,' I said firmly. 'No, we two must sleep in the same room. We must.' I shouted until Mother cried and Grandpa Brian came upstairs to tell me to think of others for once, because I was ungrateful wretch. I kicked and yelled, but it made no difference, everyone had decided it was for the best.

So that night and every night after I simply waited until everyone had gone downstairs, then crept across the landing to Helen's room. I crawled under the covers of my old unmade bed, dislodging clouds of dust from the musty candlewick and muffling my sneezes in the damp, stained pillow. Helen didn't say a word. Every morning I tiptoed back across the landing, so they'd find me in my room if they came looking.

Then, a month later, the seventh stair squeaked, late at night. Helen gasped and sat bolt upright.

I slipped out of bed and stood against the door just as the thick wooden latch slowly lifted from its notch.

'Go away,' I said loudly.

The latch stopped moving.

'Cassandra? What are you doing in there, girl? You've been told, now get back into your own room,' said Grandpa Brian's voice.

'No. Go away.'

Behind me, Helen moaned. I felt the latch fall outside its slot as the door moved inwards. There was nothing to stop him now. I closed my eyes and wished that one of Dadda's heroes was here to help us: Ajax or Achilles, under a bronze helmet a-sway with vast plumes, armour chinking confidently in the moonlight. Suddenly I felt a surge of inspired bravery. With a cheerful thumbs up to Helen, I shoved the door back a little and slipped two chubby fingers into the gap where the latch had been. I took a deep breath and shouted loudly, 'Grandpa Brian? Can you hear me? I've bolted the door with my fingers. If you come in, you'll break them.'

'What?' The voice on the other side of the door was startled, 'Don't be ridiculous, Cassandra, open up.'

The door gave an exploratory inward push, and my knuckles bent back.

'Owww. Stoppit, GB.'

'Cassandra, I'll not tell you again. Get out of there right now, do you hear me, girl? Back in your own room. Helen? Tell her to get out.'

But Helen was sitting up in bed, her hands around her face, staring at the door where my fingers made a fleshy, horizontal V-sign against the wood.

Perhaps he was drunk. Or perhaps he just didn't believe me. Anyway, suddenly the door jerked forward and I heard the crack a second before I felt the pain. It hurt much more than I'd imagined it would. I screamed, and then Helen was gently pulling my fingers from the latch and I screamed again. Unhampered now, the door swung open.

I felt cold and dizzy and thought I was going to be sick. The room went patchy black and then I was lying on the floor. I looked up and saw mother's slippered feet running across the worn carpet on the landing. While I swam in and out of the room, I could hear Helen shouting. I couldn't remember ever hearing her shout before, but here was this weird, carrying voice accusing Grandpa Brian of hurting her in bed.

GB was shouting her down, ordering her to be quiet and telling everyone else to ignore her because she was hysterical. But Helen wouldn't stop. Then he swore loudly. It was all a bloody lie, he said, and called her a filthy-minded whore.

My mother took two strides across the room and slapped her father's face.

Then, as everything fell horribly silent, the air seemed to swirl and drain away from me. When I woke up, Mother was kneeling beside me. I felt dizzy and sick and my fingers were throbbing as if they were caught in a giant mousetrap.

When I could stand, Denise took Helen and me down to the kitchen and bathed my hand in witch hazel. Then Mother sat the pair of us in front of the range, which was still warm, heated up milk in a pan and made three mugs of hot chocolate. We drank them in silence. Mother just kept dipping cotton wool into the witch hazel and squeezing the liquid over my swollen blackening fingers. No one said anything at all.

We slept three in a bed in Mother's room that night, and it was almost worth the pain to be sandwiched warm and safe in the bed between them. In the morning Mother took us to the hospital in Reading and held me tight while the doctor taped and strapped my two broken fingers together. 'Caught in a door, eh?' the doctor said. 'You won't do that again, will you, young lady?'

My eyes wide with bone-ache, I shook my head. They made me swallow two dusty pills which stuck to the roof of my mouth and made me gag. But when they put my arm in a big white sling I felt like one of Dadda's heroes after all, and I walked out of the hospital with my coat draped over my shoulders like a battle cloak over my honourable wounds.

At first, back at The Beeches that lunchtime, life seemed set to go on exactly as before. Grandpa Brian stood in his usual place at the head of the table, pharaoh-like with crossed carving knife and steel, waiting for us to bow our heads for Grace. He affected not to notice that I only had one hand to pray with.

In the silence, his voice intoned, 'Dear Lord, bless this food to our use, and us to Thy service. Amen.'

Astonishingly, no one said 'Amen'.

I squinted around from under half-shut eyelids.

Denise and Grannie Christine were already sitting down. I tugged at Helen's hem with my good arm, and we sat down, too, our eyes goggling in surprise. Wordlessly Grannie Christine poured gravy over my chicken and helped me to vegetables. For once she heaped up the roast potatoes and didn't insist on my having carrots like everyone else. I was ravenous, but cutting the meat one-handed was difficult. Noticing that I was struggling, Mother reached over and cut my chicken into bite-sized portions. Everyone ate in silence: five mouths chewing stolidly up and down.

When Grandpa Brian speared the last drumstick and offered it to me as a second helping, I snorted and shook my head: I was on the winning side at last and would make the most of it.

'No *thank you*, GB!' I said, in Helen's sweetest voice.

That night Mother made up my bed next to Helen's and moved all her things up to the room opposite us. Grannie Christine helped her, and they tramped up and down the stairs, passing each other on the landing in charged silence.

A TRIUMPH OF WOMEN

Grannie and GB shared a large bay-fronted master suite on the first floor, so I was surprised when next morning I saw GB come out of the back guest-room with a towel over his shoulder. As I stepped out of his path I made a point of sheltering my bandaged arm, but he pretended not to see me and strode off down the corridor to the spare bathroom whistling some tuneless hymn. I hugged myself. It looked as though there was going to be a punishment after all. No one heard what Grannie Christine said to GB when they finally spoke, though later that day I heard her thoughts buzzing around her head like furious wasps: *animal, bastard, shame.*

Within a few days it became clear that there were ripples of change running through the entire household. I overheard Grannie Christine on the phone telling people that Brian had suffered a slight stroke and would be convalescing at home for the next few months. This simple lie deterred visitors and explained his absence from the bar of the Fox and Hounds, the Masons and the golf club. But I was pretty sure that Grannie Christine simply wanted him where she could see him. Overnight, Grandpa Brian had been tried and sentenced to become a live-in ghost, existing on the margins of our lives. I crowed to myself, nudging Helen each time GB was scolded or criticized by his newly assertive wife and daughter. I couldn't wait for Christmas so that Uncle Derek and the boys could see how low the mighty head of the Forrester clan was fallen.

Helen didn't join in my glee. She didn't want to look at Grandpa Brian, sat as far away from him as possible at mealtimes, and shrank back against the wall if she passed him in the hall. Interestingly, I noticed that she was also reserved and distant with my mother. At first I brightened, thinking that Mother might turn to me for comfort instead. But, however kind she'd been on the night of the drama, Denise's attitude towards me soon reverted to the familiar eye-rolling distaste.

But at least I'd gone up in my own esteem and in Helen's, too. My dramatically broken fingers had more than redeemed my past silence; that summer she almost forgot I was her ugly, embarrassing sister and treated me as a loyal supporter and even, alarmingly, as a friend. This new, uneasy closeness didn't fill the dreadful space left by Dadda's absence, but it was a comfort of sorts.

Mother and Grannie Christine also became closer that summer, united in unspoken disgust with GB. Encouraged by Grannie

Christine, Mother grew stronger and more independent. She found a job as assistant to the membership secretary at the golf club. She learned to drive and bought a little car. Grannie Christine spent a good deal of time out of the house doing voluntary work: she was Chairman of the Pensioners' Lunch Club and a tireless supporter of Meals on Wheels. On Saturdays in summer she and Mother went clothes shopping together in Henley and came back with a flock of brightly coloured carrier bags. They bought pretty dresses for Helen and even managed to find a new frock for me: good-quality dark blue wool, with tiny gold buckles on shoulders, pockets and cuffs. I was rather proud of my new military elegance and toyed briefly with the idea of going into the services, saluting myself each night in the wardrobe mirror.

It was around this time that Grannie Christine also decided to have central heating installed in the attic bedrooms and to have them redecorated. GB was not consulted. Mother and daughter bought new beds and bedding, mattresses, wardrobes, dressing-tables, curtains and carpets, and by the end of August Helen and I were sleeping under crisp modern duvets (mine had planets and shooting stars on the cover) and the smell of musty blankets and mothballs had vanished from The Beeches for ever, replaced by cotton and fresh paint.

Grandpa Brian still spent most of his time immured in his cell in the back guest room, which he called his 'den', and emerged only at mealtimes. He seemed diminished somehow, his eyes watery and pale, a shiny pink bald spot gleaming through the grey-blond hair when he bent his head over his plate at mealtimes.

No one said Grace any more.

In September Helen and I started at the local secondary school in Marlow. Denise dropped us outside and gave both of us (yes!) a cheery wave before speeding off to the golf club. We were wearing our smart new uniform: maroon blazers with piped cording and a badge with a Latin motto. I remember how impressed my new teachers were when (thanks to Dadda's long-ago teaching) I translated it enthusiastically on the first day.

'Touch me not with impunity.'

And I knew what it meant, too.

12 October 1999, 8.00 a.m.

HONEYMOON

That summer it felt as though our lives were about to restart.

With Mother newly confident and independent, her self-esteem shored by Grannie Christine's unshakeable moral superiority and the public disgrace of GB, I began to feel more optimistic. Perhaps we were emerging from the disaster and misery of Dadda's death and would now become ordinary, happy people or at least as ordinarily unhappy as we had once been. Perhaps, despite all the evidence, the world could still be promising and fair.

But I spoke too soon: within a few months it was apparent that Mother didn't enjoy her new independence and self-reliance nearly as much as she claimed; and by the following spring she was engaged to be married.

Anthony Colindale. More than a quarter-century later, even saying his name is enough to make a gulletful of vomit swill into my throat. (I can visualize Helen's grimace of distaste – she always deplored what she came to call my 'tabloid vehemence'. Even now I can hear her murmuring reproof, 'Oh, Cassandra, *please* . . .')

But then I'm not Helen. Unlike her, I haven't chosen to glide over the surface of life making as few ripples as possible. And anyway she isn't here to shake her head, is she? So why hold back?

Why indeed? A quick surge of hate has left me charged and energetic. Though I've been dreading this part of the story, now I find I actually relish the opportunity to say how irredeemably, undeniably, irreparably bloody awful Mr Anthony Colindale really was.

Anthony Colindale wore vividly patterned sweaters, that's what I remember first about him. Vividly patterned sweaters and bulky cord trousers, and his hair was combed across his head from a low parting, above a face that was as soft and freckled and unfinished as the Pillsbury Doughboy. He smoked a pipe.

Tony Colindale was a widower. He had met GB fifteen years earlier, when he had joined Forresters' estate agency as an ambitious and hard-working junior salesman. From the outset he worked with stubborn tenacity, arriving at the office a good hour before his colleagues and staying behind long after the other young men left to walk across the high street to the pub. He wasn't missed there by his work-mates, who grew to detest Tony's cliché-ridden speech and earnest, toadying manner. Tony ignored them. He worked through lunch at his desk, keeping his contact files rigorously up to date and building close links with anyone who could help his career: local government officials, politicians, journalists and developers. Soon Tony earned more commission than any other salesman in the group. He lived in a modest modern flat close to the office, saved his wages and bided his time.

After seven years he was ready, financially and professionally, to move on and left to set up his own small business in the centre of Henley, managing somehow to obtain GB's blessing for his venture. In the same year Tony married an MP's daughter, moved to a large new bungalow on the outskirts of the town and began to build Colindale Associates into one of the fastest-growing estate agencies in the area. Shrewdly, he continued to keep in touch with his old mentor and made sure that the Colindales and Forresters dined together every few months. GB and Tony played golf together regularly, and the older man sometimes suspected that his protégé was allowing him to win.

When, two years before Dadda died, Tony's wife Jessica was killed in a road accident, Grannie Christine felt sorry for the stricken, young-middle-aged widower. She invited him over for dinner, initially on his own, and then to partner one of the growing band of divorcées among her friends. Tony was affable and paid flattering attention to his hostess and his fellow guests. As a result, Tony Colindale was one of the handful of friends Grannie Christine allowed GB to see after his Disgrace.

However, her pity did not quite extend to inviting him to the new-style Forrester-Byrd family lunches. So Tony would drive up to The Beeches every Sunday afternoon in his vintage Bentley, swerve to a halt in a hail of gravel and honk the horn to tell us he had arrived. If he mistimed his arrival and found us still eating he would pace around awkwardly in the hall, lobbing clichés through the doorway to the dining-room. 'No, don't worry about me, I'm fine out here, absolutely. Don't hurry. Yes indeed, Christine, better in than out today. Weather for ducks out there; raining cats and dogs as far as the eye can see. Still, behind every cloud, eh?'

I pulled a face. Dadda had always given us funny, explicit warnings against the use of clichés – though as you can see I've become more tolerant with age and now accept, as a writer-lover once ruefully told me, that some words stick together like two dogs fucking . . .

When the meal was finally over and we all emerged, Tony fished in a carrier bag and dispensed the gifts he had brought, which were the same every week: half a bottle of scotch for GB, flowers for Grannie Christine and Mother, a carton of Quality Street (which she never shared) for Helen and a thoughtful box of

Maltesers (the chocolates with the less fattening centres) for me.

'Thank you, Mr Colindale.'

'Uncle Tony, please.'

Christ.

That done, he and GB would retreat to 'the den' for an hour's whisky and chat. Later, he began to stay on for tea. In fact, his presence seemed to bring about an Early Release for GB, for after a few months, whenever Denise and Christine settled down in the drawing-room to watch the television, Brian and Tony were invited to join them. Soon Tony's vividly patterned arm was resting casually along the back of the sofa behind my mother's neck.

In spring the following year Tony left his mentor GB to his own devices after lunch and began taking Denise out for long Sunday afternoon drives in the country.

Ha! Tony Colindale . . .

Yes, there are many wax dolls on the shelves of my memory and I make sure I still twist the pins now and again, in passing. The crude likeness of 'Uncle Tony' is still recognizable after all these years, with its tuft of greying hair and cravat of brightly coloured wool.

My mother married Tony Colindale in July 1973 at Reading Register Office. A friend of Grandpa Brian's took the official pictures and several of Brian's old cronies came up and congratulated him on his excellent recovery, though on close inspection I could see that GB and Grannie Christine were still not holding hands. I fidgeted with the seams of my blue wool frock which was by now uncomfortably tight under the arms. Helen was stunning in cream velvet. Mother leaned on Tony's arm, slenderly erect in a tailored grey suit. The couple wore matching white gardenias. After the reception at the golf club Mr and Mrs Colindale – where did that leave us,

Cassandra and Helen Byrd? – departed for an extended honey-moon in Cyprus.

Helen and I stared glumly after the Bentley as it disappeared around the corner. She clutched my hand. We hadn't thought to ask, but perhaps Mother intended *our* summer holiday to be two tedious months at The Beeches in the company of Grannie Christine and the partially rehabilitated GB. I looked at the crooked tip of my finger, wondering if I would be brave enough to do the same thing again. Surely once was enough?

Happily, my courage was never put to the test.

A few days later, following a series of mysterious phone calls, Ariadne Vassos suddenly appeared, scooped up Helen and me and took us to Ithaca for the summer. It seemed Mother had not entirely abandoned us after all.

14 October 1999, 2.00 p.m.
And so we came to Ithaca for the first time, twenty-six years ago, in the summer of 1973.

As we came over the hill on the road to Peloros that July after-noon, we would have passed below this very convent where I lie now. Did a shiver of presentiment rise up young Cassandra's nape as she went by? It should have.

ARIADNE

Ariadne had inherited the house called Peloros from her second husband, a shipping magnate. His fortune had somehow allowed him to keep mention of the place off most post-war maps of Ithaca, so even at the height of her fame as a film and stage star, Ariadne spent long summers there largely untroubled by the attentions of paparazzi or celebrity-hungry tourists.

Helen and I arrived with her by private boat from Athens in the mesmerizing heat of late July. We were met by Susie Musselbergh, a London friend of Ariadne's, who at thirty-five had suddenly found herself divorced, childless and unemployed and had embraced the idea of becoming the housekeeper at Peloros.

Together with two porters, Susie brought us and our luggage across the island's central ridge in a pair of horse-drawn wagons, protected from the heat by swaying white canopies. The track led gently upwards through sandy-floored woods, heady with the scent of pine, and then descended to the sea again, winding between terraced hillsides of twisted grey olive trees. An hour after landing we were passing under a stone archway into an echoing courtyard, where a vine-shaded cloister ran around three sides and, at the far end, a flight of steps with a metal railing led up to a square Venetian tower.

'Darlings, welcome,' said Ariadne, putting an arm around our weary shoulders.

Susie showed us to our room, which, excitingly, was on the top floor of the tower. I pushed open the shutters and let in the hot late afternoon sun, and the sound of goat bells floated down from the hillside on the breeze.

Ariadne herself had designed the interior of Peloros. Our room had white walls, two carved wooden beds with crisp white linen draped about by a film of mosquito muslin and a fine antique dressing-chest and mirror. A floor of worn and polished tiles was cool to my feet (bare, ah yes, what bliss), while a door hung with shading louvres opened out on to a balcony, bright with red flowers.

When we had washed Helen and I went down to the terrace and sat for the first time in those wide rattan chairs under the vine, and we drank iced lemonade and talked to Ariadne like grown-ups, while appetizing smells drifted out from Susie's kitchen and the sun sank with wonderful slowness into the sea.

In the morning, because there was no one to tell me not to, I went down to the beach at dawn. I lay on my back in the shallows, watching the sun rise red-gold behind the mountain while my hot pee ebbed out into the pale chill of the sea.

When I got back Helen was still asleep.

Her face was sad even in repose, but still so perfectly beautiful it was hard to be sympathetic. I leaned over and let water drip from my hair on to her cheek and she started awake, not knowing at first where she was. I shook my wet head at her like a dog, and she rolled out of the way of the deluge, cross and laughing all at the same time.

Then Ariadne called up the tower stairs, telling us to come down for breakfast, and we pulled on shorts and T-shirts and raced downstairs and out into the sunshine.

It soon became clear that Ariadne had more than a temporary change of scene planned for us. She was observing us, pondering what she saw. Perhaps she realized that Dadda's death, and also something else, had made us cling together too closely. I think she saw that our claustrophobic relationship could easily become destructive: we needed space between us to grow healthily. Like a surgeon beginning a long, delicate operation she began to separate us emotionally, to give us the confidence to stand apart.

It was intelligently done. It should have worked. Of course, none of us knew then how long and difficult a process that separation would turn out to be, neither could we foresee that life, and also death, would wash us together repeatedly, like bodies inextricably tangled in wreckage.

Sometimes I wonder if all Ariadne ever achieved was to put us in a stronger position to damage each other. But, then, *we* chose to do what we did. We alone were responsible for the pain we inflicted on each other.

*

Francis.

No. Not yet.

I can't talk about Francis yet. Sometimes I wonder if I ever will. But in the moments of calm lucidity, here in the last white room of my life, I accept that if I want to float free, human and unembittered in whatever time remains to me, I must one day talk about Francis.

But not yet.

So I tell myself to go back, go on, ignore the debris that is everywhere, stretching to the horizon in all directions. Pick a route through the littered past – aim for the open sea and keep going.

Though she may occasionally have been impetuous and wrongheaded when she intervened in our affairs, I have to believe that Ariadne always acted for what she perceived to be our good. And that first summer in Greece she opened doorways to a future richer than we would have ever have known without her.

The library at Peloros, for example.

The library was a vast book-lined room, smelling of leather and brown-edged pages. The tall windows were hung with muslin to diffuse the bright sunlight. There were deep chairs and a broad leather-topped table and reading lights which gave out a soft golden glow when the book you had opened in the morning carried you through an afternoon and on into the dusk.

Many of my old talismanic favourites stood guard along on her shelves, more expensively bound than Dadda's perhaps, but still containing the familiar, soothing words.

Hera turned their chariot back. The Hours unyoked their long-maned horses for them, tethered them at their ambrosial mangers and tilted the chariot against the burnished wall by the gate, while the two goddesses rejoined the other gods and sat down on golden chairs.

There were pictures, too; art books: Mediaeval, Renaissance, Baroque, Impressionist, Abstract. There were collections of photography, from early sepia valentines to high-magnification fibre-optic pictures of the heart. I pored over them all, left them around the room propped open at favourites: Raphael, Monet, Cézanne, Doisneau, Man Ray, Cartier-Bresson. In my thirteen-year-old mind I began to understand that images could be more valuable and vivid than anything we experience in real life, that they have a power to touch and shape our innermost selves. And, most important, they could be there whenever we needed them. Occasionally I found new titles lying on the table, carefully book-marked at pictures that pointed me towards ever more exciting mental journeys.

Which is my excuse for the fact that I 'borrowed' several of Ariadne's books and hid them under my bed, planning to take them back to England with me at the end of the summer. At night, I liked to reach under the bed and run my fingers over their smooth-ridged spines, and if Ari ever noticed their absence she never mentioned it. But sometimes my cache of volumes mysteriously disappeared, and I decided that Susie Musselbergh had discovered them and replaced them on the shelves. Certainly I often found her in our room when I came back unexpectedly. Once I caught her lying on Helen's bed, her face buried in the soft white pillow.

'What are you doing?' I asked.

'What do you think?' she said, hastily springing to her feet and clutching at a copy of the *Iliad* which I knew I had hidden under my mattress the previous day.

I pulled a face. 'Naughty Helen! You'd better tell Ariadne.'

Susie flushed brick-red. 'It's not Helen,' she said, raising her chin. 'She would never do anything like that.'

I sighed, sensing another wasp buzzing around my honeypot sister.

'Suit yourself,' I said. 'But can you go now? I want to change.'

She stalked to the door, and I made a note to steal the same volume back, but to put it in a safer hiding place next time.

One morning in the middle of August I came downstairs (early, always early after that first dawn bathe) while the rest of the house was asleep. As I thudded out over the cool tiles of the living-room I saw a large gift-wrapped box on the table. It was addressed in Ariadne's bold black hand to me.

I undid the paper and discovered a camera.

It was black and silver, not too heavy, not too light. It had a small zoom lens and an assortment of buttons, figures and levers. I held it up to my eye and saw nothing. I inspected the camera and removed the lens cap, blushing and glad of the empty room. Then I tried again, and for the first time saw the world through the harmonious, selective frame of a camera. I pressed my finger against the smoothly engineered resistance until I heard a satisfying click.

There was a film in the box, but I wasn't ready for that sort of commitment yet. Instead of running down to the beach I walked slowly around the courtyard, peering through my new iris, noticing lines, angles, the light and shade of the vine against the stone walls, the terracotta urns' spillage of scarlet salvia, the cat curled perfect in sleep on Ariadne's wide wicker chair. I slid in and out of focus until I was dizzy with images.

At breakfast Ariadne raised an expectant eyebrow. I stood on one trunk-like leg, hot-cheeked and embarrassed. Worried, she held my chin and stared into my face. Then she smiled. 'You like it. Good. Take pictures and enjoy, Cassimou. You will have the eye, I think.'

My mouth dropped open. What did she mean? Would this be another blemish to add to the big feet, the heavy head, the unruly snake mass of hair? I pulled away nervously, but she was still smiling.

Of course, she didn't mean a real eye. (Later, though, I thought she might have been right in a way, for when a picture's composition struck me, I sometimes felt its warmth like a chemical reaction in the small, bony crucible between my brows.)

But back then I was not yet ready to see, I couldn't yet commit myself to taking real photographs. For days I carried around an empty camera, content merely to see the world in this new way. Two weeks later, after several sweating attempts, I loaded the first roll and began taking pictures.

I have them still, somewhere. Ariadne sits on the terrace reading a script, her gold-rimmed glasses perched halfway down her nose, her mouth bracketed with fierce lines of concentration. My sister, slender, lightly tanned, hair white from the sun, poises on a rocky promontory – a nymph deliberating whether to return to the sea. Susie Musselbergh stands in the kitchen surrounded by simmering pans, her face shining in the steamy heat.

And one, just one, of me.

Flushed with the triumph of getting the automatic timer on my camera to work, I stand full square and serious, staring out at my *alter ego*. I am wearing bulky green shorts, my developing breasts push out the front of my ample yellow T-shirt, and my hair, tangled and stiff from sun and saltwater, is scraped back in a wiry black puffball.

I have stared into my stony face many times since, trying to decipher what was already there, wondering if I would recognize my thirteen-year-old self as a twin spirit if I met her again. I think I might, now. But then, from my vantage point in this white room, I'm beginning to see that there are many Cassandras. They appear from the past as I write, passing before me in a slow, sinuous line, like dancers on a Greek vase, each one different yet the same. They share the same dark stare, though their big-featured faces alter subtly over time. I have scanned them looking for a smiling, happy self, but so far there are none; perhaps the happy ones are among those who stand further off, glimmering on the edge of memory, their faces still turned and hidden from me.

Having set me off in one direction, Ariadne had decided to point my reclusive sister down a different path. Because she was due to begin filming *Antigone* in Paris that autumn, Ari usually spent the mornings in what she called her workroom, rehearsing and scaling down her stage interpretation to suit the intimacy of cinema. One day Helen crept in to watch, and Ariadne welcomed her, explained what she was doing and encouraged Helen to try it herself: to imagine and express emotion, to act. I was outside the open window, ostensibly photographing butterflies with my empty camera but actually eavesdropping.

'That is very, very good, Helen,' I heard her say. 'Now, more. Fill each word with meaning till it overflows.' And then Helen's voice tentatively declaiming, then Ariadne clapping, 'Excellent. Helen, that was excellent. Now begin again.' And Helen began again.

The hot days and weeks of summer flew past. Our bodies grew tanned and smooth. Our minds put on weight and muscle. And then it was all over. We said goodbye to Ari and to Peloros, to sunshine and sea and happiness, and on 5 September we sailed to Cephalonia and thence to Athens, from where we flew home to Grannie Christine in damp, grey Marlow and to school.

Mother and Tony returned from their extended honeymoon a week later, and shortly after that Helen and I moved out of The Beeches and went to live with them in our new stepfather's house.

*

They let me sleep on this morning, which I find quite disconcerting – normally their rules and rituals are unchanging and give bracing, reliable form to my days. This new laxity is unsettling; it gives me a bad feeling and, suddenly anxious to show that I am still healthy, I drag my body against its inclination up the pillows, touch a spoonful of egg to my lips and eat a good-sized morsel of bread. Sister Andrew is very pleased when she comes to take away the tray. Her face, surrounded by its lappets of white, beams with wholehearted pleasure.

'You ate your breakfast, Miss Cassandra. That is very good. You are very good today.'

I smile faintly, then when she has gone, I sip the ever-welcome fragrance of tea. The day is once again my own.

I close my eyes and turn my mind back to a place I thought I had blotted out of my memory for always.

LA CASITA

La Casita was the coy name Tony Colindale had given to his large, sprawling bungalow on the outskirts of Henley. It was, as his fellow estate agents would say, 'well presented', with a bank of triple-glazed picture windows at the rear flanking a terrace that ran the full length of the house. Inside there were expanses of loudly patterned carpet, ornate, ranch-style fireplaces and living areas punctuated by chilly leather chesterfields. There were three televisions of gigantic proportions and there were no books at all.

I hated it. I don't think Mother cared for it much either. She had too much Forrester snobbery in her to be able to enjoy the crudely landscaped garden, the pink pavioured drive and the pair of rampant concrete lions flanking the door.

Inside La Casita the rooms smelled overpoweringly of air freshener. Clutching my British Airways travel bag, I stood under the fancy brass-and-crystal chandelier in the hall, missing the warm

Ionian sunshine and our plain white bedroom at Peloros. I missed my new friend Ariadne. I missed Dadda. In the kitchen my mother's ghost-like figure was reflected in the glass cupboard doors and antiseptic work surfaces.

Tony Colindale's voice rang down the corridor, summoning my mother to help Helen unpack. Denise skittered out of the room on uncharacteristically high heels. My shoulders hunched, I scowled at her retreating back. Suddenly I missed Grannie Christine's snobby, reassuring briskness very much indeed.

Tony had had separate bedrooms decorated for Helen and me. Helen's was papered in pale blue, with powder-blue carpet and sky-blue curtains. It looked like a fairy grotto. My room was pink like a gumboil, and I hated it. There was a pink furry stool in front of a pink-skirted dressing-table and a pink nylon eiderdown on the bed. I think Tony hoped I would become more feminine surrounded by such pastel perfection. He was upset when I demanded to sleep in the same room as Helen.

'Time you grew up a bit. You're not a kiddie now, Cassandra, are you?' He lit his pipe, a long detailed process that involved teasing bits of yellow tobacco out into individual threads and then squashing them down ruthlessly into the bowl with a brown-stained finger. 'You've got your own room here, so you won't *need* to share with Helen any more, will you?' His yellow-green eyes flicked up at me and returned to the absorbing task in hand. I stomped off down the corridor to my hated room and slammed the door.

That first lonely night Tony sent me back there three times. When, yet again, he found me out in the corridor turning the handle of my sister's door, he finally lost patience, manhandled me roughly back inside my pink prison cell and locked the door. I'd never been locked in before. I sat huddled in a corner, shuddering. Helen and I had slept together every night since our birth – and for the nine months that had preceded it. I couldn't bear her being separate, distanced. Who knew where she was? I wanted to be with her. Now. Suddenly I threw back my head and howled.

That was better. The Big Bad Baby was back and it was as if she had never been away. I screamed until my voice cracked and my throat was raw. I screamed and screamed and screamed. I screamed until I ran out of screams.

Incredibly, no one came.

At last, ignored and exhausted, my hands bruised and grazed from beating on the door, I stretched out on the floor and lay silent and blank-eyed in the dark. I became conscious of the cold, of the smell of wool carpet beneath my head. I hoped the cold would bring a peaceful death and that I would be found in the morning and wept over by my mother and a remorseful Tony Colindale. Faraway church bells chimed small hours. Willing myself to die wasn't working. Desperately I searched for Helen's thoughts and found her breathing evenly next door. How could she? How could she sleep when I was teetering on the lonely unexplored rim of the world? A new sense of isolation broke over me and I crawled around my room, whimpering with fear. The pink walls were slabs of dark grey rock. Now, scenting victory, they began to slide inwards. With the last of my strength I pushed them back, my palms flat against their clammy surfaces.

And then a revelation came.

I knew how I would survive.

The Big Bad Baby had the answer.

Early next morning I was sitting in the corner with my head between my knees when a key clicked in the lock and my mother's feet came slowly into view. I heard her mumble something, then retch and retch again. Talking to me from behind her hand, she told me to stand up. Then she made me walk down the corridor to the bathroom, where she peeled off my clothes, rolled them in a towel and threw them into the corner. Then she stood me in the bath and showered me until the worst had gone and she could bear to scrub my skin. I was shivering too much – I let her do it. After that, she filled a bowl with hot soapy water, poured in half a bottle of disinfectant and tried to wash down the walls of my room before Tony woke up. There wasn't much she could do about the floor: the muck and stains were too deeply embedded into the swirly embossed pattern of the new pink carpet.

Ha!

What happened then?

I can't remember.

I can't remember anything much at all.

But, forcing memory to its limit and then further still, there is something, I think: a glimmer of a small room with white grille over the window and beyond it a view of a strange, wintry garden that was not Marlow or Henley; a white frilled paper cup that held red pills instead of the expected chocolate; a slim blonde lady with a floating smile and scarves who called me Cass-ahn-dra and asked strange questions about my dadda.

I may have bitten her, or I may have dreamed I did.

Later there were walks in the winter garden, where I linked arms with someone strong and took tiny, tiny steps like a child.

When I woke up it was early January and I had missed Christmas altogether. Mother drove me to La Casita in her new Triumph Stag and it was a long way back from wherever I had been.

Ah.

Suddenly it's difficult to breathe.

Tiredness and jags of pain – probably stress. Though it's not yet time, I need more morphine. Right now.

I press the buzzer and wait, allowing myself to gasp a little. Is childbirth worse than this?

Ah.

Oh Lord. Something's gone terribly wrong. Pain. Pain.

Clear the screen.

Close down.

Shut the eyes.

Sink in pillows.

Breathe. Breathe.

God.

16 October 1999, 6.10 a.m.

Cushioned by drugs, I've slept through an evening and a night surprisingly well and woken muzzy-headed but relatively free of pain. They've decided they must increase the dosages now, and they assure me that once they've found the correct levels, yesterday's torture is unlikely to recur, at least for a while. I'm relieved, though it's tedious having to be grateful for something as ordinary and essential as a manageable amount of pain.

I badly need tea, to clarify the body and the mind, but it's too early yet; so I slide gingerly out of bed to prove to myself I still can and totter over to open the windows and the shutters, noticing as I do so the swell of my belly and the contrasting thinness of my arms and legs, which were once brown, strong and smoothly muscled as young seals.

Resting elbows on the sill, I breathe the cold dawn air of Ithaca deep into my lungs. The broken hilltops are already rimmed with pink. Between the olive trees, bells clank the progress of the unseen goats. Far off to the right, a skein of mist lies over a grey sea like cotton wool over silk.

Life in this present, perfect moment is so beautiful that I am tempted to linger at the window. It would be good to stand here all day, watching each infinitesimal change of light on the hillside and feeling each new degree of warmth on my skin as the sun climbs into the sky.

But I wrote very little yesterday and must make up for lost time. Resolutely I turn away from the window and face the past.

DEATH IN WINTER

So in January 1974 I returned from wherever I had been to La Casita.

Mother watched me carefully and made sure I took my pills (no frilled paper cup at home, just a row of small brown bottles, neatly labelled). Helen was already back at school, so I spent my days alone at home, poring over a Diane Arbus exhibition catalogue that Ariadne had sent me for Christmas. I turned the pages, lost among strange warped faces, empty rooms and abandoned Coney Island fairgrounds, recognizing a kindred spirit behind the lens – and sometimes in front of it.

Eventually, when I found it had become tiring to turn the pages back and forth, I took scissors to the brochure and pinned the photos around the room, until the pink walls were covered with a frieze of glossy black-and-white prints and the room was peopled with harrowed faces. I liked them. When I looked into their eyes I could see that these people were even further adrift than me. Appalled and fascinated, I turned around slowly in the middle of the room, then faster and faster, until we freaks all joined hands and whirled around together in a crazy freaksome reel.

Notwithstanding such lapses, in late January I was pronounced fit enough to return to school and a normal routine of sorts.

After each day's school Helen and I came home to Mother's slapdash cooking (no more ambrosial broths, no more of Grannie Christine's filling roast dinners, our diet now consisted of spaghetti hoops, fish fingers, white sliced bread, baked beans and sweet corn). Denise gave us our tea early so that she and Tony could sit in the dining alcove (yes) at eight o'clock for a candlelight supper *à deux*. She changed for dinner and wore smart rustling dresses and perfume that was stronger than the smell of cooking.

Whenever it was on I made sure I finished my homework in time for *Coronation Street*. Sitting alone in front of the television, I would hold up my hands to crop the screen to a portrait and click an imaginary shutter on those English Arbus faces. At the weekends I took my camera and wandered around Henley, taking pictures of old people, dogs, empty shops and churchyards.

By April I was largely recovered from what had probably been my first breakdown.

I was certainly calmer and once again sensitive to time passing.

And so. How does passing time affect Helen and me?

Well, puberty comes – at last.

It arrives that spring, before our fourteenth birthday. Helen's takes the form of tiny, budding breasts and I glimpse sun-gold frizz between her legs as she stands under the shower. Mine brings me even more puppy fat (joy) and a rash of pimples on my forehead, chest and bottom. My already large breasts grow even more prominent and I now have a triangle of black silky-strange hair around and above my cunt.

She doesn't say, but I suppose Helen bleeds every month. I now do. Copiously.

And how is time treating the ineffable Tony, my stepfather?

Well, apparently the Colindale estate agency is thriving. He has three branches now, he says. As a mark of his success and proof of his devotion to his new family, he has decided that Helen and I should be summarily removed from the state school we have just got used to and enrolled for expensive private education at the all-girls Marlow Court School.

We join in the summer term that year, when everyone, but everyone, has already made friends. This doesn't worry me too much, as I have low expectations of friendship and do not seek it out. Instead, I march into my place at assembly, standing a good foot above the row of puny classmates. They shuffle nervously on either side and whisper their silly girly things behind my back. I stare straight ahead, ignoring such Lilliputian antics and bellow out the words of every hymn. But Helen cannot cope with mild dislike, let alone bullying, and, when she is tormented by a clique of fourth-formers who resent her looks and her softly spoken efforts to make contact, once again I find it has to be Cassandra to the rescue.

This time I make subtle (see how I am growing up?) use of my ability to peer inside their scheming little brains. After a few unnerving (for them) conversations and incidents, they apologize abjectly to Helen and give me a wide berth.

Once I have saved her from harassment Helen adapts easily to the new school and begins to immerse herself in work. In fact, soon she no longer needs my help and relegates me to my long-standing role as the odd, ugly, unconnected twin, condemned to watch my sister's comet-like progress through the school heavens.

Take our English lessons, for example.

After her summer with Ariadne Helen's voice, unlike every other girl's in the class, is self-consciously different depending on whether she is playing Othello or Titania or Juliet or reading Auden or Wordsworth or Yeats. Miss Hancock is so impressed that every time it comes to that part of the lesson where we read aloud she smiles, puts her head on one side and simpers, 'Helen Byrd, would *you* read this play/poem/page for us, please?' And the girls nudge each other and roll their eyes, because Helen is so embarrassing and yet so impressive. I note that, though she is touchingly modest and shy, she never refuses the limelight.

I, on the other hand, am never chosen, though I feel sure I read just as well as Helen. But Miss Hancock does not care for my voice, which is deep and booming. In revenge, while Helen reads I make little grunting, snuffling noises under my breath, and the class is soon helpless with laughter. I am regularly sent to the head-mistress's study for this and similar examples of bad behaviour.

My mother says that my problems are due to what she calls my 'hormones'. I'm not sure what she means, but I know that I miss the physical release of a good old co-educational wrestle with the boys: at Marlow Court confrontations are verbal rather than physical, which can be frustrating. But thanks to D.H. Lawrence, Grandpa Brian and the Lennox brothers, I have amassed a vocabulary of excellent and cathartic swearwords, any one of which, when said at volume, reduces my classmates to shocked silence and produces a frisson of detentions from panic-stricken staff.

Denise is regularly summoned to school to be told about my misdemeanours and has to sit through galling meetings with the headmistress, in which Miss MacVicar informs her that I am 'failing to shine'. It's true: though my reading outside school is quite voracious (I collect library books and secretly burn the letters that come demanding their return), my school reports are dire. They tell my mother what she knows but prefers to ignore, that I have no brilliances, am lumbering and odd and have a tendency to fiddle with my acne during Home Economics. (Thank you for your frankness, Mrs Barrington – another wax doll on Cassandra's shelf.) From my chair outside the oak-panelled study door I can hear Mother's tightly apologetic voice, offering excuses for my latest offence. One day, when she comes out looking particularly reproachful, I grin and confide that I have grown bored waiting and have peed on the red damask chair to pass the time. Mother glances nervously at the spreading maroon stain and ushers me out of school.

They must have been worrying times for her.

*

And talking of Mother . . . Let's stop and take a look at her for a moment.

Here she is: Denise Forrester Byrd Colindale, still slender, still young and now entering the second year of her second marriage. Buoyed once again by money and increasing social prominence, she enjoys the proximity of The Beeches and her mother's open approval of her choice . . . but, really, how is *she*?

Well, Helen is worried about her, that's for sure.

For my part, I observe dispassionately that Denise is no longer the confident harpy of my youth nor the shaky young widow of Kilburn days nor the embryonic career woman of our year at The Beeches. What I also notice is that since she married Tony Colindale she often injures herself. At breakfast she often wears heavy eye makeup over a puffy lid or winces as she reaches up for the cereal.

Helen and I exchange glances.

Oh, we weren't fools of course, we knew what was happening. The walls in La Casita were flimsy, and the sound of shouting and thudding and moans had already reached us in our separate bedrooms. But, though I had once defended Helen against Grandpa Brian, when it came to my mother my emotions were far more complex. Whichever way you looked at it, I'd had to suffer years of injustice and unfairness – what my shrinks would later describe as 'a deliberate withholding of love'. Whatever. All I know is that I now decided, quite unemotionally, that it was Mother's turn to discover how much these things hurt.

DOUBLE JEOPARDY

Ha!

The year 1974 was one of terrible, mythic events.

Though not all of them were bad, come to think of it.

No.

In April of that year Grandpa Brian died of a massive stroke on the seventeenth hole at Wentworth, a passing unmourned by most of his family – though perhaps Denise did shed a tear or two. GB's funeral, like Dadda's, took place on a rainy spring day, but this time we had the benefit (as Tony would have said) of an overheated crematorium, and sang doleful hymns in company of sweating estate agents and sombre-faced acquaintances from the golf club. Wisely, Grandma Christine declined to have his ashes on her mantelpiece, and instead they were eventually scattered among the hybrid teas in the Garden of Remembrance.

Anyway, would you believe it? A scandalously short three months after her husband had been laid to rest, Grandma Christine announced that The Beeches was too big for her on her own. Ignoring her daughter's tears, she sold the place for a thousand times more than Brian had paid for it and retired down to a sea-front flat in Hove on the profits.

Good for her, I thought. Good for her, the old battleaxe.

She had changed, adapted. She was a survivor, and so was I.

A picture in the folder shows that I was changing, too.

Yes!

My spots are clearing up. Suddenly I am four inches taller (five foot ten and rising) and my Buddha tyres of fat are undergoing some sort of continental drift, so that, amazingly, my large breasts are now in approximate (and majestic) proportion to the generous swell of my hips. Of course, I am still what is euphemistically known as 'a big girl', but now my belly looks less like a sack of potatoes and more like a large, softly rounded, biblical heap of wheat. (Yeah, OK, the pictures show that my feet, hands and head are still unfeasibly large, but what the hell?) These physical changes, together with my reputation for bizarre eccentricities, mean that I am now accorded a certain wary respect at school, and in recognition of this I decide to abandon farting in favour of more intellectual ways of asserting my individuality.

Helen is also changing. At fourteen here she is, immaculate in her first and completely unnecessary Maidenform bra: a sprite-like beauty. Through the bathroom keyhole I watch her undressing and wonder whether she remembers Dadda's stories about what inevitably happens to over-pretty young maidens: Psyche, Niobe, Andromeda. I want to breathe ghostly (if clichéd) caution through the lock, 'These things end in teeears . . . wait and seeeee . . .'

But there's no need for Cassandra-like warnings – in the autumn of 1974 Helen will be reminded all too forcefully of the consequences of her beauty.

Late one Saturday night in October, through a crack in my never-quite-closed pink bedroom door, I spy Tony Colindale, in luridly patterned pyjamas, tiptoeing down the corridor to listen at my sister's bedroom door. With exaggerated care, he turns the brass doorknob, hears something (oops, pardon me), glances around, changes his mind and slinks back the way he has come.

This sortie becomes a nightly event.

One night he is so quiet I do not hear him pass but am woken by the sound of Helen's door closing. Later, there are squeaks from her bed as a heavy bulk climbs aboard.

What happened?

Did anything happen?

I never saw, I can't say for sure.

But now, if I force myself to imagine, to think back with my adult's knowledge of men like Tony Colindale, then I have to picture his hand clamped across her mouth and his supporting arm rigid beneath his upper body as he thrusts upward, so that my sister's head is crushed deep into the pillows. His grip hurts her neck and makes faint ambiguous bruises fruit around her mouth.

And how did Cass-ahn-dra feel about that?

Different. Indifferent. We were young women now, not children. She's brought it on herself, I thought, as I wedged my pillow around my ears like a giant coif. If she'd wanted to make herself uglier, she could've. No one would bother her then. But often one thought led to another. Sometimes I lay next door and wondered: what if one night Tony Colindale tired of beauty and it was my bedroom door which opened quietly in the middle of the night, my leg which his groping hand encountered and followed upwards, fondling?

I decided I would be ready for him. Under my bed, among the dustballs, the piles of curling paperbacks and the shrivelled apple cores, I hid a bright skewer from the kitchen drawer, long enough to pierce a turkey drumstick to the bone.

Two months later the irony of its pristine shine was not lost on me.

With all this going on it would have been natural if Helen's behaviour also showed signs of deterioration or distress. Was there depression? I seem to remember a certain listlessness but certainly nothing out of the ordinary. Whatever emotion was going on within her, this time she kept it buried far below the surface.

Of course, later, as an actress, these depths were probably where she went to search for raw emotion. I've seen her myself as Lady Macbeth drag up a still recognizable handful of her bloody, dripping past and brandish it before an appalled audience in the Barbican theatre. The critics said it was almost too terrible to watch, but then they're a lily-livered lot in the main.

But I'm not totally insensitive. Sometimes it occurred to me to wonder, did the applause, the fame she later enjoyed, ever make up for what Helen experienced as a child and as a young woman? But outside television drama nobody ever actually asks these bald, dramatic questions, do they?

So who knows? Who cares?

Anyway. We're in 1974, and facing, necessarily, its end and the first hour of 1975.

This memory is somewhat daunting, I have to say.

'Get on with it, for goodness' sake,' says the Baby.

Very well. If you're sure.

I remember . . .

Oh, no.

No.

Exit . . .

'Please wait . . .' blinks the screen.

No!

Close down, right now.

The machine stutters to a halt. It takes an age to quiet. I want to fold the screen down, quickly.

I want a click of grey plastic to cut the link to the past.

Oh shit.

I lie pale and sweating, a disappointment to myself.

17 October 1999, 2.26 p.m.

I think I should abandon this disk.

I should write to Marco and ask him to send a mobile phone and modem so that I can spend pleasant hours flying aimlessly around the world on the Net. Even here in the Ionian I bet the air is alive with voices, swooping down like electronic swallows from the satellites high above, carrying the thoughts of millions of curious brains like mine.

And after all these months, there will be a distraction of e-mails waiting for me, too. There was the last time I looked.

In April.

Dear Ms Byrd, I love your work. My ambition is to become a photographer like you, and I wondered if you could help me.

(And a hundred similar notes).
And then there were icebergs of news . . .

Dear Ms Byrd, [from my solicitors] We have received this note:
(PLSE OPEN WORD ATTACHMENT)

Dear Sirs, Mrs Elspeth Coltrane, widow of the photographer the late Arnold Coltrane of Kensington Mews, London, has asked us to send you these photographs, found in his studio, which she understands are of your client Cassandra Byrd. Given their content, you can imagine how painful this discovery was for her, and we hope your client will appreciate that Mrs Coltrane requires no acknowledgement of their receipt. Yours etc.

Which is how I found out Arnold was dead.

Marco sent me the back copy of *The Times* later, and I cried when I saw that white-haired, gnomic face glaring out of the obituary column. I took comfort in one postcard from CalTech . . .

Dear Cassie,

Will you be back at Peloros next summer, do you think? Missing you this spring more graphically, erotically and entirely than mere electronic words suggest. Your adoring geek, Will.

But there was nothing at all in that long, long list of mail from Helen. Though I hardly expected there to be. Ever again.

Anyway. No. I shan't write to Marco yet. No distractions for me. Hiding away from the disk would only be another cowardice, and I can hardly face myself each morning as it is.

*

18 October 1999, 7.30 a.m.

Another day. Switch on, at least. What's the harm in that?

Password?

******* (sentimentalist).

Open Folder, Open File, Go to End where the cursor waits.

Ha!

Plunge in.

Say it quickly, if it helps.

It'stheendof1974.HelenandIarefourteenandwe'restilllivingatLaCa sita.

(OK, we're off now. The memory train is rolling. Ease up just a fraction. And *breathe* . . . as Californian Will always said, with his fatuously healing smile.)

Go back a little. Reprise.

Helen and I are in early-teenage limbo and our lives have stalled. We have no friends apart from each other and, despite our adjoining rooms, we live largely separate existences outside school. Ariadne still keeps in touch with us by means of cryptic postcards of Ithaca, postmarked Rio, Sydney, Milan and New York. Tony Colindale harangues us daily as if he were our parent. Mother still has bruises but rarely on the face.

Helen worries about Mother but does nothing.

I worry slightly about Helen, but I do nothing either. Helen stays in her pale blue room for hours and is so quiet in there that I cannot even hear her thoughts any more behind the thin partition walls.

I still have the skewer under the bed.

I am still a virgin.

Down in Hove Grannie Christine's mental health has declined unexpectedly and rapidly. Suddenly confused and unable to look after herself, she has been moved into a residential home. When Mother insists that Helen and I go down to Haven House to exchange Christmas presents, we find her in a lino-floored double room at the end of a long passageway. Her perm has grown out and her once-smart dress smells strongly of piss and stale sweat. She has no idea who we are.

I hand over my fragrant box of Black Rose Bath Cubes and earn a scowl from Denise when I say loudly that I hope they will be put to good use. Grannie Christine leans to one side on her commode chair, trying to look past me to the television where the cast of *The Waltons* are saying their sugary goodnights to each other. She doesn't have any presents to give us and seems to have forgotten Christmas along with everything else. Denise perches on a stained Dralon stool and tries to interest her mother in talk of friends and Marlow, but it is soon clear that we might just as well not be here. As we trail down the squeaky corridor to reception we can hear the music to *Hawaii Five-O* coming from every room.

Uncle Derek, Aunt Pauline and the boys are staying put in Maidstone, so our 1974 festivities at La Casita consist of Tony, Denise, Helen and me.

Ha!

At the Christmas dinner Tony is very jolly and insists we wear paper hats and ask each other cracker jokes and laugh loudly as if we were a real family. I give Mother a bottle of body lotion and she looks at me nervously when I say that it has arnica in it and so is good for bruises. I give Helen a book on Doisneau, which I know she will not like and so will not miss when I 'borrow' it later. I give Tony Colindale a pack of blank cassettes, which seemed oddly and uniquely suitable when I was wandering around W.H. Smith on Christmas Eve. In return I receive a new zoom lens for my camera (it fits; Mother has followed my detailed instructions to the letter),

117

a biography of Vivien Leigh (Helen playing me at my own game, I fear) and from my stepfather an evening bag in peach glacé kid, which I have previously noticed at the bottom of the wardrobe in the spare room and which obviously belonged to Jessica, since there are traces of face powder and lipstick inside. (Thank you, Tony, you shouldn't have . . .)

As Christmas afternoon drones on with black-and-white movies full of snow scenes and circuses, I escape out into the sharp-smelling dusk and walk down into town to try out my new lens. The shops are brightly lit and chocolate-boxy and it only needs a stagecoach to wheel around the corner in front of the inn for the Victorian scene to be complete. I ignore the blazing windows and head for the churchyard at the end of the high street, where I spend a cheering half-hour taking flash photographs of tilted headstones and weeping stone angels.

After Christmas Tony goes back to work and the days tick past, each bringing New Year's Eve another ratchet closer.

It arrives.

It's 31 December 1974: a cold morning.

I have finished the book on Doisneau and have no more money for film. There is nothing to do and nowhere to go. Denise tells me do some revision for my January exams, so I pretend to work in my room. Noon, afternoon and evening pass slowly. Then night comes. There are a few isolated fireworks going off in the distance. Denise and Tony are invited to a New Year's Eve dance at the golf club, and Mother has been getting ready for hours. Now she comes in to say goodnight, thin and smart in a black beaded dress. Behind her in the hall I can see that Tony's dinner jacket is tight around the shoulders. As they go out Tony tosses Mother the car keys and tells her to drive. Mother smiles briefly and nods. There is a whisper of tyres over gravel, and Helen and I are alone.

By common consent we sit in the big empty living-room and watch television. It is dismal stuff: quiz programmes, an unfunny comedian, a Scotsman in a kilt singing about the glens. Helen yawns and goes off to bed. It's only ten thirty. I pour myself a large sweet sherry from the bottle in the bar. At eleven fifty I decide it's silly to be on my own for the Big Moment and go along to Helen's room carrying two glasses and the bottle.

As usual her golden bedside light is on. She's reading the biography of Vivien Leigh. When she sees me, though, she puts down her book and offers me a thick bar of Cadbury's Dairy Milk (a present from Tony in *her* stocking only – even in my new hour-glass shape I am still too plump to be trusted with chocolate, apparently). Helen peels back the purple foil and snaps off large, neat-edged chunks for us. The chocolate fills my mouth and makes the sherry taste even weirder. Over the fields from Henley the church bells ring out the old year and chime in the new.

We clink glasses and drain them in what we know from Grandpa Brian is time-honoured tradition. I refill them. We chink our glasses and empty them again. At one o'clock in the morning the sherry bottle is half empty. Helen, giggling like a normal person, tops it up with water from the bathroom and goes swaying down the corridor to put it back in the cabinet.

Suddenly, she is caught in the sweeping headlights of a car coming up the drive. Shadows of stone lions prowl the walls. Helen slams the bottle down on the bar and runs back up the corridor. Her face is pale and I hear her panicky thoughts stampeding through her mind.

I shall be for it, too, if I'm found here, but, fortified by sherry, I feel unaccountably brave and reckless.

'Lock your door,' I tell her. Helen is sitting on her bed, gripping the eiderdown tightly in both hands and trembling. She nods, then shakes her head. Feet are crunching over gravel outside.

'I'm off,' I say brightly, and slip back down the corridor into my room just as voices sound in the porch. Quickly I close and lock the door. We made it. But then, I suddenly think of Helen sitting there waiting for Tony Colindale to steal down the corridor in his shiny black shoes and open her bedroom door. The Big Bad Baby feels angry on her behalf.

Noiselessly I slide back the triple-glazed french windows and creep out into the night. The patio crazy paving is so cold it's like walking on frostfire. I tiptoe to Helen's window and see her start violently as she sees my face pressed against the glass. For a moment I consider whether it will be more fun to save her or torment her, but then I relent, put my finger to my lips and signal to her to slide back the door. She joins me out on the terrace, quietly closes the window behind her and follows me back to my room. We leave a trail of melted footprints in the white rime. Two sizes, large and small.

We sit side by side on my bed, rubbing our cold wet feet. My sister is shaking, but Helen is Helen and I am me, so I don't reach out and put and arm around her. Instead we focus on the voices in the living-room.

Glasses are chinking. Tony is shouting.

'You know fucking well what I mean,' he yells. 'You stuck-up, simpering bitch.'

Helen trembles so violently that I relent and put my hand over hers in a gesture of solidarity, if not sympathy. We wait, hoping we have been forgotten.

When the sound of breaking glass comes it is without warning. It is followed by a scream, a heavy bang of furniture being overturned. Then there is a softer thud and another and something worse than a scream, suddenly silenced.

I remove my hand from Helen's and slip back out to the patio.

Beyond my darkened window and our bathroom, the vast sliding doors of the living-room blaze across the terrace. I edge closer. At first the room seems empty, then there is a movement: Tony Colindale is staggering across the room to the fireplace. He kicks out at something lying on the floor. I crane higher to peer over the sofa.

It's my mother's body. I can see her feet and legs. She's only wearing one shoe. I can't see her face, and need to, so I retreat into the icy darkness of the garden and slip across to the other side of the big window. The grass crunches loudly under my feet, and I wonder if Tony will hear me, but he has disappeared. I edge right up to the window.

Mother hasn't moved, not at all.

From here I can see that her head is lying in a black puddle, which is filling from some point at the back of her skull; it is joined by a thin lines of red running from her nose and mouth.

Have I cried out?

I think I must have.

Because almost immediately the patio door crashes open and Tony Colindale stands there dark-faced, his dinner jacket unbuttoned, his tie hanging like a dismembered butterfly around his neck. He sees me shivering in my pyjamas and reaches out to drag me into the room. I dart backwards, shock making my big bare feet unusually nimble. Tony lunges after me, careering on to the patio in his shiny black shoes. As I step back out of his reach, his feet skid on the frozen crazy paving and his momentum sends him crashing over on the terrace. His head bounces loudly against the stone.

I leap over him and run inside across the warm carpet to kneel my mother's side. The puddle is very dark, glistening through her blonde Forrester hair like engine oil. But when I put my fingers in it they are shiny and red with blood. I can't see any breathing. I watch her black velvet bodice, willing her chest to rise and fall as mine is doing, but it hardly moves. I hold my hand against her thin neck, in the place where my own pulse is hammering loud enough to make my head jerk up and down, but there is only the faintest flicker under the pads of my fingers.

He did this to her.

I stand and run back to the windows, seeing my wild reflection in the black glass.

Tony Colindale is lying where he fell. I seize a handful of his hair and gag as I find I'm clutching a crinkly rope of combed-over frizz. I gag and yank his head right back as far as it will go. Snake eyelids flicker white under a massive bruise. In a spasm of disgust I let go of the frayed hair rope and his head falls back on the stone with a broken squelch.

Then there is a movement beside me and Helen is standing in the doorway staring down at us. She has blood on her night-dress and she is clutching one of Tony's massive ashtrays. There is a strange guttering noise coming from her mouth. As I twist and stand she raises the onyx dish above her head in both hands.

No! No! I grab her wrists.

The ashtray is pivoting above our heads as we stand gasping like runners. But I am taller and stronger. Helen crumples to her knees. As she sinks in front of me, I lift the ashtray from her grasp like a champion accepting homage. Calmly, I help my sister to her feet. I take the ashtray from her hand and carry it back into the living-room. I lift my mother's right hand and curl it briefly in a grip around the rough-smooth onyx edge. Then I let her fingers open and fall, and the ashtray crashes and shatters on the hearthstone. It will look as though she fought back, though I don't know why that is important to me.

'Nine-nine-nine,' I shout to Helen who is standing, frozen, staring down at Denise. 'Helen? Ambulance. Police. Quick.'

The men in white took Mother away in an ambulance and the men in black with notebooks and the women in black-and-white check hats asked us questions. We told them the truth. That we had heard voices, late. That my parents (why bother them with stepfather?) were quarrelling and there were screams. That I had crept out on to the terrace to see what was going on and that my mother had been lying near the fireplace. My father (!) had heard me outside, rushed out on to the terrace swaying and clutching his head, slipped and fallen headfirst on to the concrete. The policeman examined the skid across rime that ended at the upturned sole of Tony's shoe. A policewoman gently ushered Helen and me away from the bloodstained hearth where we had last seen Mother and sat with us until we were taken away from the carnage at La Casita to what I suppose was officially called a Place of Safety.

18 October 1999, 4.55 p.m.
For all of us, well, no, for almost all of us, there are a few pivotal events – some trifling, some tragic – which we find ourselves replaying in unchanging detail across all the years of our life. Every few hours or days or weeks or months we disinter them, review them, relive them. We try to grasp their meaning; we struggle to understand their hidden significance. Proust's night-light slowly revolves; a bell rings in a summer garden at evening; a life turns.

I saw my mother lying still and my life turned. Yet it's only now that I understand the meaning: that what happened that night was unique only in its particular detail of ashtrays and frost and concrete, that in every other way it was as unexceptional and universal as myth. We love, we lose those we love, we suffer. We follow ancient pathways round and round, moving from happiness to misery and back again like figures in a complicated dance.

For a long while I found the process incomprehensible, sense-less, yet now I begin to understand: there is something true and valuable in the pattern itself. Lying here in the warmth of late autumn afternoon in Ithaca I can say calmly (still) that I believe death is not an experience but an event like any other. Death is around us all the time, our atoms flow into new patterns as breathing starts, stops or is stopped. Dadda and Denise died, as parents usually do, before their children. When, soon, it is my turn, I'll simply do what they and millions of people have done before. And for now, that is all the comfort I have or need.

Yes, I face my own exit with a little apprehension and only one regret. (And I can tell you that, shockingly, my possible murder of Tony Colindale is not it.)

How's that for chutzpah, eh?

But can one really dismiss guilt quite so easily, blow it away with a flip, throwaway remark? Surely I should at least apologize for what I did or may have done?

Let me turn the light around for a change.

How do *you* feel about it?

If you, reader, listener, witness, were sitting here beside my bed in that slant of Ionian apricot sunshine over there, would you wait until I slept and then steal away to make a telephone call? Does justice really cry out to be done? Would you call for statements be re-examined and long-buried bodies exhumed?

Or would you shrug and turn the page, untroubled by another's possible sin?

You must please yourself. But be quick about it, because I am already circling death here in the white room, armed only with my unflagging curiosity. And tonight, I think, a little morphine.

Mother didn't die straight away. It took her three weeks. Helen and I went to see her in the hospital, where she lay still as stone, with tubes and bags and catheters feeding and medicating and draining her body. They told us to talk to her and we did, though she never gave the slightest sign of hearing. Afterwards I thought they'd said it more for our sake than out of any real hope of her recovering consciousness. Because, when I sat on the edge of the bed, I closed my eyes and climbed into my mother's mind and looked around and saw that it was smooth and empty as a blown egg and already growing cold.

But we trailed along obediently to the hospital whenever we were told to do so, until the morning when the staff nurse took us to one side as we came into the ward and told us our mother had died in the night.

Then there was another funeral (so many, and we so young) organized by someone – I suppose it was Uncle Derek – followed by a cremation. This time there was hardly anyone to see when the box with Mummie in it trundled over rollers, and the red velvet curtains swished shut behind her and we were on our own for the rest of our lives.

Light under lids; dry mouth tasting of mould; eyeballs sticky in sockets; rags of strange dreams flying around the room. Impossible to say what time it is, except that it's early.

Or is it late? The yellow square is high on the wall. That means something. Is the sun low and shining upwards? Or high and shining down? I can't decide. Can't think. I lie here and check my body. There is a sharpish pain in my chest and stomach, but these are a mere echo of yesterday's. There is also a soreness of bony pelvis on bedsheets. And a headache.

Breakfast? No. No breakfast.

Dr Mike will be cross with me, but I shan't be forced to eat. Thankfully, it was decided months ago not to consider further invasive surgery or to persist with the enervating chemotherapy. In fact, since I moved to the hospice wing of Aghios Georghios my quality of life has improved enormously. My hair has also grown back and is now a thick black crew-cut around my thinned-down face. Two orderlies come in, strong gentle women. Today they're taking me for physiotherapy. A pointless exercise, as I try to tell them, but they are well intentioned and also under orders from Dr Mike, so I comply.

As they lift me carefully into the wheelchair (not the back-straining task it would have been a year ago), the movement jolts a memory loose.

WHERE? WHEN?

The night Helen and I were taken into care, two gentle people took my arms and lifted me from the sofa and walked with me down the drive of La Casita (I had shoes on by then, which was strange) and sat beside me as I shivered in the back of a panda car.

We arrived somewhere and were passed from person to person. Each person told us that we'd be all right and our mother would be all right, though we both knew we'd never be all right again. Later, we were taken to what they called 'a home', which wasn't really and which smelled of gravy and bleach. There were cruel people there, but I kept myself tight shut because I knew somehow that if I let go and marked the walls or cut myself or bit someone again I would be taken away from Helen, and Helen and I had to stay together now, no matter what.

For days in between visits to the hospital we clung together like refugees: Helen silent as a dead person and me answering questions more or less politely, trying not to be rude or strange or mad. The police had lots of questions about what had happened at New Year and what we'd seen and how Mother and Tony got on. Yes, I told them, able at last to tell, he had beaten my mother and tried to abuse my sister. I somehow think they knew about that already, though I don't know how.

When we weren't being interviewed or visiting the hospital we slept in our cream-walled room, which had bits of curling Sellotape and corners of posters left on the wall where someone had torn them down. We didn't have any pictures to put up. Sometimes we slept together in one bed, sometimes apart. The sheets were brown with a funny green pattern, and the pillowslips were faded pink stripes. I don't think they cared much about the colours, because anyone could see that they didn't really go together. Mealtimes were the worst, because we had to come out of the room. I held Helen's hand if she needed me to, even though it looked babyish. We didn't talk much.

On the third or fourth day Geoff came and things started to get better. Geoff was younger than the other wardens or whatever they were. What I liked about him was that he didn't ask us too many questions. He reminded me a little of Dadda, with his thin face, dark hair and tweed jacket, except that his didn't have leather elbows. He made time to sit and talk with us, and after a while I talked back, which helped me feel a little more connected to the world at least. After a longer while even Helen talked to him, though her voice was so quiet that I think at first he could only have been pretending to hear what she said.

Geoff told us what was going to happen each day: interviews and coroners and police and social workers and hospital and school and all that stuff.

We almost came to trust him.

After a week I asked Geoff how long we would stay in the home, and he said, 'It may be quite a while yet, I'm afraid.' And soon, he added, getting another bit of bad news out of the way at the same time, we'd have to go back to school. Not our old one, MCS, which was expensive and private and so not an option, but what turned out to be a sprawling concrete comprehensive two streets away from the home.

We started there the week after the funeral. Park Road was full of loud, aggressive kids who hated us on sight. In our room at the home that night Helen cried for Mother. She cried so hard that I thought she would never stop and that the room would fill with tears like Alice's. She cried until she fell asleep, but even then I heard her moaning, and when I sent my mind across the room to peer into hers I nearly cried myself. But even Helen's bad dreams were better than mine.

I hovered there and watched the flickering images playing behind her eyes.

Look.

HELEN'S DREAM

At first it is silent. We see a riverbank, a family picnic in the shade of a tree: a checked cloth, a basket of food, a Thermos flask. A kind blonde woman bends down and offers sandwiches. Egg? Cucumber? Mustard and Cress? The soundtrack whirrs, but Helen hears the vanished voice, freshly crisp with consonants and warm with vowels. She weeps for joy, and then comprehends her loss and cries back through her fourteen years, 'Mummie, Mummie, I love you. Please don't leave me.'

But Mummie is talking to the little girl with blonde silk hair and a bow tied tight on top. And suddenly Mummie has gone and the girl has gone and the riverbank has vanished into a concrete sewer pipe under close-packed bungalows and the ground is crazy paving, hard with frost.

And Helen is travelling alone through space and time, her smocked dress hardly moving in the breeze of decades, her dusty sandals brushing through galaxies. She stares, trusting, straight ahead, her eyes wide with tears, searching the trackless starlight for her mother.

I didn't cry.

Not me.

I was angry: angry that Mother had gone and that her death was partly her own fault; and even angrier that now she would never be able to change her mind and love me or be sorry that she'd not shown me more than a couple of moments' affection in all our life together.

In other words, I felt cheated. And so, no, I hardly cried at all, or not that I remember anyway.

The months passed.

I asked Geoff why everyone had forgotten us. In his most reasonable voice he told me that Grannie Christine was very ill, that after the funeral they had received no reply to their letters to Grandma Byrd or the family in Donegal, that our Uncle Derek, approached by social workers in Maidstone, had written a regretful note saying that he and his wife couldn't possibly take us on. (I didn't know whether to be happy or sad about that.)

Back in the room, while Helen was in the shower, I sat cross-legged on the floor and rocked and rocked and rocked, my arms wrapped around my shoulders. I wondered if Dadda could see me from wherever he was now. When Helen was back and asleep I stood in the middle of the room and held my hands up to the four corners of the ceiling in turn and begged him to come down like one of the gods in the *Iliad* to help us. I breathed his name over and over in the dark and held my breath waiting for a sign, but nothing came.

Weeks or maybe months later, I don't remember, Geoff knocked on the door and told us we had a visitor. A friend of the family, he said, and Helen and I stared at each other trying to imagine who that could be. We followed him down the brightly lit corridor, and there in the meeting-room was Ariadne, hawk-nosed, smiling, her perfume already filling the room with the smell of rich, scented flowers. Helen gave a little cry and ran to her and buried her face in the folds of Ariadne's soft camel-hair coat. I stood in the doorway, my face turned aside from the miracle of her presence, until Ari herself reached out her hand and brought me into their huddle. For the first time in months, even if it was only for a moment, I leaned against someone stronger than me.

And yes, Ariadne did eventually rescue us. Though it took almost a year, for even though, at fifteen, we were among the oldest children in the home and had nowhere else to go, the formalities were endless. Helen and I trudged on through the days, so turned in on ourselves that we hardly registered the fact of Grannie Christine's death. She was buried long before the news reached us anyway. Even our birthday in May was much like any other day, except that we each had a card from Ariadne with a crisp £50 note inside, which bought us records and books and a few luxuries to lift our spirits when we next went into town.

Then, in November, unexpectedly there was an invitation to lunch from Mother's solicitor, Mr Cornish. He picked us up from the home one Thursday morning, blanched at our institutional smell and our scruffy appearance but gallantly kept to his plan and took us out for a meal at a smart hotel by the river.

Afterwards he sat us in down his office and told us he had important news for us.

At the end of her rational life it appeared that Grannie Christine had taken a dislike to men in general and had cut her son Derek out of her will, leaving her estate to Denise. Six months before she died Mother herself had made a will in which she left everything she owned to us. This was a little odd, said Mr Cornish, staring at us over his gold half-moon spectacles, because not long before her marriage she had come along to the office with Mr Colindale and together they had asked him to make the surviving partner sole inheritor and Mr Colindale's will had not been changed. What all this meant, he said, staring into our baffled faces, was that since Mother had died after her husband, Helen and I had inherited all three estates and were, he said, nodding cheerfully, really quite wealthy young ladies.

I sat staring at Mr Cornish, taking in his honest schoolboy face and buttoned blazer. I looked at Helen, all her prettiness hidden under a bedraggled track-suit. I glanced at my own reflection in the mirror and saw the weary, adult-child face, the snake-tangle of hair and the snagged, stained jumper.

With commendable restraint, I think, I said, 'Mr Cornish, could I use your phone to make a long-distance call? I'll pay you back, promise.'

By the end of the year we were living in Paris with Ariadne in a first-floor apartment near Les Invalides, with a view of the Eiffel Tower and a glint of the iron-grey Seine from our balcony window and a faint scent of roasted chestnuts coming up from the street below.

20 October 1999, 7.47 a.m.

I've been lying here for hours, enjoying the most delicious weariness, like someone who's come through white-water rapids and now drifts, exhausted but whole, on to a gently shelving beach. I'm through 1975 and there is calmer water ahead, at least for a while.

But, stretching myself a little now, have I learned anything from the act of remembering?

Yes. And something has changed.

In fact, something quite unexpected has happened.

I no longer feel anger towards my mother.

Really, Cass-ahn-dra? I can hear the psychiatrist's drawl.

Yes, really. Though if I'm truthful, and for the moment I am, I don't think I would even have liked Denise Forrester Byrd if she hadn't been my mother. All the evidence – real and imagined – suggests she was a shallow woman who was dangerously free of guilt. She also failed in love. But then so many people do, don't they?

How mild, how reasonable I am.

Shall we test this new generosity of spirit?

Were you and Denise equally to blame for your failure to love?

Ah, no.

Because this wasn't a debatable issue, wasn't a chicken-and-egg impasse. Whichever way you look at it, it's the parent's job to love the child. I agree with those who studied me – and why not, they charged me enough for their views – that, however unlovable I later became, beneath my bad behaviour lay a lifelong reaction to my mother's lack of love. Oh, yes. The way I see it now, the parent *must* love, unconditionally and selflessly, like Dadda. Mother didn't follow the pattern, she broke the necessary circle and cycle of family love, and I and others suffered as a result. That's all.

Now I stretch my arms out like the Rio Christ.

I forgive her.

And am, in turn, absolved.

Ah.

How mellow I am now. I hardly recognize myself. Forgiveness brings the peace of mind that must flow down upon someone emerging from the confessional.

I want to sing out like a Handel chorus.

Marvellous!

Glorious!

I lie in radiance.

Yet – and here is a first wriggle of recurring doubt – I am the pardoner and the pardoned. I decide the terms of my absolution, and they are, unsurprisingly, lenient. Other sins are less readily forgiven.

The mellow languor is dimming, fading now.

Let me drift across my Paris years – of the *lycée*, which was pleasant enough, and a single lonely year at the Sorbonne, which was not – and come ashore in London, in 1981.

I can see her now so clearly.

JULIET

At twenty-one, my sister Helen Byrd is poised on the brink of fame, with a face that is destined to light a thousand flashbulbs before the end of the year. She is dressed in plain black, knowing, I'm sure, that it sets off her figure, which is slender as a medieval princess and emphasizes the beauty of features so finely drawn that they might have been etched in silverpoint. Her fellow students, both male and female, are openly in awe of her, and yet she has spent three years at drama college without exchanging more than a few words with any of them.

Inevitably she had become a figure of mystery. La Snowbird, they called her. Rumours abounded: La Snowbird was still living with her parents; she was the mistress of a married man or a French millionaire or even another woman. Helen herself maintained a sphinx-like silence and shrugged at every wild speculation. Her remoteness was especially frustrating for James Garrison, a burly young drama student who, as Romeo to Helen's Juliet in the first-year production, had actually got to kiss La Snowbird twelve times in the course of one gruelling afternoon's rehearsal.

James had been the envy of every heterosexual male in the class that day, because by then everyone knew that somewhere beneath Helen Byrd's bleached fragility lay unimaginable depths of passion. It was there, you could hear it in her voice. 'Young Helen Byrd is capable of alchemy,' said *The Times* after the college's third-year performance of a new stage play of *The Dubliners*. And when the production transferred to the West End, on the opening night crowds flocked to watch and marvel at Helen's rollicking Molly Bloom filling the stage with hallucinatory vividness. They marvelled even more at curtain call, when a slight blonde girl stepped forward and tranquilly and modestly acknowledged their applause.

How predictable, I thought, as I clapped slowly in the darkness, that my sister's extraordinary acting talent should be innate, unearned and complete. Everyone agreed it was so. 'Helen Byrd is an astonishing and dazzling young diva,' said the *Telegraph* and continued, 'Last night's *tour de force* established 21-year-old Helen Byrd as the most impressive newcomer for years.' You would have had to be very Christian indeed (and I wasn't) to read all that about your sister and simply smile with unselfish pleasure, especially when your own career was as embryonic as mine and your talent so underdeveloped.

So I was pleased to see that, despite her growing fame, Helen herself remained aloof and rather isolated. She never lingered backstage or chatted in the dressing-room, never sat in a late-night café with her fellow students discussing plays or people or swapping gossip. After three years no one even knew where she lived. Some people said she had a flat somewhere off the King's Road, but others claimed she'd been seen in Camden and even Isleworth.

They were right about Chelsea, as it turned out. Helen and I shared a flat off Cheyne Walk throughout our three student years. Why? Because we were each other's only surviving family, I suppose. On an emotional level, I was Helen's vulgar ballast, her sheet anchor. Though later she became confident and even strong, in her own way, back then she was so detached that without me I doubt she could have got through those first independent years.

And why did I stay with her? That's harder to say. I may have seen a heroic dimension to my loyalty, like Mucius Scaevola keeping a hand in the fire, but on another level, there were other, practical benefits. Helen's tidy, compliant nature meant that bills were paid before the telephone or the gas were cut off, that food was bought and eaten at mealtimes and that, of all the many beds I slept in during those three London years, there was one at least which was nominally my own, where the sheets were freshly laundered and ironed.

The flat was large, for two people. It sat perched above the jumble of rooftops, chimneys and walled gardens that led down to the river. Though the rent was high, this was never an issue for my sister. Her needs were simple: private, uncluttered space in which to be, to rehearse and to act. Helen's room was white. White walls, white rugs, white muslin curtains and white linen created an atmosphere of arctic, austere calm. A snowbird habitat.

I don't think she ever went into my lair. She was never tempted to open the door on the appalling chaos of discarded clothes, film boxes, lenses, prints, empty cigarette packets, clogged hairbrushes, overflowing ashtrays and tidemarked wineglasses. Still sensitive and delicate, she would certainly have gagged at the smell of long-worn underwear and tights. She would also have hated the piles of dog-eared paperbacks. (Helen had a thing about second-hand books. Though as an actress she had to read hundreds of books, plays, poems and scripts, she would only work from a pristine text. Sometimes, when she opened the volume for the first time, the spine cracked under the pressure of her long, fragile fingers; when that happened she quietly bought another copy the following day.)

And Helen at twenty-one had a sense of routine and discipline that some of the nuns here in Ithaca would envy . . . Every night at six thirty – not six fifteen or six forty-five – she took a chilled bottle of wine from the fridge and drank half a glass – no more, no less – as she prepared the evening meal. She had designed the kitchen herself entirely to her taste: an uncluttered sweep of stainless steel and beech veneer, spotlit and plain. When she ate alone, Helen always chose Japanese food. She liked raw fish, sliced sliver-thin and accompanied by a small bowl of transparent noodles, with pale lychees to follow.

But when she was not alone, I mean on those nights when she cooked for the two of us, the food was very different. I liked oily stews of tomatoes and artichokes; like Dadda I mopped up sauces with giant cubes of bread, I chewed my way through lamb thick-crusted with cumin, pungent with basil and garlic. I loved seeing yellow cheese ooze shamelessly across a plate. The smell of food, rich as a kitchen alley, almost overwhelmed Helen. Some nights I saw her gagging as she cleaned the garlic press, yet she made herself do it, with that frail Forrester determination Grannie Christine had recognized in her from the beginning.

Every evening, at the start of the seven o'clock news, Helen removed her spotless white cotton apron and dropped it into the wicker linen basket in the bathroom. Then, most evenings, though not all, she sat in the chair by the window to study her lines for the following day, her head almost imperceptibly angled to catch the first thud of heavy footsteps coming up the stairs and my husky voice bellowing her name from down below.

CASSANDRA'S LOVERS

There were many, many nights, however, when I failed to show for dinner, and Helen meticulously scraped the remains of dried-up casserole into the bin.

Well, my sister may have enjoyed the solitary pleasures of her chaste monastic cell, but I didn't. Though a late starter (Montparnasse, 1977) I quickly made up for lost sexual time when we moved to London. Fittingly, one of my conquests there was Romeo himself, in the person of Helen's burly first-year colleague, James

Garrison. Intrigued by her dispassionate accounts of his kissing technique, and on the flimsy grounds of offering to take pictures for his portfolio, I invited him around to my studio one afternoon, lit his pleasant features with flattering care and then, as I held the light meter close to his face, stared into his eyes and breathed a warm and generous invitation to fuck (a simple technique which had proved one hundred per cent successful thus far). James turned out to be more than adequate in bed and I spent many enjoyable post-coital afternoons in his untidy Bloomsbury flat, smoking cheroots and quizzing him about La Snowbird.

Soon, seducing Helen's would-be boyfriends became an irresistible challenge. Of course, if I'd been her identical twin it would have been all too easy to slip into her place, but seducing these handsome, adoring, idealistic young men on my own terms was exhilarating, a positive aphrodisiac. And there were so many men to choose from: Helen Byrd left whole sex-starved flotillas rocking in her wake. Many of them were actors, of course, always ready with a pretty turn of phrase, even for me! Oh, yes. Apparently I smelled of musk, ambergris and truffles; one even recognized – bizarrely – freshly dug earth. Most of them seemed dazed, I remember, as if I had hypnotized them into bed against their will. Perhaps that was understandable when they woke with a start and found themselves lying beside not Helen's lissom body but mine, my powerful limbs entwined with theirs, my big hands foraging confidently between their thighs.

Do I remember these lovers now?

Yes. Surprisingly, I do.

Harvey Mannheim was a wealthy Jewish playwright from New York, who lived in the flat downstairs. I caught him leering at Helen on the landing one evening, and I talked myself into his bed so fast he was never even sure of my name. Afterwards I felt that Helen owed me a debt for saving her from Harvey's more lurid fantasies and (I saw the photos) a most dauntingly Orthodox mother-in-law.

Who else?

Hugo Brownrigg was a handsome, blond English actor with an oddly etiolated personality. He was so mild and unthreatening I often wondered why Helen didn't relent and let him take her to parties: Hugo was invited everywhere and they would have made such a decorative couple. But Helen didn't like parties back then, and so the mournful Hugo sent armfuls of white roses to the flat every Friday for months but never had anything more than a polite thank you in return. Hey ho.

Realizing that this particular conquest might take time, I introduced myself to Hugo as Helen's flatmate, and over a series of agonized *cappuccino* meetings in the café across the road from the apartment block offered to act as a friendly go-between. The night I finally lost patience and seduced him he fought me off with panicky vigour, until I finally managed to tie his wrists to the bed head, which unexpectedly aroused both his passion and one of the biggest erections I've ever seen.

Ha!

Yes, I went through an army of Helen's men that year. Jason (actor/model), Stanton (actor/poet), Eddie (actor/waiter), Desmond (director) . . . even those who refused me point blank at first almost always surrendered when I told them who I was. Once I had confessed, I became, in their eyes, a negative image of my twin, a Queen of Darkness to her Snowbird: my genes were her genes, albeit in a blacker, more erotic configuration.

Oh shit; in other words, they could fuck me and get closer to Helen without compromising their Grail-like quest.

But *why* did I do it?

Why, when I could have made my own choices, did I waste so

many years on lovers whom I knew really longed for, or lusted after, my sister?

Hmm. The reasons are complex.

Which I suppose means that until now I've merely avoided examining them.

Wait.

Reflect.

Well, obviously, I did it to reassure myself that I could. And to show her.

But even when I showed her, in those early London years Helen was so wrapped up in her acting and in maintaining the cloistered, pared-down perfection of her life that I doubt she ever noticed me sniffing along behind her, following her sexual spoor down seedy blind alleyways. And, because I was proud, I only ever once told her about a conquest, and that was much later, at a point when I deliberately set out to unbalance her and throw her life into chaos. And then it worked so well that it more than made up for all those earlier occasions when my little sexual triumphs went unnoticed.

Ha!

But I'm drifting too far ahead again.

Reverse. Go back.

And ask the next question: what about me, Cassandra, aged twenty-one? What else was I doing apart from sleeping with my sister's would-be lovers?

I was taking pictures.

22 October 1999, 9.02 a.m.

TAKING PICTURES

Yes. I was taking photographs: snaps, portraits, landscapes, still lives, busy lives, action shots and delayed-action shots. If it moved or if it didn't, I photographed it. Well, I had to do something. When Helen announced in 1978 that she had got her place at drama college, I felt unfocused by comparison. What I needed, I thought as I watched her fill her bookshelves with her first neat volumes of plays, was a vocation, a sense of what my own life's direction was going to be. A vision, if you will.

But October came, and Helen started classes and I was still aimless. That first morning I watched her go, standing at the window with Ari's old camera in my hands. And then the old gods sent me a sign.

As I looked south towards Battersea, watching a regiment of blue-purple clouds fill the skyline, suddenly I saw a double rainbow form and hang, glistening and perfect, between the two towers of the power station. I threw open the window, lifted the camera, focused and shot. And again. And again. And again. The sun came out and set the rainbow alight, a current of colour between the two yellow spires. I changed position slightly and shot again. And again. Suddenly it was essential that I capture this one moment, this tiny ephemeral beauty. I was panting, sweating, galvanized. When the camera stalled and rewound, I took out the film, grabbed my bag and ran down the stairs to the street. A few hours later, as I walked home through the autumn evening, I held two perfect rainbows safe in my hand, while back on Parnassus the goddess Iris was slipping off her coat, putting her feet up and reporting mission accomplished to Ariadne and that old slave-driver Zeus.

Photographs, I thought, staring at their gold and indigo perfection, amazed that I'd been so blind. So that's what I am then, *a photographer.*

Within a week I'd enrolled for a six-month course, bought an armful of books from the stalls in Charing Cross Road and a second camera for black and white. A woman with a purpose now, I walked around London all day long, my Pentaxes strung around my neck, a satchel of film over my leather-jacketed shoulder, my dark, wiry hair scooped up under a black leather butcher's boy cap. That first day I strode through the college, my great black leather thighs whispering together, a raggy scarf streaming behind me, my boots marching me along like a giant crow about to take flight.

College life was predictably uninspiring at first. Most people seemed to be there because they hadn't qualified for something else. There were wannabe film directors, artists, journalists, public-relations misfits and the terminally bored. Our tutor, Mr Marriott, was a balding man who expected the worst of his students and was rarely disappointed. He handed out sheaves of notes together with a reading list and a summary of the sort of 'assignments' we would have to complete to earn our diploma.

The subjects on his list were dull – 'portrait', 'texture' and the anodyne 'contrast' – and I stayed behind afterwards and told him so. He shied a little when I towered over him but brightened considerably when he relaxed enough to understand what I was saying.

'Oh, yes, you're quite right. They are. Though I have to say you're the first person in two years to point it out.'

It explained a lot.

'Well, Ms er . . .'

'Byrd'

'Ms Byrd. What would *you* like to photograph?'

I knew the answer already. 'Lists.'

Lists were definitely my thing that year. One of my last thefts from Peloros had been Gide's *Les Nourritures Terrestres*, and I'd been mesmerized by those incantatory, tottering citadels of lists. Gide's idea that art could be an exaggeration of an idea appealed to me, and now, through the camera, lists would be the spell I put on the world to make it reveal its pattern.

Gordon Marriott looked baffled. 'Lists of what?'

Well, I said, I thought I'd start with shoes.

In November I photographed nothing but shoes: dancing, working, high-heeled, low-slung, brogues, slippers, cutaway, bunioned, dainty, waterproof, sequinned, velvet, peep-toes, sling-backs, fur-trimmed, patent, suede, silk, sandals and stilettos. At the weekends I flirted with boots: riding boots, ankle boots, thigh boots, button boots, working boots, desert boots, astrakhan bootees, winkle-pickers, cowboy boots and galoshes. Chelsea boots carried me home through London on Sunday night, and on Monday it was back to . . . shoes again: maribou, caribou, seal-skin, pony-skin, snake-skin, rubber, neoprene and glass . . . and, finally, my own large bare feet.

Gordon may have suspected fetishism but confined himself to a professional and generally encouraging critique of the results.

'What next?' he asked, as we sipped coffee in the students' bar early one January morning. 'Fish, is it, or bicycles?' I smiled but told him straight. 'Neither, Gordon. I'm going to photograph London from A to Z on foot.'

'Amazing,' he said weakly. But I was serious, of course.

I began, naturally enough, in wintry Albemarle Street, from where it was a short walk to Beauchamp Place. After that I struck out for the Caledonian Road and then zigzagged west to Drury Lane and Eaton Square, trekked east again to Farringdon and back to Gees Court. I shot Smithfield laid out under its blood-spattered blanket of sawdust and Tower Hill overrun by tourist hordes. Hidden behind my lens, I talked to everyone: doormen and stockbrokers, whores and pimps, street kids and rabbis, florists and tramps, milkmen and draymen . . . By the time I finished (spring in Zealand Street, from memory) my journey had taken me more than a hundred miles. Some of the resulting photographs were dull, but there were plenty of good ones, even though I say it myself.

*

I still like this one. See? Tall trees in Lincoln's Inn Fields, their branches holding skeins of mist and the ghosts of hanged men. And this one of Petticoat Lane in the morning, with the stallholders sheltering from rain, is pure Doisneau, don't you think?

When I arranged the pictures around my room in Chelsea I was surrounded by a subversive London: essentially truthful and assimilable. Gordon agreed, but the examiner didn't: I got only a mediocre mark for both my projects. It didn't matter. At the end of the six months I kissed Gordon on the top of the head (which I had refrained from doing until then, knowing how unsettling he would find it), shrugged, picked up my folder and walked out into the street with a sense of excitement and purpose. There were more lists out there. Soon they became the obsessive rhythm of my life: an intricate, impermeable network of personal connections, private jokes and unlikely resonances. It never occurred to me that other people would find them of interest.

Nine months later a friend of Ari's called Nicholas Millais saw six of my photographs in a sparsely attended post-diploma show at St Martin-in-the-Fields, where a selection of 'Feet' and 'London A to Z' were on view. I ought to have recognized him. If I'd read the right magazines I'd have known that round, owlish face belonged to the most influential photographic gallery owner in London. But I hadn't and I didn't. In fact, when this plump, little man in a well-cut suit came up to me and whispered about possibilities, I almost reached for his crotch. But then, smiling up at me diffidently through his heavy horn-rims, he asked me if I had thought of putting my two photographic series together and calling them 'London, Foot by Foot'.

I liked the idea.

Liked it? I loved it. He understood! My mind raced out to the end of its chain and barked for joy. Immediately I saw a new list. We could hang them with street maps of London, I said, have street maps on tissue paper floating overhead like a river mist of developing prints or ancient banners in a church: Tudor maps, medieval maps, Roman maps, Victorian maps, imaginary maps.

Nicholas put his hand over his mouth and giggled. I loved this man.

'Why not?' he said, his frog eyes sparkling. 'Excess and exhaustiveness: an endless, encyclopaedic, essential, eccentric, endearing vision of the city . . .'

'Oh yes,' I said, grinning all over my Big Bad face. 'Exactly. Entirely. Everything. Except for endearing, that is.' And laughed my loud laugh.

Nicholas tilted his head on one side and stared hard into my face. For the publicity shots of me, he said thoughtfully, he would get Arnold Coltrane.

I raised an eyebrow. Coltrane? Arnold Coltrane had photographed Lennon, Franco, Kennedy. He was in town shooting stills for the latest Keith Hamnett film. Coltrane was an eccentric, wilful tyrant, a legend.

Yet I liked Arnold almost from the moment I met him. Fifty-five, short, dark-eyed, nut-brown, sexy and lined as Picasso, he welcomed me to his Kensington studio a week later with a brief appraising nod and went back to fiddling with a lens. After a long silence he said, without looking up, 'Ah've seen your stuff, lassie. You've got an eye of sorts. It's a shame you're so pig ignorant about technique.'

That caught me off guard and I let out a suitably porcine snort. 'Oh yeah? And what do *you* know, Mr Coltrane?'

Arnold threw his head back, and his answering shout of laughter bounced off the studio walls like a flashlight. '*Everything*, you stupid child,' he roared.

And then he smiled at me.

My legs parted a centimetre. Oh Christ.

'I'm ready to learn,' I said humbly, smiling down at him.

ARNOLD

Filters, lenses, composition, lighting, timing, film, paper, grain, tone – Arnold was right, he knew everything and Everything. And that day he started to teach me. He got me just in time, too, because Nick Millais' prediction was also correct: my first show was a flukey, providential success; without Arnold I would certainly have been rumbled next time around and my career would have been over and done in a day. But tutored, lectured and bullied by an expert, I quickly built a reputation as someone to watch: 'See the world through the bizarre, troubling lens of Coltrane's new Amazonian protégée,' said *Time Out* of my first solo exhibition. Arnold laughed his head off over that.

We were lovers on and off for two years. I moved out of Chelsea and for the first time rented my own place, an ancient, grimy, forgotten set of rooms near Chancery Lane. God, how I loved Temple Vane. I followed many generations of untidy tenants into the place, which was forgiving of slovenliness: generous gaps between the floorboards swallowed the dust I allowed to accumulate, while mice or larger rodents helpfully finished the scraps in the dark cold-water kitchen. Yet from my mullioned window I peered down on the tidal flow of Fleet Street pavements, watching for Arnold, while the lamplighter walked down the alleyway as evening came.

My bed at Temple Vane was a crudely carved four-poster bought from a Clerkenwell junk shop. Curtained in faded purple velvet and set around with sconces which held dangerously flickering candles, I was in my own setting at last. Arnold photographed me there as I lay naked, wrapped in stiff folds of crimson brocade. In

Temple Vane I was the archetypal sensual woman, my monumental hips athwart an ancient, ruined bed. He posed me against the window with my backlit hair waving like electrified clouds. In my favourite shot I stood in the primitive bathroom, my body slick with water poured from a tilted clay jug.

I remember Arnold, his camera poised and ready, prowling around the bare floor naked as a brown-skinned ape, watching me like someone intent on prolonging pleasure until the perfect critical moment. The guy made love to me with that fucking camera: I was half in love with it and half with him.

I've often wondered since how my life would have turned out if Arnold and I had stayed together. I've tried to imagine us working together in our studio: master and pupil gradually becoming equals, quarrelling and making up all day long, alight with ideas, laughter and imagination.

But we didn't.

Because Arnold Coltrane became hopelessly infatuated with my sister.

24 October 1999, 8.43 a.m.

Sister Andrew says there was a telephone message from a Signor Bertone last night, asking if I will please return his calls, since my mobile telephone appears to be permanently switched off. Marco obviously worked his charm on the unworldly sister, for she adds her own pleading look to his words and is affronted when I shake my head.

One call to Marco will open a door to the other world – the one outside this white room – and in will come all the things I've tried to cut loose, the things that no longer signify. Poor Marco. He must wonder why I don't go back to Peloros, where the surroundings are more civilized, less institutional. But no, I'm better off here in

146

Aghios Georghios, first, because I now know that if I am in pain I cannot write, and, more importantly, because this isolated place must be one of the most peaceful anywhere on earth. From this quiet room I can see back as far as I need to and forward as far as I dare.

So for a while Marco will have to be content with unproductive, flirty conversations with Sister Andrew. I have work to do.

Shall we dive again? (I'm getting the hang of words now. I enjoy arranging them, playing with them, teasing out their hidden meanings. Everything is possible.) So. Let's have fun this morning. Let's slip into a tightly fitting extended metaphor, buckle on the battered old memory cylinders, hold the breath and descend through the years . . . deeper and deeper, deeper still, until we touch down in yesterday's place in the past.

LOSING ARNOLD

Though she never mentioned it, I know that Helen had been more than ready for me to leave the Chelsea flat. The next time I saw my old room she had had it scoured of my presence. Entirely white, with shelves of once-used books in strict alphabetical order marching around the walls, it proclaimed its new owner. But I suppose my sister was happy with it, and who was I to argue? At first, out of habit, I had called her every few weeks or so, but with work and exhibitions and travel and Arnold life was fuller for me now and gradually the intervals between my calls and visits lengthened. Helen never once came visit me in the City – perhaps I described Temple Vane's antique squalor a little too vividly for her fastidious soul. No, the next time we met was New York. It was the time of The Birds.

The Byrds.

Arnold knew my sister's face from magazines, of course, but it was through me that he first saw her naked. I came back from the States just before Christmas that second winter and, without thinking, showed him the photo I had taken: *The Byrds*. He held the matte print carefully, his head cocked to study the feathered heads and the gleaming bodies. I should have heard the Siren's call.

'Is *this* Helen?' he said finally, and I nodded. When his stillness lengthened into a foreboding silence I turned away.

There were many rational reasons why we went to see her in *Othello* later that year. After all, the production had been much praised: Christopher Roper was a virile and tragic moor and Helen was, the critics said, the best Desdemona of the decade. And she was. Her innocence even touched me, and Lord knows I've never had much sympathy with that particular quality!

But when the moor took the pillow away from her face and I turned to Arnold for a quick riff of whispered banter, I saw that his cheeks were running wet with tears. Horrified, I looked away. In the dressing-room afterwards Helen was her usual contained, beautiful, fascinating self. I watched Arnold watching her and waited stoically until he invited her to lunch with us in his studio the following week.

I remember she wore blue jeans, a white cotton shirt and a suede waistcoat and small, irritating turquoise earrings that jangled when she turned her sleek head. I had cooked a meal for the three of us. (I know. I never cooked. Why did I do it that Sunday, of all days?) Caught in my own trap, I toiled to and from the kitchen, a lumbering unhappy Martha to Helen's Mary, as she sat and talked and then sat and smiled at Arnold. They were discussing masks, and Arnold asked her whether, like him, she thought the soul was visible even if the face was hidden – and I suddenly knew that Arnold was seeing her naked bird body through her clothes.

He laughed.

She laughed.

*

He didn't hide his first set of pictures from me. Perhaps it didn't occur to him that I would be jealous. But, Lord, oh Lord, I was.

Yet, to be objective, which even now I can sustain only for a second and with effort, the photographs of Helen were some of the finest portraits Arnold ever took. Somehow he got her to act to his camera, without masks or makeup or costume, just with the power of her amazing, mutable face.

And her body.

Her naked actress's body.

You probably saw the pictures: they were in the Sunday papers and every bloody glossy magazine on the shelf, page after page after page of them. And, of course, Arnold was so fucking resourceful, so intelligent, so experienced. He knew just how to attract, to please. He could change, faun-like, become a heart's desire. Instinctively he adopted a far more cerebral approach with Helen than he had with me. The brown-skinned, foul-mouthed grinning ape I had loved would hardly have appealed to Helen Byrd, would it?

Ha!

See, even after all this time there's still pain there, like a bloody splinter, hard and foreign under the skin. So forgive me if I don't linger or try to imagine exactly how Arnold coaxed my sister out of her celibacy and persuaded her to share his bed.

Anyway, share it she did.

Because that's where I found her one rainy Friday afternoon, around the second anniversary of Arnold's and my meeting, when, telling myself I didn't want to disturb him at his work, I let myself in quietly into the studio flat. Finding the place unnaturally quiet, I crept up the stairs, my heart already pounding with the knowledge of what I would find.

They didn't see me, though I hung just above their heads in the big pine mirror behind the bed, my black hair plastered wet about my red cheeks, my body filling all the frame, my chocolate eyes and my purple mouth in three hurt circles. As I watched, Arnold sighed, turned in his sleep and stroked my sister's creamy pippin breast with the palm of his hand.

Oh. Oh. Oh.

I wanted to cut and maim, but instead I stood and watched, just as I'd watched Mother kneeling beside Helen's cot all those years ago, when her own breathing went in rhythm with the quiet rise and fall of the sheet.

Then I lifted the Pentax and pressed the shutter release.

Arnold stirred once more and for a moment I froze. When all was still again I let myself out as quietly as I had come. I hailed a cab and went to Heathrow, caught a plane to Athens and a ferry to Cephalonia, then a smaller one to Ithaca and didn't stop until twenty-four hours later, when I was in my own white room in Peloros with a startled Susie Musselbergh scurrying around downstairs lighting a fire to warm the house for me because it was so cold outside and I was shivering and I had only the clothes I was wearing.

24 October 1999, 5.10 p.m.

Dr Mike came in just now. I deflected his curious glances and cleared the screen. (In the late afternoon light he had something of Arnold's physical, simian charm, though, of course, I haven't yet seen him naked.)

Yet.

Ha!

Sometimes I forget how illness has changed everything.

Odd, isn't it? I've almost always been taller and heavier than my partners, yet gloriously uninhibited in my choice of lovers. But now that I weigh just eight stone instead of twelve I am, incredibly, shy. Perhaps it's not so surprising: for three months now Dr Mike has been the only man to see me naked, and even he has shown depressingly little interest in me as a woman. Of course, he has lifted my night-dress and fingered my belly and breasts – by now he must know them more intimately than many of my lovers ever did – yet he's never once cupped an appreciative hand around my bottom or ruffled my crew-cut or breathed on the nape of my neck. In other times I would have seen his professionalism as a challenge. But now?

I think I blame this new, late mellowness of mine on – what shall we call it? – the 'decline' of my physical appeal. Perhaps I should resurrect my piercing, eagle-eyed stare: the old direct invitation/challenge which always worked far better than a smile. It's worth a try.

I close my eyes, biding my time.

Dr Mike holds my arm, taps a vein, gives me a professional warning nod, then ejaculates his opiates deep into the scarred crook of my elbow. As he straightens, I move my wrist, catch and hold his gaze, connecting briefly and wholly as *me*: original, individual, sexual, interested, available.

He starts, then quickly looks away.

Ah. I am now definitively and exclusively a patient. I exist fully only in this recreated world of memories and myths.

25 October 1999, 5.55 a.m.
A full night's sleep seems to be beyond me now. Every day begins early, as if telling me to make use of it while I can.

So. Beginning swiftly. What were we discussing?

Lovers.

Ah yes.

SINS AND LOVERS
After Arnold there were many, many men in my life.

Unsettled by loss, suddenly unable and unwilling to work, I

became a fully predatory Byrd, ruthless in pursuit of sex on my own terms and territory. For that purpose I bought three more lairs, all oddly similar in their antique, eccentric decrepitude. In New York I prowled around a vast shambolic loft near the Hudson. In Paris Ari's agent found me a cobwebbed suite in the Place des Vosges. Having moved out of Temple Vane, which held too many memories (sentimentality again: oh, dear), I searched for, found and bought an even odder, older little house in the City. At the bottom of a narrow medieval alleyway off Threadneedle Street, Number 17 Cage Street had survived the Blitz and probably the Fire and the Plague. Behind its narrow stuccoed façade, hardly wider than a doorway, three panelled rooms stood on each other's shoulders, linked by a blackened staircase. There was a cellar too, a cave, deep and dry, with Roman arches that disappeared beneath the earthen floor. My neighbour in number 19 was a cheerful whore called Gina, who ran a brisk lunchtime relief service for pressured market traders.

Once I had found it I rarely left Cage Street. All business matters were handled by Marco Bertone, whom I had told to stall or progress projects as he thought fit. I was taking a break, I said. Marco knew why. Only one other person had the telephone number there, and when eventually she rang Ariadne's voice had all the husky unchanging warmth I remembered.

'We missed you at Peloros this summer, Cassimou. How are you now?'

'I'm fine.' The 'now' told me she knew. I had to ask.

'Have you seen her?' I couldn't say her name.

'Last month, here.'

'Here?'

'Ithaca, darling.'

There was a silence.

'Alone?'

'No. With a friend.' Ariadne's voice gave no hold for resentment or pity.

Suddenly I hated her generosity, her unfailing tolerance. What I wanted was something partisan and primitive, a champion. But there was only Ariadne, ruthlessly neutral. I suppose I could have pretended that the line was breaking up, but she would have heard the lie in my voice; she always did. So we both knew it was deliberate when the line went dead.

For a year, I emerged from one den only to drag myself to another and hide. Wherever I was, my only contact with people was with those I slept with. I was like a gambler riffling cards. I slept with so many men that sex became like brushing teeth or swallowing a daily vitamin – a brisk unemotional hygiene. I slept with workmen and felt their broad hard bellies; I lay awake beside fidgeting stock-brokers; I writhed on top of stoned artists; I fucked short, tired waiters in the warmth of late afternoons.

I showered three times a day, sluicing away the smells of other bodies and traces of sweet salty sperm.

Pleasure was rarer, and I almost always found it alone anyway – my orgasms were a private matter, too intimate to be shared with people I'd hardly met, who didn't know my name. Instead, alone in the darkness of Cage Street, or, later, in the charged calm of a Paris five o'clock, I spread my legs, closed my eyes and imagined – what?

Oh, secret pain inflicted on weaker women than myself is all I shall say, I think.

It worked for me every time.

Ha!

The months passed blurrily by. Eventually I began to take pictures again, though the few photographs from that period look as though they were shot through the bottom of a glass – smeared and greasy and as harshly lit as an Eastern European bus-station.

The following winter a letter arrived from Helen. Her distinctive italics were still visible beneath the scrawled redirections which had finally brought it to Paris. There it sat one January morning, a pale blue airmail time bomb, ticking away in the mailbox labelled simply 'BYRD Cassandre' – somehow the title Mademoiselle never fitted. I tucked it into the pocket of my duffel coat and strode out into the square, where the central gardens were almost invisible through whirling clouds of snow. Soft flakes landed on my face, hair and eyes, and the cold made breathing difficult. Head bent, I struggled across to the café on the far side of the arcade, beat off the worst of the snow and stepped into the warm, smoky interior, where I ordered a *chocolat chaud,* found an empty table and pulled the envelope out of my pocket.

Did I really want to open it? I held the searingly hot cup in frozen palms, ignoring the pain. What would she have written? An apology? A description of her (or worse, *their*) happiness and a plea for forgiveness? An airy 'I never wanted this to happen'? Or perhaps just a few sisterly enquiries after my emotional health following a long silence.

Ha!

The chocolate cooled. When I reached the thick sweet dregs at the bottom I paid the bill, picked up the letter and went out again into the blizzard. Halfway back across the square I tore the flimsy thing into pieces the size of snowflake and let them take flight from my hand. Several bits clung to my coat, still pathetically anxious to be read. I brushed them off violently and jogged heavily back through the snow to the felted warmth of the attic apartment.

The following spring I returned to London. The smeary bottle-glass shots had not been popular, and Marco called me and asked to meet. Marco Bertone was an excellent agent: educated, sensitive, likeable, tough and gay; and, now, worried. We sat by the river, drinking coffee on the terrace of the National Film Theatre. It was Marco's favourite view of London. Seagulls planed between the bridges and there was a smell of wet mud and concrete on the breeze. Marco spooned up *cappuccino* froth and studied me carefully. Finally he sighed, unclasped his hands and said, 'Cassandra, let's walk.'

We stood and strolled east along the riverside towards Blackfriars. Early spring sunshine caught the spires of St Clement Danes, blazed from the windows of King's College and glinted from lawyers' chambers beyond the Temple lawns. Arnold and Helen were in New York, she on Broadway, he to promote a retrospective at the Museum of Modern Art. London was mine for a while.

I shivered and wrapped my voluminous black coat closer.

Marco walked slowly beside me, his chin buried in a red cashmere scarf. As we neared the bridge, favourite among London's suicides for decades, he grinned. 'Your girder's over there. Got enough stones for your pockets?'

I shook my head. 'Don't need them. I'm plenty heavy.'

Marco shook his head and sighed again. 'I never figured you for despair, Cass. Why don't you stop being the Woman in White and get back to work?' He rubbed his gloved hands together. 'You've got dependants, remember. Lord knows, Algy and I could do with a trip somewhere warm this summer and you haven't sold a picture since September.'

I smiled and felt tiny muscles strain, stiff with disuse. Marco always knew how to make me laugh.

'How far do you want to go?'

'Bali is nice, we think.'

I snorted. 'That's not a picture, it's a whole new collection.'

'A new collection? Yeah, well, perhaps I should increase my percentage, too.'

I looked at his sharp nose, his amused, crow's-footed eyes.

'One thing at a time, Shylock.'

'That's easy for you to say, sweetie.'

I swept a gloved paw at his head and he ducked.

We walked on beyond the bridge, comfortable together. On a wooden bench, sheltered by a graffiti-covered wall, a tramp lay asleep, trussed in greenish-grey coats and string, his collection of plastic bags at his side rustling in the wind. Marco stopped, caught my arm and said quietly, 'That's a Byrd picture, isn't it?'

I shrugged. 'What, black and white, layers of subtext and a message?'

Marco didn't reply.

The wind blew an empty beer can over and the tramp stirred. Under the grime and the beard, I thought, he was probably a youngish man. I felt guilty, watching empty-handed.

'*Thatcher's Eighties*? I'm no campaigner, Marco.'

He glanced at the sleeping form.

'Maybe not. Though he looks as though he could do with a champion.' Marco sauntered on.

I glared suspiciously at his tweed-coated back. 'You condescending bastard. I thought you were just interested in boosting your income. Now you're giving me lessons in humanity.'

Marco turned and nodded happily, 'I wondered when you'd notice. The time has come, the walrus said, to stop crying over the Lost Boys and get back to living.'

'You're confusing Peter Pan and Alice in Wonderland.'

'I know.'

Behind us, the tramp was sitting up now, his head in his hands, matted hair blowing across fingers black with grime. There was a gleam, and I saw he was wearing a wedding ring. For the first time in a long while I wished I did have a camera with me. And money.

Marco said, 'He'll be here tomorrow, too. He always is: that's his bit of wall.'

It was a lesson of sorts.

I went back the following day and met Karel and took the first picture. He took me to Lincoln's Inn Fields, where the gardens had been invaded by a horde of travellers and vagrants, who had set up a makeshift shanty village. Karel's sometime girlfriend Kim sat under a plastic awning, listlessly breastfeeding a scrawny baby. An older man called Lud lay in his piss-stained cardboard box, growling at anyone who approached him. Their neighbour on the other side, Ellie, was a woman somewhere between forty and sixty who wore a woollen knitted quilt like a shawl and dirty pink bedroom slippers. Her thick stockings were rotting on her ulcerated legs.

Karel's wife had died of a drug overdose soon after they arrived in London. He had worked on a building site until he broke his foot in an accident. He couldn't claim benefit because he was an illegal immigrant and would be sent back to Romania if he turned himself in. Kim had been on the streets for three years, flung out of her Liverpool home by her stepfather at the age of sixteen. I asked if I could take pictures of them and their baby, and they asked if they could be paid, which seemed sensible. In turn, they introduced me to their other neighbours, Jockie and Beano, two gaunt, morose young men from Dumbarton who were supposedly looking for work in the building trade. At midday they went off to the West End to beg.

Ellie spat after them, 'Bloody Scots gits, go home if you don't like it here.' Then she turned to me and said, 'I'm a singer, you know. Was on the stage once. Oh yes, dear.' She broke into a cracked warble, breathing whiskily at the start of every line:

'We are in love with you, my heart and I,
And we are always true, my heart and I . . .

And yet my darling, if we ever say goodbye,
I know we both should die,
My heart and I.'

Weeks later, waiting in the queue outside the Odeon Leicester Square, I heard that voice again. The few people who knew the song tried their best to pay her off before she made a last screeching assault on the impossibly high note of 'heart'.

I developed the Lincoln's Inn Fields pictures myself. And Marco was right, because they were photographs of people isolated and alone, and their faces were the Arbus faces I had admired in my teens. I was fascinated by what the camera saw in their eyes: a gaze stripped down to the bare metal of nature. It made me curious. Were the watcher's eyes any different? One night I set up the tripod in the cellar of Cage Street, wadded myself in my voluminous black coat, bounced a test flash from the ceiling and took a single shot.

Later, floating in the developer tray I found a big sad face that stared out at me with utter impersonality. I pored over it with my magnifier, examining the dark pupils, the curve of the nostril, the thick arching line of the brow. I tried to see myself as a stranger, setting aside all preconceptions of personal knowledge, shame or pride. Yet the deeper I stared, the more my face reminded me of someone else, and it wasn't until I was on the point of dropping into sleep that night that I remembered a gaunt, hostile figure reeling away from the camera which she suddenly believed was going to suck the life out of her.

Ellie.

I kept in touch with Karel and Kim for a several months that summer. Then one day Karel wasn't on his bench on the South Bank. When I went to Lincoln's Inn Fields to see if he was ill, the plastic roof of the shelter was torn and flapping in driving summer rain, with only a heap of dirty disposable nappies to show that there had ever been a family there. I didn't recognize many of the squatters now. One well-spoken man in a disastrously stained camel-hair coat told me that Old Ellie had gone weeks before, off on some ancient route that she followed every spring. He thought the Scotsmen had found building sites somewhere in north London and said that the police were encouraging the remaining travellers to move on so that the gardens could be returned to their traditional summer occupants: the slender, white-skinned legal secretaries and their colleagues. No one had news of Lud.

Once their subjects had vanished, the photographs seemed to lose their vitality. I put them in a box file and told Marco I wasn't happy with them. He sulked and asked if he could borrow the file. Without asking me he took them over to a Mayfair gallery owner pal of his and they came back a month later with a design for an exhibition that would be shown on boards specially erected in the empty winter fields of Lincoln's Inn. I ranted awhile – I don't like being railroaded – but the idea was already growing on me: my travelling friends would be back where they belonged. I stopped objecting and helped Marco and Piers stage what became one of the most talked-about shows of the late eighties: 'Margin'.

'Margin' played in parks in Leeds, Bristol, Manchester and Birmingham. It spent the spring in Scotland and was in the square of the Palais Royal in Paris by summer. It paid for Marco's holiday in Bali, and I donated my share to Shelter, a gesture which was viewed with depressing cynicism when Marco let it slip to the *Guardian*. What can you do? Except that I still wished I'd done something practical for Karel and Kim, who had vanished leaving only their pictures behind to speak for them.

Nevertheless, working had helped change my mood. Feeling strangely optimistic I felt an urge to reconnect with life. From my new air cushion of confidence I decided, rashly you may think, to revisit and lay (*Ha!*) a few ghosts. So, telling myself it was an impulse, I went to see (well, yes, I knew that would mean 'sleep with') Arnold. Just one last time.

I should have known better. Not that Arnold refused. Far from it. But it was immediately obvious that our relationship was never going to resume where it had left off. Even physically there were changes. Arnold's small body seemed to have shrunk, while I had mysteriously grown and now towered over him like a giant when we embraced. Out of habit I explored his mouth with my tongue, all the while feeling confused and embarrassed that we had ever been lovers at all.

Still, having gone that far, there was nothing else to be done without hurting each other's feelings unnecessarily, so we ended up naked in the same bed where I had found him with Helen the year before. Our lovemaking was considerate and kind enough but meaningless. When I got up and went to the bathroom in search of a towel, a casual search revealed Helen's Vuitton makeup case in the airing cupboard and a pair of her virginal-white Dior panties lying unchastely crumpled in the bottom of the linen basket. I went back into the bedroom and, ignoring Arnold's outstretched hand, I picked up my clothes from the floor without word, dressed quickly in the hall and was out of the door before he realized that I was gone.

26 October 1999, 8.33 a.m.

Yesterday was a marathon session. From before dawn to after midnight. If I were healthy I would never have been able to do it: there would have been photographs to take, shopping to buy, cats to feed. But here, suspended in medical aspic, I have all the time I need for the moment, and can overwork to my heart's content.

Not that there aren't a few side-effects, though.

My thumb joints are red and hot, like overstressed bearings, which, of course, they are, after a day's thudding up and down on the spacebar. I've been resting them against the cold iron frame of the bed since I awoke and it seems to have eased the inflammation a little.

Today is Dr Mike's day off. Though he's so selfless that he's probably doing home visits to poor families in his spare time. A saint, my doctor is. When he dies, I have a feeling the women of Ithaca will pray to him as they do at the tombs of other holy men in the island chapels. (The women kneel on the stone floor, their cheek pressed against the reliquary, while the priest covers their head with his hands and takes them through an elaborate ritual of confession and entreaty. The outcome, I think, is final acceptance of the very thing they hoped the saint might change for the better.)

I myself have no expectations of anyone or anything – saints, angels, God, gods, fate, magic or destiny – intervening to save me. And, in a way, I'm pleased: miracles have always seemed such an illogical proposition. Why should God interfere on a Divine Whim (I like these Divine Capitals!), when He has already decreed a Perfect, if unpredictable Cycle for Everyone and Everything in Creation? OK, enough: upper cases read like hiccups. The point is that if, as believers say, the Creator gave humankind the inestimable gift of Free Will (sorry, last time, I promise) so that they might choose whatever things are choosable in life, then why should anyone beg for it to be superseded by direct intervention in the form of a last-minute miracle?

I'm not a believer, but even if I were, it's fairly clear that health and recovery are no longer choosable options in my basic free will package! And even if I did believe, I still wouldn't pray for a miracle, because that would mean setting aside the most valuable clause in the whole damn contract as far as we humans are concerned. And for what?

Just to postpone the inevitable for a few more days or months or years.

We all die.

Like my Sorbonne professor, I love those lines from Montaigne: 'Les plus belles vies sont, à mon gré, celles qui se rangent au modelle commun et humain, avec ordre, mais sans miracle et sans extravagance.' And I'm with Montaigne there – no miracles for me either (though I think by the end he might have relished the odd swish of extravagance now and again). But no, I won't be praying today or on my last day either, provided, of course, that I'm still in my right mind and not being floated out of life on a floodtide of opiates.

They may do that. Sisters and priests love to round up departing souls and shepherd them into their religious fold for eternity, in my case consigning me to dispiriting aeons in Purgatory in the company of perfect strangers . . .

Ah. Poor taste. Sorry. *Pace*, Sister Andrew. For though I am glib and flip, with slices of snide, I'm really not as cocky as I appear. In fact, I'm beginning to understand why so many people opt for conversion on their deathbed (such a bleak, ancient word: is there a sanitized modern term, I wonder?), though it seems unfair that an accident of last-minute confession should deliver an eternity of anything.

But, then again, very few of us are so virtuous or innocent that we can afford a high-stake, win-only, 'take-me-as-I-have-been-or-leave-me' bet on redemption. I certainly wouldn't risk a flutter. After all, my own admissions already include: (a) promiscuity, (b) real, contributory or imagined manslaughter, (c) incestuous desires, (d) assault and (e) adultery. And then there are minor sins and generally antisocial behaviour to be taken into account: jealousy, farting, greed, snorting, sadism, violence, peeing, biting, coprophilia, spitting. I'd also have to own up to murderous thoughts concerning my sister.

And there's worse to come.

Yes.

Pass by quickly, don't look yet.

For I have done some things that I know are unforgivable. At the very thought of them I turn away from myself in horror. There is nothing to say. Never has been.

Until now, as I find myself working my way towards them.

For I have come to realize how important it is that before the end of our life we reach an understanding of our true condition. This answer can only be found deep within ourselves, and we reach or approach it only by drawing conclusions from our own and other people's experience of life, however brutal and unpromising it may appear.

And to understand my own truth I must first remember.

So. No choice.

I descend.

Of course, not all memories are dignified.

LOW PLACES

In the months that followed my final disastrous encounter with Arnold I fucked so many men that even I lost count, though I noted without amusement that certain sociological patterns emerged even from this activity: businessmen preferred to keep their boxer shorts on; bureaucrats checked their watches after lunch; tramps stole and left a stench of unwashed bodies on the sheets; students asked me for payment; and aristocrats regularly handed me cards and proposed weekends of orgiastic excess in Long Island, Neuilly or Maidenhead.

I was beaten up several times, occasionally threatened with knives and woke once with an Algerian stevedore's hands around my throat. I fucked instead of eating, instead of drinking, even instead of taking pictures. Ariadne grew concerned, found pretexts to drag me out from my lair in whichever city I was in so that she could feed me healthy meals, sobering coffee and good advice.

Eventually, I saw my addiction for what it was and admitted I needed help.

The treatment, I was told by my new East Side therapist Dr Louise Manners, a surprisingly frank and sexually explicit woman in a neat blue Jean Muir dress, would involve lithium and abstention from sex for a total of six months, at which point a gradual re-entry into normal life could be effected. *Ha!*

It was not going to be easy, she said, briskly and with a good deal too much relish for my taste. And she was right: it wasn't, though, as it turned out, there were certain compensations for a lifetime Big Bad Patient. When Dr Manners' 'colleague', a middle-aged male analyst called Leonard Potts, questioned me (as he often chose to do) about my penchant for older men, I avenged myself by making his trained eyes flicker with each restless, celibate shift of my mini-skirted thigh.

Here's a piece of free advice. No matter how much you are tempted, never tell a psychiatrist, policeman or journalist your whole truth; it's far too valuable a commodity to be squandered on experts, especially when you are paying them so dearly to listen. I never told either of my sex shrinks about Georgie or Jeanne or Michele or the fact that after losing Arnold to Helen I bedded a succession of carefully chosen women, several of them fragile blonde actresses and almost every one of them a Gemini.

Well, they could have, should have, guessed, really, shouldn't they? Any textbook will tell you that if a child is deprived of (or, in my case, never really knew) a mother's love, a sister figure is natural substitute.

I'm wandering from the point. Am I talking too much; telling too much? Perhaps I should delete these last few pages. Beginning at . . . 'Here's a piece' and ending at 'substitute'.

There, it's highlighted and ready to go into a cyber bin.

But even as my middle finger hovers over the key I know that's wrong.

The only way to see the truth is to peer into the constantly distorting mirror that is me. Its deformities are my own, and I'm bound to reflect them, blackly and deeply, if not truly and madly.

Ha!

Ha!

Laughing tires me, too, now.

End.

Save.

Let the humming stop for a while and the overstressed machine cool down.

If I turn on to this side, a different set of bones make new depressions on the sheeted bed. The pillow, turned, is smooth and cool as marble under my head.

What bliss.

28 October 1999, 8.10 a.m.

Christ.

You know, even though I began this story in search of self-awareness, a grain of worth and meaning behind my life, I'd have to say, looking back, that so far it's a pretty unedifying tale. In olden times I'd have ended up hanging from a tree in Lincoln's Inn Fields: a crow-pecked warning to others.

But no one, not even me, can know the truth until the end, can they?

So?

So.

It's time to leave sin and guilt behind. Instead, let's dally for a while with the Sirens on the Isles of Pleasure.

THE SIREN'S CALL

Less than three years after my last visit to Arnold's studio and bed, I was pleased to read in the papers that his affair with Helen was over – though even now I still come across those old luminous Coltrane pictures of Helen Byrd in newspapers and magazines. My sister is the sort of person who regularly appears in those 'faces of the year/decade/millennium' features so beloved of lazy editors, and, of course, her two great love affairs, first with Coltrane and later with her husband, were the stuff that media wet dreams were made of.

So, yes, there is a picture of her somewhere in my bedside cabinet. It was a *Time* magazine retrospective: we see Arnold's Helen at twenty-three staring out at us, bare-shouldered and fabulously beautiful. (I came to pity gallant old Elspeth Coltrane in the end: at least Arnold's photos of *me* naked never appeared in her breakfast broadsheet.) I often wonder if Elspeth, like me, was secretly relieved when, shortly after parting from Helen, Arnold suffered a stroke that left him paralysed down his left side and temporarily unable to speak.

After this calamity Arnold was in hospital for a long time; when he had finally improved enough, Elspeth took him back home to Finchley and nursed him for years with what I imagine was the most touching and unwelcome devotion.

(Despite what you're thinking, I never wished Arnold ill. OK, OK, I admit, during the first months after Helen took him away

166

from me I *did* make a rather stumpy brown wax doll and kept a supply of sharp pins in readiness. But, no, I could never bring myself to press them into the doll's rudimentary limbs or to pierce its round blank head.)

Did Helen suffer much when their affair ended? I've no idea. I expect so. I certainly hoped and imagined she did. We hadn't spoken for years by then. Oh, I'd heard news of her, of course. I knew that her career blossomed while they were together. She was in demand both in Hollywood and in Europe, often made two or three films a year and was becoming known for her golden touch. It was true: she seemed to step from *succès d'estime* to commercial blockbuster in an ever-upward direction, her smooth progress followed by a claque of salivating producers and studios.

So I was interested to read that after Arnold (unlike me!) Helen had apparently gone back to her old reclusive ways. The studio PRs in LA must have had sleepless nights over that: here was a star who shunned publicity, never slept with co-stars, rarely gave interviews and never appeared in tabloid gossip columns. But, being Helen, after a while her very reclusiveness came to fascinate the media, and I began to see carefully hyped shots of her in hotel lobbies or airport concourses, looking pale-faced but still ethereally lovely.

'Does this face belong to the loneliest woman in the world?' cried *Vanity Fair* one month.

'No it bloody doesn't,' I yelled out of habit and buried myself still deeper in work.

Restored to a more even sexual keel, I was travelling the world taking pictures, racing from country to country as if pursued. My passport in the late eighties shows I was in Nepal, Korea, Greenland, Madagascar, Chad and Peru, all within the space of a few months.

Wherever I went, my camera gravitated towards strange locations and bewildered people. In one three-month period alone I did projects on prostitutes, plastic-surgery patients, caravans, butterflies, blood, dwarves, beaches and car wrecks, and my pictures appeared regularly in Sunday colour supplements and journals in Europe and the States. I took thousands of pictures and was fanatical about quality, destroying each less-than-flawless negative with a perfectionist zeal worthy of La Snowbird herself.

Marco Bertone had come up with a strategy that made sure that there was a launch of a new Cassandra Byrd exhibition somewhere in the world every six months. I liked the plan: it kept me moving. And Marco was right in other ways. Ingeniously he insisted that my fabled 'Geisha' collection remain permanently in Kobe, where it proved a remarkable tourist draw and resulted in me being honoured by the city fathers.

Other shows were specifically designed to go on journeys of their own. I criss-crossed the planet in 1991 to promote the 'Cathedrals' series (yeah, that one was brazenly commercial, I admit: but I'd queued to see Monet with everyone else) and followed it with a UNESCO urban arts project, 'City Deserts', which helped raise a quarter of a million dollars for homeless kids in Brazil – my emerging quixotic streak, see? Then there were the glossy books. *Penis Envy* appeared in 1992: it was great fun and extremely sociable. I followed that with the rather more cerebral *Artists at Work*. Then came my year of unlooked-for courtroom drama when I was sued by a top American restaurant chain over three pictures in my controversial 'Fast Food World' collection – an unusual case of photographic libel that I won with costs and which made me a hero and a vegetarian for a while.

So, no, I didn't mope after Arnold, as you can see.

In fact Helen and I were each rising in separate worlds, she famous for her face and me for my pictures of other people's faces. Our names were linked only occasionally by the few gossip columnists who remembered *The Byrds*, had heard we no longer spoke and were curious about why twins would quarrel.

It wasn't that difficult to discover the reason. One Sunday a British tabloid phoned me up to ask me if Arnold had ever slept with Helen and me at the same time. The idea made me so angry that I got the most terrifying libel lawyer in town to issue a writ which shut them up immediately but kept the 'did they, didn't they?' story bouncing around the papers for weeks. Helen, of course, put out a cool, dignified statement saying she had no comment, and afterwards I wished I'd done the same. But I guess when you are Beauty, the idea of being in bed with your lover and big ugly rival is so preposterous that it's hardly worth fighting and, after all, she knew which of us Arnold had chosen in the end.

I had a dream once where Arnold stood at the end of my four-poster bed, looking down at me, and I knew I was big and cumbersome in my nakedness. (What had he called me when we were together? His C-cow. Not 'sea', you understand.) Then in my dream I turned and saw Helen lying next to me, her fragile, desirable body angled upwards at him, waiting for him to choose her. They laughed together with the intimacy of lovers.

When I awoke I hated my sister even more than the day I had found her and Arnold together. Yet I suppose there were advantages in our being estranged. After all, just as Ariadne had planned for us so many years before, we were now truly separate individuals rather than twins. And, ironically, during this period Ari herself was the only link between us. She and I met two or three times a year, usually in New York or in Paris. I knew she bought many of my photographs and that some of them had already found their way to Ithaca. I also knew she went to see Helen perform whenever she had a West End run. She was like a grandmother scrupulously observing the visiting rights in a divided family. She should have been satisfied with that.

But she wasn't.

It troubled her that Helen and I had quarrelled and no longer spoke. What would Dadda have thought? So in 1992 Ariadne revised her views on our independence and made up her mind that we must be reconciled. (As Odysseus could have warned us, that's the trouble with having a *dea ex machina* on your case: capriciousness is a characteristic of interfering divinities.)

In July that year she invited both of us to her white-pillared house in Notting Hill.

I arrived late. Deliberately? Yes, of course. I'd got out of the cab in Knightsbridge and walked slowly through Kensington Gardens, delaying the moment of meeting for as long as possible. When I arrived I stood at the foot of the steps for several minutes before acknowledging that the thing could not be put off any longer. Slowly, I climbed the steps, rang the bell and, when the door opened, bent to embrace the rich-smelling Ariadne.

'Why are you doing this, Ari?' I whispered as I patted her flat little back.

'What do you mean, why?' Ari pushed me away, her hooked nose flared with pretend anger, 'Eh, Cassandra. *Someone* has to, and who else would?' She slipped my leather jacket from my shoulders and put her arm around my waist. 'Come on now, my big brave girl. You can do it.'

I looked at her sharply. Sometimes I thought I heard a trace of well-practised Ulster accent beneath the husky Greek voice.

'I'm here, aren't I? What more do you want?' I said warily.

'Ah, much, much more than that, Cassimou,' she said, pinching me gently on the cheek.

Ariadne brought me through the house to the candlelit back garden. And there under the tree, curled in a wide wicker chair as on that first night at Peloros so many years before, was my twin.

Her hair was shorter than when I last saw her asleep on Arnold's pillow.

Helen rose and held my gaze as I walked down the path towards her. She was wearing a short, jade-green dress and a white jacket. When I was only a pace away she hesitated then held out both hands. Actresses do that sort of thing. I kept my own arms rigid at my side. We stood and looked at each other.

I didn't think she'd aged much, to be fair, though there were faint lines of tension beneath those pale, appraising eyes. Defiantly I stared into her skull, prising at the edge of her mind until she shook her head. No, Cassimou, not that.

Suddenly I laughed. She smiled.

We nodded at each other and sat. It appeared our estrangement was over.

Pleased with her handiwork, Ari brought out a tray of crystal goblets and ice-cold vintage champagne. She settled herself between us as friend and mediator and poured the wine, which was rare and heady, tongue-loosening stuff. We sipped and talked, at first to Ari, then, hesitantly, to each other. Later we ate, food carefully designed to remind us of Peloros.

When the meal was over Ariadne sat back and looked at us appraisingly in the candlelight, reaching for her cigarettes. 'Darlings, well done. I am so pleased to see you together again. How happy your dadda would have been.' She flapped the match in the air and huskily, breathing out a swift smoke trail, she said, 'But I must admit now that there was another reason why I asked you here tonight. And that is because of a remarkable – what can one call it? – we need a Greek word, of course – a synchronicity of events. Yes.'

She tapped ash on to the lawn and continued. 'For the first time since we know each other, how many years now, my little ones?' (Thank you for the 'little', Ari.) 'Twenty? More? Aie, it's not possible! Anyway, no matter, for the first time we are all three of us alone and free. We are', she said solemnly, 'a waiting potential. No one and nothing holds us back from whatever we may choose to do.'

I frowned. 'I'm already doing what I choose to do.'

Ari smiled her famous crooked smile. 'Yes, Cassimou, I know. So is Helen, and so am I to that extent. But, listen. I have an idea whose time is right. Believe me. And I know in my heart,' she thumped her chest hard with the flat of her hand, 'here, that we must recognize and grasp it now.'

Ari leaned forward, and gripped my wide-knuckled hand and Helen's slender one in hers. 'We are the Sirens of Peloros.'

'What?' I pulled at my hand, but Ari's grasp was tighter than I expected.

'Wait. Listen to me. You remember the Sirens?'

I didn't forget myths. 'Half-bird, half-woman, they lured men to their island with irresistible song and devoured them, so they did.' Dadda's Ulster voice, the wavefall in my ear.

Ariadne laughed, 'I hear Feargal, too. Yes. A Siren's song was irresistible. Now, listen to me.' She let go of our hands and lit another cigarette. 'I am fifty-nine. As an actress I know my career is on its downward slope.' She flicked a dismissive hand at Helen's protest, 'Yes, yes yes, as even yours will be when you reach my age, my dear. It's no matter.

'Also, I have spent thirty-five years travelling the world like a nomad, living a few weeks here, a few months there. A film, a play, a new setting – this house, the Paris flat, the apartment in New York, none of them is home. And so', she paused with an actress's timing, 'I have decided to go back to Ithaca. Permanently.'

Helen and I glanced at each other in surprise, but Ari wagged her finger. 'Eh, no, I am not retiring from the world. Old as I am, I am hardly,' she blew smoke out in a long straight stream, 'hardly the retiring type. No. What I shall do is create a summer centre for the arts on Ithaca. At Peloros. And I would like you to help me.

'My friends,' she said, and I recognized that compelling mesmerizing voice, 'I believe that together we can make something unique at Peloros, something so brilliant that it will attract and nourish excellence from all over the world.'

There was that famous iconic grin again.

'And we three will be its guiding spirits, *Sirens*. Those whose song is irresistible. Whose call is eternal. Your dadda would have loved the idea. Siren.' The husky voice flowing over hard Greek consonants, caressed the word. 'That's what I am. That's what you are. What we will be. Yes.'

Helen turned her blonde head, white as polished marble in the moonlight.

'Who will come to Peloros, Ari?' she asked in that cool, melodious voice.

Ariadne smiled at her. 'Artists of every sort. Actors, painters, writers, musicians, philosophers, photographers, singers, sculptors. All through the summer there will be schools, workshops where the best can teach the next generation and their own. And we will be there each summer to keep the whole magical place spinning like a sphere. Do you see it?'

She looked from me to Helen and back again.

'What do you think? Shall we be Sirens together?'

I reached for my glass and drained it, playing for time, ignoring the song that was playing in my head – summers in Peloros, my childhood paradise regained. It was too seductive, too soft, too dangerous. I frowned into Ari's animated face and drawled,

'Ari, I can see *you* as a Siren, and Helen here was born one. She'd have had Odysseus swarming up the beach with his tongue out, begging to be allowed to stay, wouldn't you?' I turned to her. 'You do it, Helen. You were born for this.' Then I turned to look Ariadne in the eye. 'I'm more of a Caliban than a Siren, Ari. I'd end up dragging disreputable men into Peloros by the hair on their heads. But Helen would be just *perfect*. Wouldn't you, sis?' I threw my head back and laughed my Big Bad Baby laugh.

My sister shrugged the perfectly cut shoulders of her white jacket, smoothed a spotless lapel. 'Perhaps,' she said and somehow managed to let the word hover above the table, like a sail slowly filling with imagination.

Surprised, I gave her a hard glance. Her thoughts were still well concealed, yet somehow I knew the idea was glowing deep in her mind. I looked at her face. It had never occurred to me that she might actually like the idea, that while I was changing she, too, might have altered to the point where she might prefer the company of other people to being alone. Seen from this new perspective, Ari's idea wasn't a grappling hook lashing us together but a lifeline to pull us back into a more sociable, peopled, human world.

I drummed my fingers on the arm of the chair and stared hard at the two of them. Over the years I'd come to put a high value on my 'otherness', my idiosyncratic and bizarre bolthole life, where I made sorties, took pictures, made money and disappeared again into my lairs. Boldly staying out in the sunlight would be a new challenge. Why shouldn't I take it?

There was a long silence. Ari sat between us, her head back, looking up at the skyful of stars as if she had never spoken. She was, I knew, waiting for answers.

Helen took the smallest sip of her white wine and looked over at me.

'Should we, do you think, Cassandra?'

Over the gardens of Notting Hill a church bell struck a single hour, and I wondered how far the reverberations carried – would they hear it through the open window in the hospital near Hampstead Heath, where women struggled to give birth and new lives started with a yell?

'Cassimou?' Ari's voice was soft, and I realized that she had asked me a question.

A few moments earlier I had wanted to refuse. I'd planned to sneer, throw a tantrum, make a scene that would embarrass them both. Instead, I breathed the night air of damp grass deep into my lungs and released it slowly.

'OK,' I found myself saying. And felt as though I had set down a large weight that I hadn't even realized I was carrying. Light-headed, I took a risk and smiled at my sister, 'OK, sure, Ari. I'll give it a go. Why not?'

Ari's eyes suddenly filled. 'Good for you.' She lifted the second champagne bottle to the light, 'Oh dear, it's empty.' She yawned, and the long, strong jaw was like an icon. 'I'm too tired to think properly. We agree in principle, and that's enough for tonight. So, shall we meet here a week from now and make plans for the Sirens of Peloros?'

Finally we owed her too much.

'Yes,' we said, and our voices overlapped in the dark.

I walked back through the quiet summer night to the City, following an eastward course through the ancient twisting back streets, to my burrow.

LEAVING FOR ITHACA

I have to say that Ari had picked her time well.

The following morning I threw open the window of 17 Cage Street, sipped orange juice and sat with a notepad balanced on my knees (no laptop back in those pre-cyber days), watching with surprise while idea after idea added itself to a list headed 'Peloros'.

First, there was my own specialist area, of course. Between us Marco and I knew many famous photographers and artists who would surely agree to lead workshops and classes across the summer and attract other, newer names to listen. Photography needed

175

exactly such an injection of inspirational thought. The pencil flew down the page. There could be annual themes, a scholarship, a Peloros award for photography. I put down the pad and stared out into the misty sunshine, wondering what Helen was thinking, in her white room, miles upriver in Chelsea.

When we met a week later, Helen too had her list and of course, since she was an actress, the names on her list were far better known than the photographers on mine. Young Shakespearian virtuosi, charismatic new film stars, fashionable new directors. The only problem, she said, pleased to see that we were impressed, was that, though she herself was absolutely enthused at the idea of Peloros, her time was committed months ahead and she would not be able to come to Ithaca until the end of August. In fact, that might well be the pattern of her involvement in the future, too, since she was often filming during the summer. Would that matter?

Ariadne scanned the list. 'No, darling. Though it's sad for you. But these names you have here are so exciting. I have a very good feeling about this. And I have been busy, too. Look.'

Unsurprisingly, Ariadne had the most impressive address book of the three of us. She had already spoken to Anthony Cropper and his wife Marianne Lucas who would like to do a two-week course on dialogue. The tenor Federico Casales had called her back early this morning to say he would be delighted to come for a month the summer after next. Enrico Matteo was coming to dinner the following day to discuss a masterclass in landscape. Anita Yu and her boyfriend Malcolm Lewis had gone away to think about a course on composing for violin.

'Eh? What do you think, my little ones?'

We gaped. This wasn't a summer school, it was a renaissance movement

The idea of Peloros shimmered and took on substance.

In September Ari returned to Peloros and presented the dazed Susie Musselbergh with a sheaf of notes for their neighbour and friend, the architect Leonardo Gallides.

29 October 1999, 6.30 a.m.
Today I am well again.

If I wanted to I could climb that hill over there, outstripping every spry brown goat as I leaped from rock to rock, pursued by bells.

When Dr Mike comes, I tell him this, and he smiles with genuine pleasure and wags a finger at me.

'You see, Cassandra Byrd, I told you, there are no straight lines in illness.'

'Perhaps my illness line has stopped altogether.'

Dr Mike makes a complex expression with eyes, lips and angle of head, which seems to say, 'Maybe. Let's hope so, though it would be highly unlikely.'

He tells the sisters I may have wine with my lunch. Things are looking up.

So today is a day to seize.

Quickly. Start at once.

Skid back down through six years, and remember.

The reaction to the idea of Sirens took even the positive Ariadne by surprise. Within a month we were almost fully booked for June and July and were already turning away people who had heard about the Olympian collection of artists hosting workshops on their own particular specialism. Next season's Peloros programme had already written itself from those people who had loved the idea but whose commitments prevented them from attending the inaugural year.

In April I closed up Cage Street and handed the keys to Gina, my prostitute neighbour, who promised not to dust while I was away.

All through that summer, the boats from Cephalonia nosed their way through purple and turquoise water into the tiny port on Ithaca's western shore. The guests – those artists, musicians, students, amateurs and professionals who had responded to the Sirens' call – stepped ashore, breathed in the scent of pine and myrtle and swayed gently against each other as the wagons brought them slowly over the hill to Peloros.

In the evening they came down to the courtyard rested and refreshed and found a place at the long table set out beneath the vines. Mingling with the course leaders and other guests, they shook hands, talked, laughed and drank as the sun went down.

At nine Ariadne clapped her hands and stood. Her dark voice spread through the dusk like honey.

'Ladies and gentlemen. We make no claims for ourselves: like you, we all have flawed, imperfect lives beyond this place. But here at Sirens, we have drawn a circle of enchantment. Today, you have stepped inside that circle, and while you remain here we hope you will find and take from it whatever you need: peace, relaxation, the stimulation of excellence, a chance to watch time pass slowly, to savour the pleasures of intellectual and physical well-being.

'Let us begin.'

By September 1993 I had listened to those same words many times, and yet every time I heard them they spoke directly to me and, I think, to all of us who sat around that long, long table under the vine.

The following day I moved from class to class, fascinated initially both by the teachers themselves and, later, by the taught.

*

My favourite picture of that first year is here, in the black folder.

Wait.

Here.

See?

It was taken at noon, a time of high contrasts and sharp shadows. Under an awning Filomena Harris and Federico Casales are singing, surrounded by an audience of twenty cross-legged people, old, young, middle-aged, dressed in T-shirts, shorts, chinos and caftans. The music is written on the faces of the singers and in the expressions of the watchers, a luminous, tangible connection between them.

I had listened and watched for an hour. When I finally released the shutter I knew that I had caught more than the moment itself. That photograph, *Masterclass*, became an enduring image of the place, and many people took copies away with them.

Yes. It was clear from the beginning that Sirens was unique. In the letters that came from Britain, America, Italy, Argentina, people spoke lyrically of their first summer at Peloros. And, even better, they said, the magic had survived the return journey and was with them still; they talked of heightened perception and a sense of joyful belonging that flowed from the island itself.

Even I felt it. Each picture I took that summer seemed to hold a distilled drop of its essence. When I look at them today, the smell, taste and touch of Ithaca come back to me, and I remember the feeling: it was as if I was beginning anew.

But then, one Sunday morning in September, Helen arrived.

Pale among the tanned residents of Peloros, she was nevertheless immediately and visibly at home. After a few days' rest and relaxation she began her own set of classes, which would run through to the end of the season. She called them 'Still Drama'.

I sat in on one of them. Her brilliance was appalling. In those last few weeks the axis of Sirens changed and began to revolve around her. After a week of competing I cancelled my remaining classes, pleading a mysterious virus, and spent my remaining days down on the beach. The water lapped over my shoulders, and when I dived I swam down into a blue-vaulted, silent world where no Siren voices sang.

Eventually October came, and the last band of guests waved from the covered wagons, their voices calling out thanks and promises to return.

Iconic in white, one arm raised in salute, Ariadne stood under the arched gateway and watched them until they disappeared over the hill. Then she turned to Helen and me and put a hand on our shoulders and somehow her presence short-circuited, once again, the bitter distance between us. As we walked together under the green shade of the vine Ariadne squeezed our hands and raised them in hers.

'A triumph, my dears. Tonight we three celebrate the end of a perfect beginning.'

I found myself smiling at her. And then I smiled at Helen, too. Whatever my misgivings, for the first time in my life I was part of a circle.

Suddenly life stretched ahead of me, waiting to be discovered and enjoyed.

30 October 1999, 10.05 a.m.
Yesterday morning, when I woke and felt so well, the process of remembering seemed therapeutic. It was as if, by diving in and out of this pool of memory, I was salvaging something rare and valuable from my past, which had the power to heal the body and the mind.

But when Sister Andrew came to take my temperature at noon

she announced that I was running a fever, and I suddenly became conscious of my pulse racing fast and loud deep in my ear and throbbing in the corner of my jaw. The afternoon was plagued with headache, dry throat and agonizing stomach ache.

Dr Mike has been managing my illness so efficiently ('palliative care' – isn't it a wonderful term?) that real pain came as a surprise when it uncoiled and began to eat its way through my body. In the afternoon I slept for a while, but around dusk I woke to hear some- one wailing and discovered it was me. They brought me a jab of morphine then, and its rush of relief set me drifting on a black tide of dreams.

STRANGE PORTENTS

I dreamed I saw Ithaca far below me in a Hebridean-grey sea. Vast grey breakers crashed on the pebbled shore. Amid a mewling of gulls I flew lower, straining my ears to catch the songs of my sisters that would guide me home to Peloros. But I heard nothing. There was nothing to lead me home, and I knew I was lost.

Then, in my despair, I saw a ship with fifty oars, battling purposefully against the seas and the windblown sheets of spray. I folded my wings and plummeted down, my eagle beak slicing the wild air. Just above the wavetops I skimmed alongside the ship and read the name with horror.

The *Argo*.

I saw she carried her fatal crew of heroes: Jason and the Dioscuri, Hercules, Amphion, Theseus and Meleager. And I knew that she also carried the man who would bring death to the Sirens. Terrified, I screamed aloud to warn my sisters on the shore. But my cries were swept out to sea on the wind or were buried under the toppling waves. And it was too late anyway, for on the heaving deck stood the tall, fair-haired man, the lyre already in his hands. He lifted his yellow head and began to sing.

And Orpheus' song was the song I had always longed to hear and dreaded to hear, and at the sound of it I felt my feathers grow heavy as stone. They hung massive from my shoulders, and under their weight I hurtled down towards the waves.

The last thing I saw as I sank beneath the chill grey surface was my sisters crying together on the shore, holding out imploring hands that were already stiffening, palm to wrist to shoulder, into the barren mindlessness of rock.

I woke bathed in sweat, as if washed up from the seabed by a storm.

I knew who Orpheus was.

PELOROS, 1995

Three o'clock in afternoon on the island of Ithaca. Bushes of cystus and thyme crisp quietly in the afternoon heat.

It is the third summer of Sirens. Already the summer schools at Peloros are legendary, and our guest list goes forward to 1999. Our lives have assumed new patterns. Ari now stays more or less permanently on the island, leaving it only at Christmas, which she spends with old friends in Paris. Helen is even more famous than before, since a documentary crew followed her around Los Angeles for two months last year documenting her progress towards her first Oscar nomination and then followed her to Sirens last September.

I, too, have been busy, living out of a large black holdall chalked with the customs hieroglyphics of the world, striding jet-lagged through terminals towards the next exhibition, the next shoot. My travelling camera case has worn such a deep groove into my left shoulder that I'm thinking of mentioning it on my passport as a distinguishing mark.

Yes. For me the last two years have been one of the most creative periods I remember. Wherever I am, hidden away from the world or jetting around it, new ideas and themes are always jostling in my mind. I put this down partly to the influence of Peloros. Exceptionally gifted artists, musicians and actors come to Ithaca, and our late-night conversations under the vine spark ideas which become reality over the winter months.

In spring I worked with Jethro Mullings on the setting for his new opera *Penelope,* while James Garrison (remember Romeo?) began reading excerpts from the *Odyssey* for a tape that will play during the London exhibition of my Peloros photographs next September.

Marco is pleased to see that I am suddenly so prolific (of course he is – his earnings have increased dramatically over the past two years, as have mine). And yet the biggest change in my life is one that would surprise most people: I now have friends; friends from Peloros who seek out my company; friends (yes, astonishing) who come to stay with me, who have seen the *inside* of Cage Street and the attic in the Place des Vosges, and whom I visit in return, in their various parts of the world. I am beginning at last, it seems, to connect.

(On a more familiar note, Sirens has also proved a fruitful source of lovers, which is fortunate, since, though I have not returned to the orgiastic numbers of ten years ago, I am destined, it appears, to remain promiscuous and occasionally downright predatory.) And so when not with friends, or enjoyably alone, I dine and later sleep with many men – academics, tycoons, actors, musicians – who I know look at me and see the terrace at Peloros, who breathe the scent of its pines in my hair and feel the smooth-ness of olives when they run their hands over my breasts. I don't mind. In fact, it pleases me, for I am part of Ithaca now. At Peloros I feel that one day I may even come to terms with who I am.

But I don't kid myself: emotionally I have been, and still am, flawed. (One thing is certain: I shan't ever have children – there are far too many gaps in my emotional and genetic makeup: I'm like a swaying wooden footbridge with too many missing slats. Why pass this rickety DNA structure on to future generations? No reason that I can think of.)

This summer, Ariadne is watching me. When the Peloros becomes too crowded she sees that I usually disappear off to the dark-room I have installed in one of the outbuildings or stride off up into the hills with my camera bag and a small bottle of water, returning sunburnt and pleasantly tired just before supper. And because she watches me, Ari knows I will already have cast an appraising eye over the new group. At some point during the evening, she will see me moving in on my latest, unsuspecting prey.

Sometimes, if she sees me sitting on the terrace steps, Ari glides past, ruffling my hair as she would a child's. 'Cassimou, you have dark rings around your eyes. You are living too hard, running too fast. Why don't you slow down a little, eh?'

'I'm OK, Ari. Keeping busy is good for me.'

Ari waves a cigarette around the Ionian horizon. 'Even here you give yourself no time.' She reaches down, stills my drumming fingers and looks at me enquiringly. I have no answer for her. I am a still a solitary person who was born a twin – it creates a certain tension, I suppose.

Last year we had to employ a security guard to patrol the Peloros boundary. We caught paparazzi prowling around the gardens with their telephoto lenses, trying to take shots inside the bedrooms of the more famous guests. Then one night a lunatic fan of Helen's crept into Susie Musselbergh's room by mistake and tried to attack her. The outside world has begun to intrude on Sirens and I suppose will continue to do so.

But up here, in the afternoon shade of a fig tree high above the bay, Ithaca itself is still paradise. The sea below is indigo and emerald, aquamarine at its edge. The pines shade slopes whose rocks remember Odysseus. It is hot, even with the faint breeze stirring the air. A bead of sweat rolls down from my hairline to my jaw. I roll over to check my companion's watch and shout as my foot flops outside the blue shade of the leaf canopy and touches the baking white rock beyond.

'Ouch. Iannis?'

I sit up, rubbing my ankle and feeling for my sunglasses. The boy lying naked beside me is in his early twenties, his brown body sprawled across the cotton rug. For a second I study the fronds of dark lashes flickering against his cheek and the faint smile on his face. His thoughts in Greek are difficult to follow but run like shallow water over pebbles. Abruptly I lean over him, my heavy breasts swinging carelessly as I jab him in the ribs.

'Iannis. Hey. Time to wake up. The boat will be here soon. Iannis, come on now.'

The boy rubs green eyes awake. 'Miss Cassandra?'

'It's four – the boat's coming in. Susie will be looking for you.'

I have made progress over three summers and speak in rapid colloquial dialect, which is muffled by fabric as I draw a white cotton shift over my head and shoulders.

The young man rolls away from me, his fingers scrabbling across the rug for a pair of faded red swimming trunks. 'It's OK. She won't mind if I'm late.' He stands, runs a hand back through sweat-darkened curls.

Briskly I sweep my mass of hair into a topknot and secure it with a wide silver clip. 'Maybe not, but Ariadne will. There's a special guest this evening.'

'Special?'

I can see that Iannis is looking uncertainly at my nipples, which are swaying under the thin, embroidered lawn. 'Yes,' I say firmly, folding my arms. And then, relenting, I reach up and pull the young man's head down to my mouth. 'Look, it was very nice, Iannis.

We'll do it again some time, maybe. Yes? See you later now.' I slip thick unvarnished toes into white flip-flops, hook my leather satchel over my shoulder and stride off down the hillside.

Iannis watches me pick my way down through the shimmering olive grove towards the main building and the sea beyond. '*Efharistó*, Miss Cassandra,' he murmurs, his voice a mix of pride and relief. Of the few women Iannis has slept with in his short life I am probably the tallest and the scariest. Perhaps the oldest, too, for, though he knows I'm in my thirties, alongside him I feel aeons older. Far below him now I reach the corner of the white house. Out of the corner of my eye I see Iannis raise his right arm and wave goodbye, but I have no answering gesture for him, and turn briskly through the arch into the shade.

'Cassandra, where the hell have you been?' Susie Musselbergh brakes her headlong rush across the courtyard and glares at me over an armful of neatly ironed table-cloths. Tightening her grip on the linen she angles her bony wrist forward so that I can see her wristwatch.

'The boat lands in *half an hour*, Cassandra. *Half an hour.*'

Dispassionately I study the damp tendrils of hair plastered either side of Susie's red face. The woman is a born housekeeper, but even with her much expanded staff she is beginning to resent the extra load that Sirens' success has placed on her. She has even been trying (unsuccessfully, of course) to involve *me* in the logistics of catering.

My heart isn't in it, I tell her.

Now I roll my eyes. 'I *know,* Susie. That's why I'm *here*. And we'll be ready, won't we, because we always are, aren't we? Anyway, it's only *Helen*, isn't it? Or, rather,' I roll my eyes again, 'Helen and her *mysterious friend*.' All Helen has told us is that she is bringing someone with her this year. A secret lover, it is rumoured in the British press. A man whose identity she is keeping so secret it has not even been vouchsafed to *us*.

186

'Perhaps he's royalty,' I say and watch Susie blanch. I can sense her thoughts racing like mice through a maze and feel an impulse of pity. Not unkindly, I say, 'Hey, look, Suse, if you can't stand the heat, why the hell are you racing around at the hottest time of the day? There's no point working through the siesta. You'll just be exhausted by the time they arrive. Remember, people come here in search of calm, not sweating, stressed-out Sirens.'

Susie squints angrily up at me, trying to make out my expression. I know she has been complaining about me to Ari: somewhere in her neat little soul she disapproves of my slovenliness, my language and my wayward prowls through the male guests' rooms at night. Now, acutely conscious of her own nervy dishevelment, she hitches the table-cloths higher and says, '*You* may be a Siren, Cassandra, but *I'm not*, and I wouldn't *be* so bloody stressed out if you pulled your weight.'

I draw my unplucked eyebrows together. Now I am like a lioness circling a limping wildebeest. 'Hmm, I see. Well, if you're fed up with playing Martha, why don't you do something about it instead of moaning? Hey! Why don't *you* lead the photography discussion tomorrow instead of me? I'm doing "Lighting the Nude Body". You can ask Helen to pose – everyone will be so thrilled – especially her. How does that strike you?' I grin belligerently.

Susie reddens.

I am overstepping several previously respected marks here, notably by referring to Susie's passionate and almost certainly unrequited love for my sister.

'Shut up,' she yells. Then suddenly she drops her shoulders and says brokenly, '*Please* don't, Cassie. Just help me with these sodding table-cloths, will you?' Her eyes are brimming. I feel ashamed, and it takes a real effort not to stretch out a hand and take a few of the creased bundles from her after all. But, then, tonight's much-heralded guest of honour is only my sister. I

187

straighten my shoulders and draw myself up to my full five foot eleven.

'Fuck off, Susie. I don't do table-cloths. Ask Ariadne.'

Susie's eyes bulge. '*Ariadne*? Are you insane?' she cries.

'No, she's not, Susimou,' comes the famous gravelly voice from just behind her. 'Despite her natural crudity, I'm afraid Cassandra is often the sanest person here.'

Ariadne herself, majestic in bronze cotton, stalks across the sun-lit flagstones towards us. 'Darling,' she says, kissing Susie on both hot cheeks. 'Give me those,' she takes the pile of table-cloths, 'and come and sit in the shade for a moment.'

'But they'll be *here* in a hour,' wails Susie.

'And we shall be ready for them,' says Ariadne, settling herself into a rattan chair and draping the folds of her skirt across a foot-stool. A swallow, swooping from beneath the vine, flies low over the stone basin in the middle of the courtyard, dips its beak in the water and soars up over the wall. Ari calls back over her shoulder into the kitchen.

'Cristos? Are you there? Could we have three glasses of peach juice, please?'

Ariadne turns and pats the blue-and-white striped cushions on the sofa beside her. 'Now sit. Both of you.' Susie slumps down, kicking the sandals from her hot, damp feet. I stand for a moment, hands on hips, making a point; then, shrugging at Susie, I ignore the sofa, hitch my skirt indecently high and lower my thighs on to a delightfully chill metal chair.

Ariadne reaches for a packet of cigarettes, takes out a long gold-tipped menthol and lights it, drawing heavily. Her eyes narrow in the rising smoke and the lines around the hook nose deepen as she smiles her peacemaker's smile.

'Better, my friends, eh? Yes? So. Helen arrives this evening.'

Susie's frown unclenches slightly; she adores it when her idol is here. But then she remembers that this time will be different and her face clouds over. 'Who's she bringing with her? Do *you* know, Ari?'

'She didn't say, darling,' replies Ariadne vaguely, clearing newspapers and magazines from the table. Cristos arrives with a frosted jug and three tall glasses and lifts each one in turn to fill it with red-flecked peach juice. He sets mine down last, with a petulant bang, and a thin wave of orange liquid spills over and runs across the tabletop towards me.

'Sorry, Ms Byrd. Enjoy. Please,' The voice is as frosty as the glasses.

'No matter. Thank you, Cristos.' I grin, and light a cigarette.

Ariadne watches the tight, narrow-hipped walk as her major-domo stalks off.

'I told you not to go after Iannis,' she says wearily. 'The island is too small.'

'Bollocks, Ari,' I say comfortably, 'He came after me. Almost. And, anyway,' I grin and roll my eyes maniacally, 'I don't think Iannis is lost to the cause. I frighten him far too much for that.'

Ariadne frowns. Nowadays, despite her praise of my sanity, she finds some of my pronouncements worryingly obscure.

Susie gulps at her juice, then, refreshed but still anxious, she picks up her linen and rushes away.

Ari looks after her fondly and turns to me with a sigh. 'Eh, Cassandra. Why do you tease poor Susie like that? She is kind and good and loves you very much.'

Uh-oh. I don't want this conversation now. I stand and drain my glass. 'She's fond of Peloros, Ari, and very devoted to you. But it certainly ain't *me* that she *loves*.' I raise a hand, half in apology, half in warning, 'Look, I'll see you later.' I'm already halfway across the courtyard when Ari calls after me.

'Cassie, will you be here when Helen comes?'

Without breaking stride I say, 'Don't think so. I've still got notes to do for tomorrow's class. And after that there's the ritual evening swim. No rest for the wicked Siren, eh? Bye.'

'Goodbye.'

The thoughts Ari sends after me are disappointed and full of foreboding.

Of course, I have already prepared the class, but for form's sake I spend half an hour in my room jotting notes in the margin of notes until the pages are unreadable. In the end I have to print off a clean copy of the first version and work from that. It's five thirty. On the other side of the island the boat from Cephalonia will be nosing into the little bay.

I slip out of the house, which, thanks to Susie, is ready and expectant now and hurry down the sandy path through the pines to the sea. Slipping on my mask, I glide out over the urchin-studded rocks and into deeper water. Grey-and-yellow fish weave above the sandy seabed as I swim on steadily out into the ruffled blueness of the bay. Turning around and treading water I can see the tall fig tree on the hill where I fucked Iannis this afternoon. His sperm is slowly trickling from me out into the Ionian. Perhaps it will fertilize Neptune's daughters and cause them to bear handsome Greek mermen. I float on my back, looking up at the blue curve of the sky over Ithaca.

Then, suddenly, I glimpse a white swaying canopy, and the first covered wagon crests the ridge on its way to Peloros. Almost immediately it disappears down through the pines again, and the second wagon appears at the ridge and pauses at the top. There is a tiny glint of gold, and I know that Helen is there in the front. I kick out gently at the water, keeping still, trying to focus on the minuscule figures half a mile away. Is that a tall fair-headed man next to her? The wagon passes into the trees.

I hang motionless over the deep water, suddenly afraid to swim back to shore.

Let's start with the bare facts, shall we?

FRANCIS

I met Francis Hammond at half past eight on the evening of 5 September 1995. As usual, I'd joined Ariadne, the leaders and guests for a pre-dinner drink in the courtyard and was moving smoothly between them, a seemingly relaxed giantess but in fact uncomfortably aware that with Helen's arrival my equilibrium was under threat.

I knew she was there when I heard that murmur run through the crowd. Glamour had entered the room – the star was come among us. Without turning, I heard Ari's voice welcoming Helen and her companion. I listened intently, straining to catch his name, hoarding every advantage I could get. I heard Ari's voice rise in surprise and then soften to murmurs of surprise and pleasure. There was a pause while kisses were exchanged. But at that point the guest on my right chose to ask me about my latest exhibition, and by the time I listened again the murmur of voices had faded.

Still I didn't turn around. She would have to come to me.

Minutes passed. I spoke to guests and was spoken to in turn. Then, suddenly, there was Helen's voice, silvery soft just behind me, and this time there was no mistaking what she said as she introduced her companion to Casales and Filomena Harris.

'Federico, lovely to see you again. Filomena, may I introduce my husband, Francis Hammond.'

My companion asked me a question, but I stared through him, aware only of a new, oddly familiar voice behind me.

'Thank you. Yes, in Venice, three months ago. She is. I know. Thank you.'

I sent my mind down into the cool deep waters of the bay to compose itself.

Then Helen was approaching. I felt the light touch of her hand on my arm, gently pulling me around to face her. I was almost ready for them or, at least, for her. There was the usual chill of her perfume, the perfectly burnished cheek, the fall of gilt hair.

'Cassandra?' Her eyes blue and wary, reflecting a lifetime's apprehension of my reaction.

'Helen.'

And then she was reaching a hand behind her and saying the same words that she'd already said to Casales and all the others, giving me no choice but to look. Turning, I stared straight into the eyes of a tall, fair-haired, thickset man.

'Francis Hammond,' he said.

I noticed that his eyes were oddly shaped, almost Mongol, curved and narrow like two grey scythes.

He nodded his big shaggy head. We stood eye to eye, smiling, the two tallest people in the room. Mechanically I stuck out my arm and said my name, feeling the enormous paw of his hand, firm and powerful, enveloping mine in its warmth. He smiled.

'I know your pictures.'

Oh God, *this* was Helen's husband?

I wanted him.

I desired him.

I craved Francis Hammond with every nerve-ending in my frame.

'Hello,' I said.

'Francis and I met last year in London,' said my sister, re-entering the conversation. My eyes slowly swivelled back to Helen. 'And then again in spring at a film launch. Next thing we knew we were getting married in a tiny stone chapel with carved cherubs on the ceiling and a priest in a monk's habit. Like something out of *Romeo and Juliet.*' She laughed and squeezed her husband's hand. 'I don't know how we've managed to keep it a secret so long.'

Helen looked at me as she spoke, taking in, I supposed, my sunburnt skin and wild, salt-tangled hair. She herself was cool in a pale-green sleeveless dress, her arms shapely and slim, her tiny painted toenails resting in her sandals like perfect cherries in a basket.

I was reaching for a witty, deadpan reply and at the same time positioning myself to catch every nuance of Francis's reaction to this sickly romantic nonsense, when suddenly a group of people came up to us, surrounding the famous one, claiming her attention.

His arm protectively around my sister's narrow shoulders, Francis Hammond slowly moved away from me.

Overhead, stars wheeled crazily across the sky. The air was sucked out of the courtyard and breathing became impossible. As Ari called her guests to table I reeled out through the arch and out into the darkness beyond.

1 November 1999, 5.17 a.m.

Today is cold, cold, cold. The dawn is hours away, but the screen is throwing out its own steady glimmer, enough for me to see the keys but not their letters, and so I mistype sometimes and write in cipher. Would anyone guess that *Gtsmvod* is really *Francis*, transcribed one small place to the right? Perhaps they would, the puzzlers, the witnesses, the readers.

You. If you are there.

(Though I may still decide to delete everything, to hold the cursor above the small brown folder icon containing these all words, and at the last conscious moment type the single letter that will agree to its destruction.

Y.

Just like that.

A single Y. And everything I've lived and remembered and learned has gone for ever.

Ha!

No, I'm serious. In fact, to make sure that it remains an option I've deleted the back-up file and wiped the old diskette clean. From now on, fittingly, this is a life without a safety net. To leave it behind me I must consciously *decide* to save it and then, at the last minute, send the disk, as I once was myself, to a Place of Safety.)

Some people, especially my sister, would prefer that my story vanished with me. They may be right. Personally, I'm still not sure. All I know is that at thirty-nine I've already outlived all the people who might once have read this out of loving kindness. So if I go on writing it's for my own reasons, because somehow it's become important to find small truths and leave them behind me, like a homing trail of pebbles through the forest. Will anyone follow? It doesn't matter. At least if I save them, the words may keep my pictures company after I'm gone. They might even outlive them in the end. Who knows?

So.

Continue.

Go back across four years and three hillsides and drift down to Peloros, where on the terrace, the following morning, I am having my first breakfast with Francis Hammond.

I was up at six, ravenous. The house was peaceful and I tiptoed down to the courtyard to breakfast alone. Cristos had laid out fresh fruit, bread and yoghurt on the tables under the vine. I picked a fig from the basket, dug my fingers through the ripe skin and pulled it into crimson gobbets. When I looked up from my plate Francis Hammond was sliding into the seat opposite.

He nodded hello.

I put down the torn fruit, folded my hands over it and managed an awkward nod, trying to fit the man to what I'd heard of him. Of course I'd known his pictures for years. A few of them had hung on the walls of the lairs so long they'd become almost as familiar as my own. Not that they were anything like mine: Francis's photographs were hard-edged, spare, with something distinctive in them, a kind of moral vehemence, in a hungry child's face, an old woman's outstretched hand, a soldier's swagger. And his pictures charted the course of late twentieth-century conflict: Colombia, China, Belfast, Russia, the Falklands, Yugoslavia, Lebanon, Israel, Pakistan, Afghanistan and Ethiopia. Last winter I'd watched his images of internecine violence come in from Bosnia, and they'd been as harrowing as anything from Dachau fifty years before. He'd been interviewed on television after that and, with the rest of the country, I'd watched a naturally taciturn man making a supreme effort to describe in words what he had seen. St Francis, the tabloids called him now and showed his face as often as his pictures, like a badge of authenticity.

I watched him eat. He was a big man, broad-shouldered, with a boxer's broken nose. He looked around forty-five, those long narrow scythes had sheaves of lines below them.

My sister's husband was holding a bread roll, his broad hands tearing it apart, scattering crumbs over the table like snow. He saw me looking, laughed, quickly brushed the debris on to the flagstones for the sparrows, then pointed to my own red-stained plate.

'Messy eaters, aren't we?'

I couldn't place his accent: it had a burr that could have been West Country or Liverpudlian, a drawl that was Irish or Californian. He poured orange juice into a glass, reached across to offer me some. His forearms were thickly covered in blond hair and his skin smelled like hay. I shook my head. I was breathing dizzyingly fast. There was a long silence while we ate.

195

'Would it be OK if I sat in on your class on Friday?' he asked suddenly, and I felt my stomach lurch under its content of half-chewed fig. As he looked at me my shoulders expanded to the size of an American linebacker while my hands swelled like giant bananas on the table in front of me. I was Alice in Wonderland, growing through the fabric of her surroundings. Inwardly I groaned. Was it possible I could stand up and give my standard talk on 'The Nude' while Francis Hammond, his skin fresh with the memory of my sister's body, sat there and watched me do it?

'No,' I said tartly, 'it wouldn't.'

He looked taken aback. Rubbed his big crooked nose with his index finger.

Don't ask why not, I thought. Don't ask me, because I can't say.

'Why not?' he asked stolidly.

Oh shit.

I'm usually good on my feet. Even then, despite this uncharacteristic panic, a squad of serviceable excuses rushed into my head and quickly lined up. All I had to do was pick one, for God's sake. In the space of a second I'd run though them, weighed them up, discarded the weak ones, shuffled the remainder and chosen. But it was while my mind was racing along in idle that I made a bad, bad mistake.

Carelessly I looked into his face.

It's hard, even now, to say exactly what happened. I remember it like a blow under the ribs. All I know for sure was that in the space of a second I decided to derail the past, bend the future to my Big Bad will and claim what was rightfully mine. Suddenly I was super-calm, my clever brain racing away.

'Why do you care?' I said nonchalantly.

He grinned, which did terrible things to my heart, lungs and legs. 'Are you always like this?'

Sulky and paranoid, he must mean. 'Like what?' I said insouciantly, wiping my lips on the back of my hand. (I was rallying now and stronger.) 'Surely the famous Helen told you all about me?' I bet she did, I thought. 'Cassandra, my "twin" sister, Francis. Just wait till you meet her – big as a bison and certifiably bi-zarre.' But strangely he's still smiling, though his face looks unused to that expression.

'She didn't say much. But I knew that you were twins, of course. And, as I said, I'd seen your pictures.'

Yes. He'd seen my pictures.

'Really? Which ones?' Well done, Cassandra. Except he's still bloody smiling.

'Well, *The Byrds*, of course . . .'

Oh Christ, he's already seen me naked.

'. . . and your pictures of the homeless.' He paused, hesitated and went on, 'Arnold Coltrane was a good mate back in the eighties. I'd already heard about you from him.'

Great. This man and I had been orbiting within fingertip reach of each other for years. I must have walked through his thought-waves on Arnold's stairs. If I'd arrived late or early or unannounced I might have met him before Helen; I might have caught those grey scythes and watched my whole life reel off in a different direction.

I stared at the shiny red-gold ring on his left hand. Then I peered closer. It looked a little tight and new for comfort. And despair had never really been my thing.

I leaned forward.

1 November 1999, 11.25 a.m.

The pain came back half an hour ago. If Dr Mike were to ask me I'd tell him it felt as if someone were peeling my stomach open from the inside. When it came on I had to clutch the computer and cling to it as if it were a tiny life raft. After a while, with difficulty, I freed one hand and shook the bell, and a few minutes later Sister Andrew came bustling in. She sat with me while I moaned and kept mopping my forehead and squeezing my hand in sympathy.

'We'll wait for Dr Mike to prescribe the new dosage,' she said. We? *Ha!*

'He's coming soon,' she said. 'He won't be long, I promise.' Then she checked the watch she had pinned on the front of her scapular. Prayers called. 'I'll come back, Miss Byrd,' she said in her thick peasant-soup Greek. 'And he won't be long now, believe me.'

Alone, I closed my eyes against the pain and typed anything that came into my head. I have the page on screen now. Looking back on it is unsettling.

He won't be long.

She won't be long.

It won't be long.

I can do it. I can take it.

Write. Write. Write.

He's coming now, coming soon, making the sign of the blessed needle outside the doorrrrrrr

Sweet Jesus

Help me Help me Help me Help me Help me..hlllllp me eeeee.

AAAAAH HELLP

hhhhhhheeeeeeeeeeeeeeeeeeeeeeeeeeeeeeeeeeeeeeeeeelllllllllppppppppppppppppp

Gtsmvod   gtsmvod gtsmvoddddddddddddddddddddddddddddddddddddddddddd

Later

I'm floating here.

Pain-free.

Swinging in the air. Up and back. In the ticking of a clock, in the

198

clicking of a shutter, in the winking of a scythe, I'm floating through a blue day in Illyria. Over the hills and far away a lute is playing. Over the hills and a great way off an enchanter is walking through the olive groves. The goats fall silent in the afternoon sun and my heart is turned to stone.

Francisssssss my snake in paradise.

My paradise.

I can't fly any more

Forgive me

Dadda

Gtsmvod

2 November 1999, 8.10 a.m.

Still darkish – the days are shorter. How fitting that I'm fading with the year.

Some time during the long, wakeful night Sister Andrew returned. I remember she gave me cold water to sip and spoke to me when I tried to move. She said Dr Mike told her that predicting the correct morphine levels for me was difficult now. Too much and I hallucinate; too little and . . . well, now we know. My body is going down fighting, apparently. Good for me!

When Dr Mike called I asked the How Long question, but, thankfully, he just smiled and wouldn't or couldn't say. So I lie here as the sisters come and go, smelling the incense that drifts up from the chapel prayers, hidden in the folds of their robes.

High up in the corner is the yellow square, paler now, awaiting next summer's butterfly.

I slide my hands down under the uncreased sheet, feeling my xylophone ribs, stroking gingerly over the grotesque, taut swell of the belly, gently so as not to wake it. Its southern slope ends abruptly in the bony dish of the pelvis and clump of springy black curls between my legs.

Francis's blond head, lying on my thigh.

Ha!

Shall we sleep now?

2 November 1999, 2.18 p.m.

Resume.

If you study any couple for long enough, and especially if you are looking for it, you will eventually notice a tiny tic of imbalance, an almost imperceptible difference between two partners, a nuance which separates the one who loves from the one who is loved.

In those first days I studied my sister and her husband surreptitiously for hours on end. I noted the line of her neck when she looked up at him, the way her hand reached out and touched him like a lodestone every few minutes, the grateful curve of her hip against his body when they walked hand in hand. I watched her talk and him stand silent at her side. And I watched a flicker of distance and abstraction in his eyes, an irritation with the people who now followed Helen everywhere, just to be close to the star. I saw the way he twisted the new tight gold ring on his finger and, when he smiled at her, the faintest tinge of regret. By Thursday I was sure: Francis Hammond was an introspective, solitary man who had been briefly dazzled by my sister's interest in him – and, of course, by her irresistible beauty. While in this state of blind grace he had acted out of character and married her. Now, he realized he was trapped. Now, as they say in the movies, I had to think for the two of us.

And I did.

In the heat of the afternoons, while Peloros and its guests slept, I climbed high into the hills, to think, to plan, to scheme, to plot. I tramped up and down lonely defiles, my head filled with the buzzing of crickets and the smell of burning bushes until, at last, I saw how it could be done: a little, invisible incision, a first tiny prising apart.

I was so pleased.

But before I could begin, later that same night someone knocked at the door of my room. My bed was covered with photographs of and by Francis Hammond and I hurriedly swept them under the pillow before opening the door.

'Cassimou,' said Ari, 'can I come in?'

One must never refuse one's patron goddess anything, especially when one has embarked upon a dangerous project whose outcome is eminently unpredictable.

'Yes,' I said. 'Come in, Ari.'

She came in and sank into the old tapestry chair near the window. I was surprised to see how tired she looked and wondered why I hadn't noticed before. There were streaks of white threading back through her hair from her temples and, under her eyes, odd tobacco-brown shadows. I poured her a glass of whisky and waited.

Cleverly, she didn't tell me straight away why she'd come. Instead she acted (who better!) as if she'd just dropped in for a chat with a fellow Siren, and for a while we gossiped mischievously about Federico Casales' dislike of Enrico Matteo, about Anna Yu's visibly swelling belly and Antonia Clayton's blind passion for Susie Musselbergh. Out of some sense of delicacy, I noted that she didn't mention either Francis or Helen.

'Here at Peloros we offer people art and truth and beauty and peace of mind,' sighed Ari, lighting a cigarette, 'and all they can think of is sex.'

Was this an oblique criticism of me? I shrugged. 'It's natural. They're talented, attractive people living close to each other. They're enjoying themselves.'

Ari looked hard at me. 'And you, Cassimou. Are you enjoying yourself?'

I knew from a tightening of her jaw why she had come, so I scowled. 'What d'you mean?'

Wearily, Ari raised her eyebrows. We can make this difficult or easy, her eyes said. Which shall it be?

Don't give me hassle, I frowned, getting ready to send her packing. But as I glared into those steady brown eyes, which shone almost purplish in the soft glow of the lamps, I suddenly heard Dadda's voice asking me, 'What's wrong, kidda, eh?'

'I love him,' I said, and was amazed to find my big broad shoulders heaving up and down helplessly like a child's and my eyes spilling tears.

'I know,' said Ari, and she put her arms around me.

SERPENTINE MANOEUVRES

Afterwards I was grateful to Ariadne.

That one breakdown, one confession of weakness to someone I knew would never tell a soul, actually made me stronger. Naturally we ended up reassuring each other that I would get over it, that Francis was not for me, that I would find someone else, that I had my career, my life inside and outside Sirens. In other words, I comforted Ari as best I could. But nothing changed in *me*. I was set on a course now and would follow it to the end.

Would I have done what I did if I'd known what the end would be?

Probably.

Yes.

In the same way that, offered two cups of poison, one would still choose the sweeter tasting of the two.

The following morning I was once more up at six, in time to meet

Francis at the empty breakfast table. Seating myself opposite him I smiled engagingly (or as near to it as a Big Bad Baby can get).

'Sorry I was so temperamental the other day. A crisis of confidence, imagining the famous Francis Hammond sitting there while *I* talked about photography.'

The scythes widened in surprise – see, a tiny grain of truth works wonders, like homoeopathic medicine. Quickly I went on, 'Look, come along this morning, if you want. It's not a problem. But do me a favour in return, yeah? Take next Tuesday's session?'

Francis edged back warily.

I reached forward and rested my hand on his, ignoring the orgasmic delight that immediately leaped across every synapse in my arm. 'Don't say no straight away, will you?' So light. So unconcerned.

Ari would have been proud of me. Or perhaps not.

Francis was still looking doubtful. I had to get closer to him, to block out more of my sister's natural brilliance, eat away her advantage of looks and time.

'It can't be worse than shooting pictures under fire, can it?' I said, my gaze innocent. 'Look, OK, just imagine for a moment you say yes, what would you choose as your subject?'

'What would I talk about?' he said slowly.

I wasn't fooled: he'd already decided. I knew it for a fact because, while we were talking, I had gently, oh so gently, climbed the walls of his mind and taken a quick first look around his inner self. Predictably I liked what I found there. Of course, he didn't yet know what to make of me. But he had certainly made his mind up about talking. His subject would be 'Truth'.

'Yes,' I said. And then, amusing myself, I let my mind speak directly into his, *'That's good.'*

He started as if he'd had an electric shock and then rubbed the back of his neck and stared at me. I watched expressions race across his face – alarm, fear, mistrust – and then, as the rush slowed, the one I'd been hoping to see. Fascination.

'Yes. Truth is good,' I said aloud. Cut and run, girl, my instincts told me, quit while you're ahead. I rose to my full height, smiled generously and told Francis Hammond to let me know if there was anything I could do to help. He nodded and shook his head as if to clear it. Then – joy – he looked at me and laughed. With a wave I hitched my leather bag over my shoulder and strode off down to the beach, whistling a jaunty Greek love song as I went.

Ha!

2 November 1999, 10.25 p.m.

By the time I stood in front of my group that morning I was ready for stage two of my plan.

There would be a change of programme, I said, noting the gratifying sag of disappointment in their faces: they were looking forward to spending two hours discussing 'The Nude'. But they brightened again when I explained that the change meant our special guest Francis Hammond would be talking on Tuesday instead of me and that his subject would be 'Truth and Photography'. Heads turned to where he sat at the back of the studio, his big form supple and relaxed. (I was gratified to see that he was alone. Helen's morning session had already begun: she was with a large group out on the terrace, talking about 'Close-up Tragedy'. But he had chosen to be here with us.) Francis raised a broad hand in acknowledgement of the room's murmured appreciation and returned control of the meeting to me.

It was time to begin.

I picked up a stack of mounted prints from the table and arranged them on a ledge around the walls. Soon we were surrounded by every kind of nudity: skin tanned and beaded with sweat, bodies singular and entwined, muscles like running mountain ranges, downy arms, veined breasts, legs braced like classically turned columns, tumescent penises and the shadowy deltas of cunts.

'The Nude,' I said, looking around the room. 'The point at which the human condition of nakedness becomes art.' A shiver of prurient excitement ran through the fifteen faces around me. I kept my own gaze steady.

'Would everybody stand, please.' With sideways glances at each other the class scrambled to their feet. It was a typical Sirens group: Matthew and Debra (two Californian postgraduate fine art students), a brilliant young violinist from Birmingham, a French philosopher, a pair of lesbian sculptresses from New York, a famously irascible English novelist, a prima ballerina called Penelope, two student photographers from Camden who had received a Siren's Award to finance their stay, a fabulously wealthy Greek widow who illustrated children's books, a Swiss businessman who had had several exhibitions of his pictures, a supermodel who had produced a book of (extremely poor) photographs of body piercing and Julia, an actress refugee from the drama session who openly resented Helen Byrd's unquestioned diva status.

I smiled briefly at her.

'To illustrate this I should like us to study the difference between the two conditions. In detail. Will everyone please take off their clothes?'

There was a horrified intake of breath. The English novelist, red-faced, called out, 'Predictably outrageous of you, Ms Byrd, but no thank you.'

I nodded peaceably. 'I understand, Mr Falmouth. Some people can only face the nude, not nakedness. Please rejoin us tomorrow, won't you? Good morning.'

Crossly Henry Falmouth shouldered his way out of the room. One of the photographers, a plump man with a babyish halo of ginger hair, had also reddened. 'I'm just too shy to do this, Cassandra,' stammered Leon Masters.

I shrugged. 'I sympathize, Leon, but if you want to stay, then nakedness is a condition, I'm afraid.' I was unzipping my skirt, kicking off my big dusty sandals. I looked around the room. It was a lot to ask of people – and I was hardly the sort of person who inspired trust – but then I saw that the French philosopher Jean-Paul was already bare-chested and that Whitney and Muriel, the two New York sculptresses, were looking steadfastly towards the front while they unzipped their shorts. The rest of the class began to follow their example. T-shirts were pulled over heads, chinos and sun-dresses rustled to the floor. I was pleased to see that Leon Masters had stayed and was soon down to an intriguingly bulky pair of Y-fronts.

Facing the group brown and bare-breasted, wearing only a pair of black cotton briefs, I smiled encouragingly. 'Let's do it, shall we?' At no point did I look towards the big blond figure at the back of the room. I didn't have to. I knew he was calmly hooking his thumbs in the waistband of his shorts and pushing them down over his hips.

We were all naked. For a moment every gaze flickered left and right at pelvis height. Then they looked at me. I had brought them this far, they were trusting me not to make them feel foolish. The Big Bad Baby was sorely tempted, though, I have to say. But, instead, I perched cross-legged on the table at the front of the room and talked about bodies.

I said how ordinary and how odd bodies were, serving as our point of connection with the world and yet also as our shield against other people and against danger.

'Think of the words we use: thin-skinned, a *fleur de peau*, skin-deep, thick-skinned, flesh wound: all terms that tell us staying on the surface is good and going deeper is dangerous. Some scientific photographers work with surgeons, sending tiny fibre-optic cameras inside veins or wombs, but as artists we operate without anaesthetic: getting below the surface is our *job*. And today is all about getting below the surface, to reach out for beauty and expose truth.'

I divided people into pairs, asked them to study a stranger's body dispassionately for one minute, then talk to him or her about it for another minute, perhaps comparing it with the face which was all they had seen of the other person until then. Then they would swap. Yes, it might be their worst nightmare, but that was why we were getting it out of the way first. There was a murmur of soft, awkward conversation. I heard Debra, paired with Jean Paul, say that he had a philosopher's face but a schoolboy's body. Julia told Leon Masters she liked the way his belly sloped down in a flat triangular plane, like a statue. Then a different set of voices spoke up. 'What's strange is . . .' 'I like the way . . .' 'See that line . . . ?' 'That scar, how . . . ?' Everyone changed partners and began again. I kept the groups moving, reforming, talking. After ten minutes we were relaxed; curiosity was satisfied, embarrassment had eased and physical beauty had lost its unfair advantage. Everyone was eager to take pictures. I resolutely avoided the eye of my prey.

'The Nude' turned out to be one of the best Sirens sessions ever. Once everyone was over the shock of seeing the private places of each other's bodies I put them to work. The task was to get below the surface of the naked body, to let it speak. They were free to use whatever film they chose, black and white or colour, fast or slow, and I encouraged everyone to swap cameras and experiment with lighting.

Groups formed and ideas sprang from collective thought and collaboration. Julia posed the Greek widow and Leon gazing into each other's eyes, as if the stills camera had followed Clark Gable

207

and Vivien Leigh into the bedroom at Tara. The supermodel made the American lesbians look like catwalk icons and they took their revenge by laying her on a table and lighting her as cruelly as an illustration from a gynaecological textbook. In Francis Hammond's Pietà composition, the violinist became a woodcut Christ, arched across the lap of naked, mourning Debra. Julia, Penelope and I stood entwined as the Three Graces, our bodies smooth as marble under a lighting rig devised by the Swiss businessman and the other photography student.

It was well past one when Ariadne herself came to find us. She stood still on the threshold, startled by the throng of naked bodies.

'Cassandra?'

I turned to face her. ' "Nakedness and The Nude",' I said agreeably. 'We'll develop the black-and-white pictures this afternoon, then you must see.'

There was a clamour of agreement from the others.

'Brilliant.'

'Wonderful session.'

'You should have seen the Pietà, Ariadne.'

Ariadne, resplendent in royal-blue silk, wasn't fooled. She glanced at me and then around the room, lingering briefly on Francis Hammond's impressive nakedness as he leaned against a floodlight by the door.

'That's good. But lunch is served now, my friends. And for lunch', she smiled sweetly, 'we dress.' She turned and bumped into someone standing right behind her. As she moved out of the way I was pleased to see Helen's face staring in astonishment at where her husband stood, Adam-like, beside my immense, resplendent Eve.

Poor Helen! (What a wonderful thing to be able to say those words at last!) Poor Helen!

I took a quick peek into Francis' mind as he walked to the back of the room in search of his clothes. There was no embarrassment, no regret, just sheer enjoyment – and a vivid image of Cassandra Byrd, a bronze giantess, reaching up to pull a spotlight into place.

Ha!

3 November 1999, 5.55 a.m.

In the circumstances it seems a waste of time to sleep.

Instead, but equally unproductively, I've been lying here thinking about Helen.

'Poor Helen!' I said the words again, wondering if I'd feel a tug of remorse or regret. But there wasn't a flicker of either. Does that make me a bad person?

Hmm.

Listen, there were weaknesses in our sisterly ties long before I tested them to destruction. There had been little respect between us or love or even liking. I'd sat in theatres on many a night while Helen took a standing ovation up there in the spotlight, bowing towards me with her actor's fake humility. And I'm sure there must have been times when my sister ducked into a gallery to walk around one of my exhibitions, stared at the pictures of odd faces and inhuman places and experienced the anxiety of someone who realizes they share lunatic genes.

We simply weren't born to love each other. And when adulthood pressed on the already strained connections they splintered and shattered, broke apart entirely.

See?

That was why Helen took Arnold away from me and stole Francis before I had a chance to claim him.

That was why, in my turn, I took him away from her and why he died.

Whoa.

No. No way, girl. Halt now. Stop right there.

Ah. Yes. That's better.

Slowly now. Take it slowly, baby. Breathe.

Wait until you're ready, more than ready. Then, carefully find your way back to that long ago summer's afternoon in Ithaca, when the future was simply a bright gleam of intention in your scheming mind.

DEVELOPING SEDUCTION

Over lunch Francis (modestly clothed again) and Helen sat on either side of Ariadne at the top of the long table. It was so hot that the air shimmered, even in the shade of the courtyard, and the bees hovered above the blazing marigolds as if afraid the petals would scorch their tiny black feet. We all ate sparingly. The white wine grew warm in the glasses and the salad wilted on the plates. Ariadne sat in her high-backed chair, fanning herself thoughtfully; Helen talked to her neighbour about Greek tragedy. For a while Francis appeared to be listening, but then his attention wandered, and I smiled, hoping that he was remembering this morning's press of naked bodies under the lights. And me.

Whatever was on his mind it was some time before he noticed that his wife was watching him in silence, a strange expression on her face. He gave her a brief little smile, more of a wry grimace, and pretended to eat. Perhaps he was suddenly wary of her: as my twin she might share my ability to infiltrate his mind. Then the meal was over and it was time for the siesta. People began to drift off to the shady peace of the Peloros bedrooms. Helen and Francis had always been among the first to leave the table: the honeymoon couple's departure was usually followed by indulgent or envious glances from the rest of the company. I'd already had to spend a week imagining their lovemaking: Francis and my sister embracing on the white bed under the slowly revolving fan.

But now when Helen raised an eyebrow Francis shook his head. My sister murmured something, but he shook his head again. Obviously put out, she rose and walked quickly from the courtyard into the house without a backward glance. The table was emptying fast now. Discussion of the nude session had stimulated everyone's sensual appetite, and I could see that many of the guests were sending eye signals to each other or openly holding hands. (One got used to seeing new couples form and dissolve at Peloros. I had watched Jean-Paul work his way through the available females of all ages, though he had lingered at Julia's side for the past few days and did so again now.)

It took a while, but eventually everyone had gone, except Francis Hammond and me.

I sipped my water (oh yes, I was stone cold sober this afternoon, by intention) and waited. A few minutes later I felt him slide into the chair next to me.

'So. Are you still planning to do some developing this afternoon?'

'Uh-huh.' I nodded, sipped. 'Cristos takes the colour into Vathi, but I like to do the black and white here.'

'Want some help?'

I put down my glass. 'If you like,' I said, not trusting my voice for more than that.

'Where's your dark-room?'

'Follow me,' I said and led the way through the outer gateway into the sunshine. Stepping outside was like walking into a furnace, and I took shallow breaths of burnt, aromatic air as we climbed up the track a little and then turned right to where an old stone building stood in the deep shade of a chestnut tree. The wooden door was freshly painted, its Our Lady blue gloss blistering in the sun. I fished in my pocket for a key, turned it in the newly oiled lock.

The familiar chemical dark-room smells greeted us as we

entered a large cool room with roughly whitewashed walls lit by high windows. In one corner were untidy piles of gardening equipment: hoes, spades and forks, ladders and balls of twine. To the right stone steps rose to a wide wooden gallery that ran halfway across the room. Casually I locked the door behind us. Then, followed by Francis, I climbed the steep stone stairway up into the light.

Was he watching my bottom sway from side to side as I went up? Was he imagining it naked, as he had seen it this morning: broad, brown and unashamedly monumental? Was he imagining holding its two ample cheeks and gently sliding between them . . . ? I closed my eyes and leaned a hand against the rough stone wall for support.

The gallery was lit at either end by circular windows cut in the thick walls: round columns of sunshine slanted down through the dusty air. I lowered the blind on one side and walked across to the dark-room itself, which was a shed-like construction some ten feet square. I opened the door and the chemical smell became stronger.

Hanging from wires the length of the room were the last batch of photographs I'd been working on. I stepped back and watched Francis walk down the row, his hands on his hips, studying the prints. He held up a picture of Ari and Helen and me. We were dressed entirely in black, staring hypnotically into the lens.

'When was this one taken?'

I shrugged. 'Here, last summer, I should think. Ari wants to use it for a brochure.' I peered at it. 'Yes. The three Sirens. Did you realize that was what you'd married into? Too late now to be sorry now, though.'

He flickered a glance in my direction, checking. 'Too late?'

'Homer,' I said. 'The *Odyssey*. "First thou shalt arrive where the enchanter Sirens dwell, they who seduce men. The imprudent man who draws near them never returns, for the Sirens, lying in the flower-strewn fields, will charm him with sweet song; but around them the bodies of their victims lie in heaps."'

Francis winced, then rallied. 'Could I have a print?'

I looked down at the photograph. It was a good one of Helen and Ari and, though I loomed over them like something from a freak show, my presence somehow added an indefinable, bizarre gravitas to the whole thing. 'Sure. Take that one. I have plenty.' At least he would have a picture of me. The other pictures were mostly portraits of people currently at Peloros. I watched him smile as he identified Leon, Julia and Whitney. I'd caught Muriel and Henry Falmouth in mid-argument: you could see her wide-flung hand, the strands of spittle stretched across his angry mouth. In another shot Susie Musselbergh stood forlornly at the foot of the main stairs, waiting for someone to appear. And there was Ariadne, enthroned on her peacock chair, head cocked, long cigarette in hand, a goddess amused at the puny goings-on of mortals.

Towards the end of the row he came to the picture I had intended him to see and stopped. Slowly he reached up and unclipped it from the wire to get a better view. Yes, Francis, that's right, I thought gleefully, just you take a long hard look at that little beauty and then tell me honestly why you're here this afternoon.

I didn't have to look at it: I knew every detail by heart.

I'd taken it three days after they arrived. In late morning light Helen and Francis stood on the terrace. She was leaning against him, her head nestled against his shoulder, her left hand just visible at his waist where it clutched at his white cotton shirt. My sister was staring up adoringly into her husband's face. But her husband was looking firmly out of frame – and his expression was unmistakably that of a man bored rigid by the woman at his side.

That photograph had told me all I needed to know. After all, the camera couldn't lie. I hadn't had to scan, crop or distort the image in any way. No, it was incontrovertible evidence, would convince any objective witness that Francis Hammond was the beloved in this impulsive marriage, not the lover. It said that he had been caught up in the romance of Venice and found himself standing at a dimly lit altar making promises to a woman he'd never planned to wed. The message of this picture was inescapable, wasn't it? Now, it said, the honeymoon was over. Morally and emotionally Francis Hammond was available.

For me.

While Francis gazed at the picture I kept my back turned to him. I guessed he was wondering how I could possibly have seen a truth he'd tried so hard to conceal. For all her stark physicality, he must be thinking, Cassandra Byrd is a surprisingly perceptive woman. He was still staring.

'Sorry, but it's time to turn out the light,' I said, reaching for the first film.

In the dark I worked in silence. It felt odd to have someone there beside me in a place that had always been like another safe and lonely lair. I busied myself with the familiar ritual of take-up spool, canister, developer and fixer, concentrating only on detail.

When everything was done I switched on the light and held up the strip of wet film. At first sight the exposures looked good. Then I gestured to Francis to help, and he hung the film to dry, clipping a weight to the end to keep it from coiling. He handed me the next film, and I plunged us back into darkness.

'Did Arnold teach you this?' he asked.

'Arnold and others,' I said. I didn't want him to see me as a tyro. 'Where did you learn?'

'Local newspaper. Photographic club. I was a sad teenager,' he said, though I could hear the smile in his voice.

'Me too,' I said.

We worked our way through the films, and by the time I'd finished the last one the first two were dry. I switched the light to infra-red. 'Want to do this one?' I said, handing him a strip. We worked side by side to produce the contact prints. He was fast and deft.

Together we watched as the first images swam on to the page of photographic paper.

'Which ones will you enlarge?' he asked.

'Dunno yet,' I murmured, scrutinizing the tiny pictures. 'There are some good ones here, though. Look. Anyway, let's do the rest, then we'll take a break and make some choices.'

It took a while. Which was nice. For the most part I ignored him, kept a satisfied grin strictly under control and busied myself with developer trays, reaching down the bottles, setting trays in position, quietly pouring fixer. I hummed to myself. The silence was becoming overlong. To break it I had a choice of two questions: the small one or the big one. It would be sensible to choose the small one. But then again, when had I ever been sensible? It was time for Cassandra to take a Big Bad risk.

I put the last sheet into a plastic page and cleared my throat. 'Why did you marry Helen?' I asked, leaning back casually against the sink.

Francis picked up the folder and studied its contents carefully. I began to worry: the silence was now much too long.

When he finally spoke, his voice was flat and odd. 'Jealousy's an ugly thing, Cassandra,' he said.

Christ. Suddenly the dark-room was stifling. I opened the door and blinked into the afternoon glare of the gallery. 'I'd s-still like to know,' I said, managing a hastily improvised stammer. Francis followed me out into the sunlight.

'Is that why you asked me here?' he asked curtly. He turned to face me, and the circular window behind him silhouetted his body against a disc of light. I shut my eyes against the dazzle.

'No,' I said, 'of course not.' And waited.

After a moment he said in a softer voice, 'I'm sorry. Look, I'll tell you. If you really want to know.'

Ah no, suddenly I wasn't sure I did. I wasn't sure at all. The picture was a lie, after all. He loved her and I must disgust him. I held my hands up to stop him, stepped back, almost tripping over the pile of cushions I'd arranged against the wall to await our blissful coupling. The situation was flatlining. I had already forgotten how to breathe and now my heart stopped.

Then, suddenly, gloriously and just in time the Big Bad Baby came to the rescue. Dauntless, full of panache and bravado, she stood at my side, firing warning shots over the head of my scattering wits. The Baby said, 'Breathe, Cassandra', and I did. After three deep lungfuls I was as calm as clay, and wise.

'Hey, relax,' I said, 'I was just curious, that's all. Nothing more.'

To reassure him, I even patted his arm, though it took all my willpower and a stern look from the Baby to ignore the intoxicating brush of hair against my wrist. Then I drew another, deeper breath and began to fight back.

'Francis, you saw the photo. It seemed to be saying something. So I asked the question. I was out of order. I apologize.' Oh yes, I deserved an Oscar, I really did. And apparently it was possible to go on in this same even tone. 'As for this afternoon, you said you wanted to help with the developing. If you've changed your mind that's no big deal. Just leave.' I walked back into the dark-room, leaving him standing in the sunlight. Then, with a hunter's instinct, I turned and gave a brief, casual smile. 'But if you decide to risk staying, perhaps you'll make yourself useful and choose a set of contacts for the enlarger.' Even as I spoke I knew I'd accomplished an impressive swerve away from the canyon edge. What would he do now? Only an undignified wimp could leave. Peaceably I let the silence linger. I had things to do.

Then Francis was standing behind me in the dark-room, his sheer bulk intimidating in that confined space. 'Cassandra, sorry. I'm not usually so . . .'

I turned, eyes locked steady, stomach tensed, thoughts marshalled. 'Married?' I said.

'Married,' he grinned. 'Rewind?'

It was capitulation of sorts. The Big Bad Baby crowed and I allowed myself a grin. 'Absolutely, *brother*.'

'Friends?'

'Of course.'

'Good.' He reached across, took my hand and kissed it lightly on the back. His mind was curved like polished steel against me, I noticed. Shit, shit, shit. I didn't want that, I wanted my thoughts in his, my legs around his neck, my hands holding fistfuls of his hair. A kiss on the hand was a pretty hollow victory by comparison. I licked dry lips. It was hot in here.

'Come on now,' I said briskly. 'If we want these for this evening there's a shedload of work to be done.'

I remember every moment of that afternoon. It's engraved in minute detail in Cassandra's book of hours. My *très belles heures* with Francis Hammond. I was conscious of his every movement. When he stretched to reach something from a shelf I watched his muscles tense, bunch and relax. When he poured developer I watched the frown lines on his forehead deepen then vanish as he sluiced the liquid around the print. I admired the steadiness of his hands as he held up the dripping paper. Outside, the sun moved slowly over the roof and set it shimmering. By four o'clock we were almost done; the tension had eased, talk ran easily between us and we were friends.

Except that I was sweating with the sheer physical effort of staying away from him. As I washed up the last trays and set them to dry I yearned to touch his arm, to put my cheek against his face and whisper Siren's talk: Come with me down to the beach. Let's swim naked out to sea and around the headland to the little cove, where a tree overhangs the water and there's a patch of soft green grass. Let's stretch out there to dry ourselves in the sun. Side by side and separately, of course, like brother and sister. No touching.

No, no touching at all. Oh. The Big Bad Baby and I clasped heartening, blood-sister hands. We would have to rethink. And quickly.

'OK, looks like we're all done here, Francis,' I said. 'Thanks for the help. I'm off for my afternoon swim now,' I added smoothly. 'If you'll lock up I'll see you tonight at dinner. Bye.'

Then I was gone, down the stairs, through the wooden door, striding down through the thrum of crickets and the pines, peeling off my shirt as I reached the beach, then wading, sinking, drowning while wishing all the time I was being fucked senseless in the cool transparent waters of the Ionian sea.

Ha!

3 November 1999, 7.08 p.m.

Twelve hours have flown past. I can hardly move my fingers to type. I have to write in short bursts – half an hour, ten minutes, two – then rest. My constricted lungs barely inflate, there's a feeling of suffocation, like being trapped in a sealed vault. Each breath is a tiny, exhausted sip: another depletion.

Reliving the past is so strenuous: the batteries of my body are beeping an ominous, steady LOW warning. And, because of this, every interruption is unwelcome. Washing my face, peeing, brushing my hair (I am going grey so rapidly I refuse to look any more), changing my nightshirt, pretending to eat, cleaning my teeth, swallowing pills: all of these actions take precious time. But they earn me remission for words, and so I do them uncomplainingly.

Now, in the peace of early evening, nuns' voices in harmony are rising from the chapel. I fumble on the panel behind my bed and switch off the overhead light which has been burning my sore eyelids. Gratefully I sink back into freshly plumped pillows. Thank you,

Sister Andrew; thank you, Dr Mike. Gentle Jesus, how wonderful it would be if I believed in you now.

So tired.

But even now, with eyes closed, the fingers still perform their fluttering dance, translating thought to electronic page.

Gtsmvod.

Gtsmvod.

A light glows in the darkness.

It grows and glows and glows and grows, until we lie side by side in a Klimt-like bower of dreams, suffused with precious gold. Ahhhhhhhhhhhhhhhhhhhhhhhhhhhhhhhhhhhhhhhhhhhhhhhhhhhh hhhhhhhhhhhhhhhhhhhhhhhhhhhhhhhh

4 November 1999, 5.30 a.m.

Better. Much better. Oh, yes. Quickly now. Run down the path to the past. Joggety-jog.

Feel the fingers bounce off the keys, vigorous, flexible, pneumatic.

Hey! Hey! Here I come! Remember me?

MIND GAMES

In the days that followed the dark-room I struggled with what I now assume was my conscience. (See, even the Big Bad Cassandra has one.) Our conversation had unsettled me in more ways than one. First, there was galling fact that Francis had seen right through my strategy. Second, even though I'd managed to recover the situation my options were now limited because I was dealing with someone who understood my motives all too clearly. What was even worse, I couldn't allow my frustration to show, since I'd assured him I had no interest in him other than as a friend and brother-in-law. Finally, and most ironically, just when I was desperate to know what he was thinking Francis had deliberately made his thoughts inaccessible to me.

In other times I'd have trusted my instincts to fill in the gaps. After all, I'd instinctively known that Francis was not in love with Helen; I'd instinctively known that he was available for my bed. So why was I suddenly hesitating now? And why the hell, after a childhood of mutual damage and a decade of healthy separation, was I now apparently unwilling to hurt my fucking sister's feelings?

In despair, I turned to the Big Bad Baby for help, but this time she laughed in my face. This wasn't the Cassandra she knew, she sneered. This wasn't the shellacked giant who'd made a virtue out of every vicious whim.

'Fuck him and have done with it,' she yelled.

Slut, I thought. OK, I will.

But it would take care and cunning. In the meantime I would have to avoid him. I would also avoid the all-seeing Ariadne and wary Helen. Seducing Francis Hammond would take a lot of planning, a lot of time. But it could and must be done.

By the following Sunday I had plan of action and, as I had contrived, it was Francis himself who set it in motion.

The day before he was due to give his talk we met at breakfast. He was tanned now. In his big crumpled chinos and white cotton shirt he looked like Fletcher Christian in Tahiti. I smiled politely when he asked if I could help him prepare materials for his session. Mild, controlled, I suggested we met at ten in the library.

In the bright morning light it was a pleasant place. Francis came in carrying a sheaf of pictures and spread them around the tables, just as I'd once arranged Ari's books to have my favourite photographs and paintings around me. Then he sat back in the same chair I'd curled up in years before and scratched his head. 'OK. So. We're talking about truth. I've got a few pictures here and I'd like your views on them, but I'm pretty sure I need more. I wondered if you had anything. Ariadne said you knew the library better than anyone. What do you think?'

Oh, Ari. Dangerous play.

Lick my nipples, the Big Bad Baby whispered at him. Dip your finger between my lips, feel the moisture running like honey. I ignored her: her brand of brazen desire definitely wasn't part of the plan. Slowly, I walked around the room, examining each of his chosen pictures in turn. It was important to show him how seriously I was taking this. After all, like the dark-room, this was common ground for us, a fitting place for a meeting of minds.

When I reached the end I turned to face him and caught him yawning cavernously behind his hand. Poor man was tired, I supposed, after a night of passion with the beauteous Helen. He needed waking up. A little light provocation should do it. I picked up one photo in each hand and stared at them.

'You don't need me to say that these are wonderful photographs, Francis, but are they good examples of truth?'

He stood up at that, came to stand beside me, looking over my shoulder. 'What d'you mean exactly?'

Concentrating hard on the photographs, I nodded at the one in my left hand. 'This young girl, for example. I see a frightened child, which may be *a* truth. But is it the whole truth? Without a caption, an explanation, the picture's ambiguous, even secretive. I don't *truly* know what to believe.'

Francis stepped back from the table, leaned against the wall and folded his arms. Careful, Cassandra, I thought, careful. But after a moment he was back, pacing up and down in front of the table, fully awake now and poring over the pictures, untidy and absorbed.

'Good. That's the point I wanted to make tomorrow. Look.' He picked up a picture. 'See this snotty-nosed kid sitting scowling on the pavement? Luis was an orphan in Bogotá. He kept following

221

me around. Every time I stepped out of my hotel he was there. He never smiled like the other begging kids, he never looked desperate to please. He just stuck his hand out and snarled, 'Give me dollar.' What made him memorable was the anger in his face, and so I took the picture. And because of this photo Luis became the symbol of a major UNESCO project to give third-world youngsters an alternative to street life. Even now when I look at it I see what I saw then: desperation, an adult's experience trapped in a child's body. It's absolutely true in that sense. But reality,' he ran his hand back through his coarse tawny hair, 'reality is more complicated. Just after I took that photograph Luis tried to sell me his eight-year-old sister for sex. He was much angrier than this when I refused. So is the photograph untrue? No. It's the truth as I saw it in that moment. If I'd attached a rider afterwards, a caption explaining what I've just told you, it would have changed your perception and destroyed the authenticity of the photo.'

I agreed but frowned doubtfully, encouraging him to continue.

'Look at these.' He beckoned me closer. I found I could stand quite close to him as we bent over the pictures: our shoulders were almost touching, his coffee-breath was warm on my cheek as we talked.

'You talk about the difference between truth and lies,' he said, 'but some of the best pictures I've taken have been half-truth, half-lie.' He picked up a shot of a thin, dark-haired man in his early twenties, his wolfish nose pinched with cold, his thick woollen jacket stained and torn. 'You know faces. What d'you make of him?'

I looked. 'He's frightened and hungry. And there's something fragile about his mouth, isn't there? But', I said, hesitating and peering closer, 'his eyes are strange. Very odd. Empty.'

I stared into the face, concentrating now, reading it as if it was a living mind. 'He may have been a kind man once, but now he's certainly capable of . . . cruelty. In fact, I'd say he was capable of anything.'

Francis reached across and picked up another photograph, this time of a pleasantly smiling Chinese woman.

'And her?'

It felt like a test now. I held the image close, struggling to discern traces of thought behind the hooded eyes, the smiling mouth, the gleaming gold-capped teeth. At first sight she seemed motherly; someone's aunt perhaps, I thought. But why would Francis Hammond photograph someone's aunt? There must be more to it than that. I held the photo closer and blurred my vision, trying to sense what lay beneath the surface. The black eyes glittered through the haze. Suddenly I felt an unmistakable pulse of menace.

'Evil.' I said briefly, putting the photo down.

Francis picked it up. 'That's impressive, Cassandra.'

I raised an eyebrow, but he shook his head.

'No, seriously, I'm amazed.'

'Why? I was right?'

'On both counts.' He picked up the first photo. 'This is Stefan. The day before I took this Stefan had carried his injured wife on his back four miles to the nearest field hospital. She died an hour later, when Croat guerrillas shelled the place. She was twenty-three. He was sitting on the steps of the ruined building, crying, when I took this picture. But later that day I met someone who told me Stefan had been a commander of the local Serb brigade. The week before, he and his men had captured and crucified two elderly farmers, brothers, in the neighbouring village.'

I looked at the face again. The young man stared stonily out at me, silver tracks down his cheeks.

'And her?' I pointed to the Chinese woman, still unwilling to touch her.

'Yes. Evil. This is infamous Mamma Cheung. A brothel-keeper

and serial killer in Manila. She . . .' he fingered the edge of the print. 'She did unspeakable things to teenage boys and girls. Over many years.' He stared at the face but spoke to me. 'This was just before she was sentenced. She asked me for a cigarette, complained about the over-heated courtroom, said how she hoped someone had given her cats a home. Sometimes what's most horrifying about an evil face is its banality.'

He put down the picture, leaned forward on his hands, talking to the pictures rather than me.

'Painters can be judge and jury. They can create a single, unmistakable truth out of a hundred thousand conscious brushstrokes. But pictures like these are unposed, instant things. OK,' he ran his hand back through his hair, 'as professionals we have the skill and the training; maybe we also have an eye for a good picture, but taking the photograph is still an act of faith. We think we glimpse something, we point the camera and press the button. And if we're right, the result is a snapshot of pure truth. When we . . .' (I loved the way the inclusive 'we' was creeping into his conversation.) '. . . get *that* a photograph is something priceless.'

He yawned again, and I wondered whether he still believed what he was saying. As if reading my thoughts, he turned to me. 'Whatever you say about captions, and I'd guess that you're saying it partly to provoke me . . .' (*Qui, moi?* I raised an eyebrow.) '. . . we don't always need words to get behind outward appearances.'

(See how close we were. That could have been me talking back then. Who better than an ugly twin to understand the importance of seeking the essential truth beneath the physical and superficial?) I could have kissed him.

But instead, as a distraction, I focused on details of his appearance, carefully noting the frayed shirt collar, the unkempt curls at the nape of his neck, the deep criss-cross lines of his throat. How old was he? Forty-five? Forty-eight? After a beat I said, 'Perhaps.

Well, that'll go down well tomorrow, for sure. "Can we take pictures that don't need captions to reveal their truth?"'

I smiled. 'I think seeing beneath the mask is partly a question of habit. OK, maybe I'm unusual . . .' (Ha! Well, I'm unique, baby, unique! Wait and see!) '. . . in that I think I have a certain insight, but there are always clues in faces, don't you think?

'Like this one.' I went over to a shelf on the far side of the room and took down a heavy clothbound book of art history. I leafed through the pages and stopped at a dark portrait.

Francis stared down at it. 'Richard III. Funny you should choose him, I've always liked that portrait. Narrow eyes and such a shrewd, modern expression.' He moved his finger over the plate like a blind man reading Braille. 'But there's wisdom there, too, isn't there? And sadness. And some physical trouble – illness maybe. It's a great face.'

'Yes. And some places show you their truth, too. I took a photo of Culloden once. There's a copy here somewhere.' Talking over my shoulder, I went in search of it. 'It was one of the most haunted places I'd ever seen.' I found the exhibition catalogue, flipped through it to the right page. I was enjoying myself now: looking at things together was definitely bringing us closer.

'I've always believed that my best shots were a sort of clairvoy-ance,' I said. 'When I find I've got inside a place or seen inside someone's head . . .' I turned, book in hand, then stopped at the look on his face. 'What?'

Francis was staring at me.

'Clairvoyance?'

I hadn't been concentrating. That was stupid.

'Yes. What? Suddenly you're looking at me as if I was Mamma Cheung or something.'

He wasn't smiling. 'Is that what you tried to do with me, Cas-sandra? That first morning. You remember, out on the terrace.'

'What?' I was so reasonable, no visible panic at all.

'It felt as though you were . . .' He was getting angry with himself now. 'Oh, look. It felt as if you were reading my bloody mind.'

'What makes you say that?' Answer questions with questions: the therapists always know best.

'Because I distinctly heard your voice. In my head,' he said flatly. 'Didn't I?'

I *knew* I shouldn't take another risk with him. I really shouldn't. Not again. He would be angry, disgusted, repelled. But he was so close now, and of all the minds I had ever wanted to scale this was the one. Suddenly I couldn't resist. Staring past his retina I slid my thoughts deep into his, like a sword blade into a lake.

Like this? I said gently.

'Christ,' he said, startled. And then, 'Wait.'

I froze and held my mind inside his, motionless. Then, slowly and deliberately, he laid himself open before me.

There, he said.

Now it was my turn to freeze. How had he done . . . ? Suddenly I was in a place I had never expected to find – and it was a place where I belonged.

I was home.

I shuddered, and as my concentration lapsed the blade of thought withdrew. Francis opened his eyes wide. 'No,' he said hoarsely, 'stay.'

'I'm sorry,' I said quickly, laying my hand on his arm. 'I'm so sorry.'

'Just stay still,' he said. 'Wait.' And he folded his hand over mine like a man steadying himself to step off into cold deep water. And for the first time in my life I felt another person do to me what I had done to others so many times before.

It was delicate pain at first, like frost beneath the skull. I lifted a hand to stop him. Any minute now he would see *my* deepest thoughts and I would be exposed, invaded. He would see the ugliness that was me. Yet still I held my mind steady. The truth was I simply couldn't let go now. Because I recognized what this moment was: this *now* was my once-ever chance to connect.

In my mind I stretched out a trembling hand to welcome him. 'Ah,' I said, aloud. 'It hurts.'

His eyes were closed. I could hardly hear his whisper. 'Yes. No. Like ice. Ah.'

Go on, go *on*, I told myself. Do it. Say it. Now.

Slowly and clearly, I spoke into the quick of him, without a sound, and said his name.

Francis?

He was still clasping my hand, and I could feel a tremor running through his body. Then in my mind, a voice replied.

Yes.

4 November 1999, 3.15 p.m.

If I had to pick a moment to relive for the rest of eternity it would be that one.

One perfect instant that made up for lifetime of anger, pain and confusion. Because, then, nothing else mattered: not the bodies I'd fucked by mistake, not the cruelties I'd done and had done to me; not the mischief or the isolation, the months of curdling boredom or moments of convulsive pleasure.

If I believed in heaven, which I don't, everyone who'd ever lived would be there, replaying their own perfect human moments, again and again, world without end. Oh yes. And the essence, the pattern, would be revealed in the diversity and sameness of those moments. A mother gazes into the knowing eyes of her new-born child; lost souls find their twin. I am standing in Francis Hammond's mind and he in mine.

4.30 p.m. – same day?

Another injection. Floating now. Lonely as a cloud. Whooooo.

Where was I? Heaven.

Heaven?

Yes.

And there they are now, the people I loved. Though I never told them – in my whole life, never told any of them. Not Dadda. Not Ariadne. Not even Francis.

Once I'd have been proud of that. But not now.

CASSANDRA IN LOVE

Oh, yes.

Sledgehammer time.

Now I *know* my sister's husband.

I walk in the fields of his thoughts, and I love him.

And he feels . . . ?

Ha!

Shock, I imagine!

What? This man walked into the room as your brother-in-law and walked out again your lover?

Well, no. Not exactly. I know I've made it sound as though everything happened that same day, within the dramatic unities of time and place, but in fact in Peloros we only took that first, irreversible, startled step towards each other. (Being Francis, he didn't run towards me, not for a long time afterwards; indeed, he struggled to keep away.) No, in reality I left him standing there in the sunlit library and walked away. I knew he would follow me now; just as I knew I would be there waiting wherever, whenever, he came.

And so, at first, everything went on as before on Ithaca. We sat in the same candlelight, dined at the same table, ate the same dishes of tender lamb, salty cheese and honey cakes. We talked to the same people and listened to the familiar old Greek tunes. And, as he had done before, Francis danced with Helen, following her gliding movement in a shambling, bear-man's version of the steps. He held her hand. He smiled when she talked to him. But I didn't need to read his thoughts to know what Francis Hammond saw whenever he closed his eyes.

His talk on 'Truth' was very well attended. Helen sat in the front row. She was wearing a pale yellow sundress that showed off her sun-bleached hair and her tan, her shoulders gleamed, polished and cool under the thin cotton straps. Francis's voice resonated through the room, sending waves of energy and emotion surging between the walls. I heard him say my name and saw Helen frown.

'As Cassandra Byrd said to me a few days ago: what *is* truth? Without a caption, an explanation, aren't all pictures ambiguous and secretive?'

The grey scythes swept over the rows of nodding heads, drawn, as surely as a blade to a stalk, to a tall dishevelled figure at the back of the room. One of them winked in the sunlight.

Ha!

It was two weeks later that Helen came to my room – five thirty on a late September afternoon. I'd been expecting her, I suppose. Surface normality had been stretched to breaking point, while beneath it everything had changed. Eventually the fault lines were bound to show. She knocked loudly at the door, as if giving me fair warning, but I didn't need it: her anger had come swirling down the corridor ahead of her like a bow wave.

I have to say, she didn't look well. Helen Byrd, darling of the lens, was pink-nosed and snotty, her blue irises swimming in angry red, her raw silk shift crumpled and blotched with what could only be tears. (In my baggy white drawstring trousers and vast black top

I was almost elegant by comparison.) Anyway, she marched straight in and slammed the door behind her.

'Cassandra, why are you doing this?' she asked wildly. 'Tell me, because I'd like to understand. Really, I need to understand.' It was that same voice from our teenage drama class: full of emotion and passionate sincerity.

'Understand what?' I said unhelpfully.

She was trembling, beating her little fists against her thighs. '*You*, Cassandra, *you*. And what you're trying to do to Francis.'

'What do you mean?'

She was shouting now, her actressy voice carrying beyond the shutters to the courtyard. 'You know. But he's my *husband*, for God's sake. We're *married*.'

I nodded. 'I know.'

'Well then?'

'I just wish I knew what you were talking about.'

Helen breathed in, placing her hands either side of her slender waist as if being instructed by a voice coach to feel the full rise of her diaphragm.

'I'm talking about you seducing Francis, you whore. Of course, it's not the first time. I should've known. Poor James; and Hugo, for God's sake. You've always been a tramp.'

I laughed. I know I shouldn't have, but it was too funny.

'*Tramp*? Oh, Helen, *please*, you sound like something out of a twenties melodrama. Grow up.'

She was shrill now. '*You're* the one who never grew up. Mother always told me you were an imbecile, and she was right.'

OK. Scorned woman or not, this was getting a little out of hand.

'Helen,' I said calmly. 'I haven't seduced your precious husband. Though, if it helps, Francis Hammond has always had a reputation for being rather temperamental. It seems to go with the job. I know a couple of American war photographers, and they both suffer from violent mood swings. Take Errol Graham, for instance . . .'

'I'm not interested in Errol Graham,' snapped Helen. 'I'm interested in *my husband*. And I think you know a bloody sight more about that than you're letting on.' Her neat hands were clenching and unclenching. Any moment now she was going to let fly.

Perversely calm, I shrugged. 'There's been absolutely nothing between Francis and me, Helen, believe me – *nada, rien, niente,* zilch – not even a peck on the cheek.' I moved into pained sincerity, 'Odd though it may sound to *you*, I haven't forgotten that he belongs to my twin sister, which I rather assumed put him off limits.' (Sometimes I wonder how I can live with myself, really I do. But I guess that's what comes of having to work out your own Big Bad strategy for survival.) I flopped back into a chair and crossed my tree-trunk thighs.

But Helen wasn't in a mood to fall for dramatic flourishes.

'That never stopped you before, Cass, so you might as well cut the crap,' she said.

I decided that Francis must have said something. Shame. And her with confetti still in the corner of her suitcase, figuratively speaking. Poor Helen. Curious to know if my guess was right, I said. 'If you don't believe me, Helen, then why don't you ask *him*?'

'Of *course* I've asked him.'

'And?'

'He won't tell me anything. All he keeps saying is that he's sorry. *Sorry.*' She took a great gulping sob of breath and suddenly all her violence seemed to evaporate.

Hoping I'd timed it right, I moved towards her, put a heavy arm around her little bird-wing shoulders.

'Helen, Helen. I'm so sorry. Poor you.' I meant it, too, in a way. 'Here,' I reached across to the chest of drawers and pulled a wad of tissues from the packet on the top. 'Here now. Look. I don't know what I can say. Except that whatever Francis has decided to do it's his decision, nothing to do with me.' Helen was blowing her nose loudly, like a real person instead of a fragile film star. I felt faintly nauseous.

'Really?' she muttered, unconvinced.

It was better for her to find out the truth later, and gradually, rather than have it break over her head in one massive comber today. 'Really,' I said, giving her a tough-love squeeze around the neck. 'Honestly, would I lie to you?'

Which was almost as good as telling her the truth, don't you think? It wasn't *my* fault if she was too bound up in her own emotions to sense the complexities of mine. Anyway, feeling a tad guilty despite myself, I dried her tears, poured two stiff ouzos down her throat and sent her off to see Ariadne.

The following day neither Helen nor Francis appeared at mealtimes, and a worried Susie found Helen alone in her room when she took her up a bite of supper on a tray. (Though Susie appeared cheered by this and offered staunchly loyal support to her idol.) But, anyway, by the end of the week the newlyweds were gone from Peloros: Helen to Mexico, where she was committed to start filming some Aztec adventure romance with Hunter Merriman, and Francis to who knew where.

Well, I soon did, actually.

But I'm rushing on, when, for once, it's sweet to linger. Yes. I stayed for a while on Ithaca, reliving, enjoying, relishing what I had found waiting for me in Francis's mind: those emotions which up until then had been denied me: understanding, laughter, sympathy, intelligent kindness, love.

5 November 1999, 8.15 a.m.
Another day. Turquoise dawn like a thrush egg and a scouring wind humming through the bare olive branches. In England the kids will

232

be out begging a penny for the guy: 'Please to remember the fifth of November, with gunpowder, treason and plot.'

I remember Grannie Christine made treacle toffee one Guy Fawkes' Night. She took a hammer and cracked the trayful of toffee into pieces, and I grabbed the biggest slab and crammed it into my mouth. Immediately, my jaws locked together as if they had been bound with iron. Everyone laughed as I gurgled and moaned in silent fury. I strained so hard to free myself that I broke an eye tooth. Under my tongue today, I can still feel its craggy, fractured surface.

THE LOVERS

Of course it wasn't going to end well, though for a while at the start I honestly thought it might.

But, anyway, by Christmas 1995 Francis and I were together.

Helen, filming in Yucatán, had suffered some sort of nervous collapse. The media sniffed a scandal and soon uncovered the fact that Helen Byrd's new husband (moody war photographer Francis Hammond, forty-five) had not flown out to see her once during the four weeks she had been in Mexico. A pack of them doorstepped him outside his flat in Camden the following day. At first Francis managed to fend them off, but then someone, at a guess Susie Musselbergh, gave them the gift story they wanted, even before it was true.

And then, 'Twin Steals Helen's New Hubby', 'Snapper Dumps Beautiful Byrd for the Beast', the papers screamed. To illustrate the anomaly of this bizarre choice they published pictures of Helen, stunning in Versace at her last première, and of me, wild-haired and dishevelled in Lincoln's Inn Fields. One paper splashed *The Byrds* photograph across a centre spread but took our masks off and replaced them with the same contrasting head shots: I looked like the bloody Elephant Twin. Soon Helen's agent was stirring the

233

pot, saying how their client was 'devastated by her sister's act of betrayal' and how she was recovering, initially at a clinic in Switzerland and a fortnight later in Phuket with Oscar-nominated British actor James Garrison. (I must say, from the photos, James had grown into a devastatingly attractive man, and he looked so protective with his arm around my sister.)

Soon Ithaca was invaded by paparazzi searching for stories about me. Someone (Susie again or perhaps Cristos?) obviously told them that I was an insatiable virago who worked her way through the famous guests, male and female, at Peloros. The journos began a gleeful trawl back through the Sirens' visitors' book.

Marco Bertone called me to report that the sales of my pictures were up three hundred per cent on the previous year. Ill wind, huh?

I hadn't been looking forward to Ariadne's call. It was late October before she tracked me down.

'Cassandra.' Her voice was strange. 'I am heartbroken.'

I was not, but I respected her frankness.

'Why, Ari?'

There was a long silence, during which I thought, as she had intended, about what I was now preparing to jettison. Eventually she said, 'I have shut up Peloros for the winter. And, of course, there will be no more Sirens.'

I shrugged. That had been on the cards.

'Where are you now, Ari?' I asked.

'In Paris.'

There was another long silence, in which I thought I heard her swallow. When her voice came again, it was twisted and hoarse.

'Did you have to do it, Cassimou?'

'Do what, Ari?' I asked.

Then I waited a long time for her to answer.

When she didn't, I finally said, 'Yes.' But I think she may have hung up by then.

That was sad. One of the worst things, in fact. But then it's obvious that sad, bad things happen when a couple is split apart. (The passive voice, you notice . . .) Anyway, later that autumn I lost all my new friends and almost all of my old ones. (Which is partly why at this late stage I find myself talking to you, my reader, and fitting words and questions into your unseen mouth. I hope you don't mind.)

So, you say, did any good come out of it?

Oh yes, I reply.

It did. Something so shining, so jubilee marvellous, that reliving it is perfect, blissful torture.

It is an early November night in London. I am in Cage Street with the telephone off the hook and the door locked and bolted. I am alone and waiting, as I have been since I returned from Ithaca. There has been no news, but tonight I feel anticipation beating in my stomach.

At nine thirty there is a knock at the door.

I slide back the bolts, already sure who will be on the doorstep.

Even in the orange sodium light he looks pale and dispirited. His face is gaunt and unshaven, his hair is unkempt and he has lost weight. The collar of an ancient leather flying jacket is turned up against the drizzle, and his shoes seem squelching dark with rain. He must have walked here from Camden.

'Hello, Cassandra.'

'Hello.'

I stand on the threshold, smelling the rush of damp night air, wondering where the next few moments will take us.

'Come in.'

He walks past me and then I lock the door and lead the way up the steep wooden stairs to the green sitting-room lit by candles, which bow and flicker fitfully as we step over the threshold. I point to the wing chair and then go out to the galley kitchen and fetch a wineglass. My hand brushes against his as I pour dark burgundy, and I feel the physical pull of him again, strong as a tidal race. Resisting, I sit down in a chair on the far side of the fireplace and look across at him steadily, my body and mind under strict control. I am wearing a huge silk shirt in the same shade of green as the walls. My hair is down, it stands out from the side of my head to the points of my shoulders, like the head-dress of a sphinx.

He says, 'I didn't want to come – until there was no reason to stay away.'

'I know,' I say.

'It doesn't make it any better, I guess.'

I shrug, carefully.

He's holding the bowl of the glass in both hands so that it almost disappears inside his hamlike fists.

'We should never have married,' he says flatly. He wants to say, but instinctively refrains from speaking the words aloud, 'But she was so beautiful, and until I met you I thought that what I felt for her was love.'

'No.' I agree. And let the silence lengthen. The City is always quiet on Saturday nights. A skyline of darkened offices towers above the empty street outside. We sit on, quiet giants, he in his shame, me in my triumph, without talking, as the wind rises and rain begins to patter again on the crooked window panes. How long do we sit? I don't know. A long time.

At first we stare past each other, our thoughts proceeding down rigidly parallel avenues. Then gradually, by infinitesimally small degrees, they converge. Francis mutely accepts his own inconstancy for what it is: mere force of circumstance. I let my preening triumph subside, to focus on the man I have won. Without looking at each other, we each reach out a hand and touch – and it begins.

So, what do you want to know?

How we talked about our childhoods? How we winced at the unhappinesses and laughed at the incongruities of our lives? How we fitted together like an Inca stone puzzle? Is that what you want to know? Oh, but I suppose you mean – since everyone is curious about such interesting things – what did it *feel* like when Francis Hammond and I first came together naked?

Ha! Well, shame on you for such a short memory: we'd already been naked together, remember? In Peloros, in the green innocence of pre-apple Eden.

No, you say, that's not the same.

Oh, come, I reply archly. Clarify. Sharpen. Explain. What *do* you mean?

Do you mean, what was it like in the early hours of a November Sunday morning when Francis and I, our two bodies entwined like giant creepers, fell across the iron bed frame and ripped the sheets from top to bottom in our frantic haste to couple? When hands and lips and breasts and tongues and arms and legs and penis and cunt did everything they are capable of when driven by love and passion and jolting ecstasy?

Well then, imagine away.

No, please. Feel free. Compare, contrast, because if the gods have been good everyone has at least one such memory to draw on in their old age.

Ah?

Ah.

Yes.

So. Perhaps I should ask you, my reader, How was it for you?

No, Cassandra, you say politely. How was it for you?

Fucking perfect.

7 November 1999, 7.00 a.m.

Nothing yesterday.

It was a nightmare day that began with unspeakable pain. At some point in the morning Dr Mike must have authorized a higher dosage, because when I woke the room was full of trees, their trunks so impossibly close-packed that even a child would have found it difficult to squeeze between them. And I was not a child. I was myself, Cassandra, but more so, vast as a Jack-and-the-Beanstalk giant. I struggled on through the forest, grazing my swollen belly against ridged bulwarks of bark, until I was jammed fast in a thicket of timber. I couldn't breathe. Imploringly I stretched my hands through the gaps, begging for help from the darkness beyond.

When I woke, later, the trees had moved back, and their branches were curling down gently towards me, offering a cup of tea. I smelled the familiar bergamot and went to sip, but then I saw the bottom of the cup was thick with mice and recoiled. Later I woke to find my hand and forearm bandaged and throbbing with scald. Hallucinatory hours followed, while the mice gnawed my wrist and the cold tree trunks rubbed themselves lasciviously against my loins.

In other words, it was a bad day. A *memento mori*.

Soon, while I can, I must write to Marco and send him the disk.

What will he do with it I wonder?

(I need hardly ask. My sweet, sleek, canny Marco – what else would he do?)

Now, as the morning comes grey at the window, I slip my arm from the sling and type as fast as I can.

*

238

We spent a week in Cage Street, coming out only in daylight hours to scavenge for food in the City sandwich bars. We sat facing each other under neon lights, our elbows propped on sticky Formica tables. We tore bites out of thick sandwiches of beef and ham and cheese and swilled down cup after cup of hot strong coffee, while our eyes devoured each other. Then, warmed and re-energized, our senses heightened by caffeine, we ran back through the cold streets until we were safe inside again. Behind the Cage Street door we stripped off our clothes and dropped them on the floor, then scampered huge and naked up the stairs.

In bed we drank sweet wines all afternoon – Sauternes, Baume de Venise, Muscat – kissing all the time, until our mouths glistened with grape juice.

At night (or it may still have been day, it was difficult to tell behind the heavy velvet curtains) we lit a fire and stretched out on the rug in front of it, like two huge lions at rest, stroking each other with soft, sheathed paws, while Francis said extraordinary things to me.

'Beautiful' he called me. And I was.

I woke beside him once and lay propped on my elbow, watching him sleep. My fingertip millimetres above his skin, I traced the crooked profile of his nose, skimming over the stubble around to the curl of his ear with a gentleness I never knew I possessed. Then I leaned closer still, studying the terrain of his face and breathing in the hay-scent of sweat.

When, at last, he opened his eyes and spoke to me, our minds embraced as neatly as our bodies had before.

Marco's advice, when I at last emerged from Cage Street, was, as ever, shrewd.

We met in a café next to his office. He sipped a latte and watched me carefully. I was wearing orange, I remember, orange wool sweater and brown leather trousers and a necklace of egg-sized amber beads around my throat. Beneath the beads my skin glowed as if buffed and polished. Blood sang through every capillary, charging my body with energy. Marco smiled and sighed.

'Every tabloid in town has been hammering at my door for the past three weeks, Cassandra. It's a good thing you have broad shoulders, my darling, because they call you some pretty terrible things.' He undid his fine leather satchel, pulled out a wallet of press clippings. There were more shots of the grieving Helen, more copies of luridly enlarged pictures of *The Byrds* and someone had stolen a blurred shot of Francis and me hand in hand in Clerkenwell, towering over passers-by. Starved of information, the papers had baptized us 'sicko snappers', and to prove their point they featured Francis's brutal shot of a wounded girl on a Sarajevo street and mine of Ellie the tramp, snot-nosed and mad in Lincoln's Inn Fields.

'So we're pariahs. So what?' I said, pushing back the rest of the pictures.

Marco stacked the photographs neatly and slid them back into the wallet. 'Yup. They've gone for the jugular, and Helen's playing it like a dream.'

'So?' I said again.

'So, you and Francis need to do something to tell your side of the story.'

I put down my coffee cup with some force, slopping black-grained espresso across the saucer.

'What do you want us to do, Marco? Invite *Hello!* magazine to take shots of our Cage Street love nest?'

'Yeah, that would do for starters. Would Francis agree, do you think?' His mischievous face grinned appealingly.

'No he bloody well wouldn't. And no one, but no one, is ever going to see inside Cage Street. Is that clear?' My voice boomed, and people turned to stare, and then a whispering began.

'Whoa, Cassie, baby. Whoa. I'm only trying to help.' Marco spread his manicured hands on the marble tabletop. 'Cassandra. I'm happy for you, believe me. But I am also worried, not just for you but for Francis, too. His agent is Meg Bruckmann, and she says . . .'

'How the hell do you know what Francis's agent says?' I yelled, ignoring the heads that turned again and the elbows that now nudged openly around us.

'Because I called her, of course, when the shit began, when the moody snapper decided to disappear, leaving your sister to tell the world what you'd done to her.'

'So what if she did. Who cares?'

Marco sat back, visibly gathering his patience.

'Cassandra, you were a minor celebrity before this, weren't you? Well, the good news is that now you're famous. The bad news is that you're famous for stealing your sister's husband. Nobody blames Francis Hammond. Oh well, a couple of papers have side-swiped him, but they prefer to see him as helpless in your hands. No, the story is the beautiful film star mistreated by her grotesque and scheming twin.'

I reached across the table, took a cigarette from his packet, lit it with his lighter and grinned. 'No, really, Marco, don't pull your punches. Give it to me straight,'

But Marco was shaking his head. 'I'm serious, Cassandra. The situation is slipping away from you, can't you see? And if that doesn't worry you – and, believe me, it should – just think what all this is doing to Francis.'

'Making him the hottest lover in town, I should think, if Meg Bruckmann is doing her job properly.'

'Cassie, Cassie, how can you be so naïve? A month ago he may have been a soulful, courageous news photographer, but now he's "The Love Cheat Who Dumped Helen Byrd".'

I snorted in my best Cassandra style. 'That sort of thing can't just happen overnight, Marco.'

'Wake up, little one,' said Marco, looking worried. 'It just did.'

I don't know what I'd been expecting. Of life after the meeting of bodies, I mean. I suppose I had some vague idea of Francis Hammond and Cassandra Byrd as a latter-day Spencer Tracy and Katharine Hepburn. We would work, together or apart, and afterwards we would come home from wherever in the world we had been to the peace of a lair for two.

I hadn't predicted that we would be social untouchables and outcasts.

But Francis just smiled when I told him about Marco's gloomy predictions. 'Three weeks don't change the world that much, Cassimou,' he said. He had started using Ariadne's diminutive of my name, which I liked very much.

'That's what I told him,' I said, suddenly sure that Marco was right. 'But do me a favour and call Meg Bruckmann anyway, will you?'

He was on the phone for a long time, and when he came back he was clutching a notepad covered in jagged doodles and scrawled schedules. Throwing it on the coffee table he slumped down on the sofa with a sigh.

'What did she say?' I asked.

'She's got a job for me,' he replied. 'I leave for Haiti on Tuesday. Voodoo and politics for *Time*.'

'And that took half an hour?' I asked incredulously.

'After that I fly on to East Timor. Meet James Troughton out there for a reportage piece.'

'And after that?'

'She'll know later next week.'

I frowned. Meg Bruckmann was known to be very proprietorial about her clients. It was my guess that, having seen the wave of bad publicity, she had decided that it was time Francis Hammond left the country or, more properly, distanced himself from the source of all the harmful gossip: me. How dare she? Angrily, I marched about living-room, firing off reasons why he shouldn't go. As I swept past him for the third time he clipped the wings of my velvet jacket and pulled me down on the sofa beside him. Keeping me pinned still, he reached across to the ebony table and picked up a large white envelope.

'These are the pictures I took of you last week. See?'

I slid half a dozen ten-by-eight prints from the envelope and, in the flickering light of candles and flames, saw myself transfigured, a sumptuous and mysterious goddess of plenty, wise and powerful. Such a woman, loved by the man who had envisioned her like this, need not feel petty jealousy and resentment. I felt calm and confidence stream out through my body. What would Katharine Hepburn have said I wondered.

'Not bad, for a newshound,' I said, airily, 'though you'd better sharpen your focus a little before Tuesday.'

Francis growled and toppled me back on to the cushions.

7 November 1999, 4.22 p.m.

The wind is rising outside.

There are creatures scrabbling through the forest beyond the bedside table. The floor is alive with grey scurrying bodies. They're all rushing in one direction, as if drawn by the sound of a flute.

Gtsmvod

*

7 November 1999, 8.09 p.m.

Tired.

Lie still and let the fingers talk.

ARIADNE ASCENDING

The following day Marco himself came to tell me that Ariadne had been rushed into hospital. I left Francis to his pre-departure meeting with Meg Bruckmann and flew to Athens that same afternoon.

During her last days Ariadne moved steadily up through the Athens hospital building, like a Madonna slowly ascending to heaven.

'No surgery, Cassimou,' she said firmly, when she reached the second floor. 'No cutting me open and patching me up for a few months more. I'm happy as I am. Truly. Now is good.'

When the news of her illness leaked out flowers began to arrive, some in big cellophane-covered bouquets, some in little posies of spring blooms. Whenever I went to see her there were visitors with her, a pair of black-dressed widows, a trio of smart-suited elderly male admirers, respectful and awestruck in the presence of a living icon. And often there were old friends, too. One day I photographed her playing backgammon with Federico Casales, her ringed fingers jabbing at the board as furiously as in the old days.

'They are kind to come.' She laughed, her eyes wincing. 'And they bring me all the gossip.'

'And cigarettes?' I said, noticing the scent of smoke around her bed. Ari shrugged.

'What does it matter now?'

In late January I had to time my visits carefully to avoid meeting Helen, who had returned from holiday but took time between location filming to visit Ariadne. I don't know how often they met or what they talked about.

I had never discussed Helen with Ari. What good would it have done? It would have solved nothing. One February afternoon I sat by her bed as she slept, watching her brown eyelids flutter and her beaked nose cut through some sedated dream. Suddenly she woke and seized my hand. 'Ah, Cassandra. Good. Promise me. Swear you won't.'

'Won't what, Ari?' I asked, hoping that her memory would fail her again, as it often did by then.

'You know.' Her grip on my hand was terrible, like someone biting on wood.

'Ari. It's too late,' I told her. 'Don't you remember?'

Her dazed brown eyes looked up at me, filled with tears.

'Oh, my poor girls. Poor Sirens,' she said, and there was an old incongruous Ulster note in her voice. Since there was nobody to see us I stroked her dry forehead and permitted myself the rarity of tears.

She reached the top floor in April, a week before her heart finally gave out. Up among the rooftops there was birdsong and the purring of cats, for people were allowed to keep the things they loved by them night and day under a regime relaxed to the point of invisibility.

I stayed nearby then and so was at her bedside, watching and waiting with her, when her heart faltered.

And stopped.

Epitaph.

Ari gave off warmth like a fire, unconditionally. She also had the two immeasurable human gifts: a capacity for love and an ability to be loved – she used both with immense and generous profligacy throughout her life. With Ari I was never conscious of size or oddness and, though I often shocked her, she never lost her faith in me.

Given what we both knew by then, it was more tolerance than I could have expected from any other human being and typical of the woman my father loved.

Ariadne.

They gave Ariadne Vassos a state funeral. I think she would have enjoyed the drama of the slow-pacing military band, the guards in their foustanellas, the speeches, the warmth and emotional out-pouring from the people who lined the route to Piraeus in the spring sunshine. Afterwards they brought her body back by sea to Ithaca and buried it in a suitably impressive marble sepulchre in the white cemetery at Vathi.

'You'll see, Cassimou, the people of Ithaca will make good money from sentimental tourists when I am gone,' she had chuckled to me, clutching my hand in her manicured, bird-like claw.

Ariadne had left Peloros to me. Her lifelong friend Demetrios Gregoriou gave me the news as we sat in his leathery office high above the noisy Athens traffic. Transferring the title would take time, he said, raising his palms helplessly to the shelves of law books, but, yes, eventually I would be the proprietor, the owner of the house and land that had once been home to the Sirens. I was touched. And curious. So I took him out to lunch in Bajazzo, and over tender lamb, honey pastries and strong red wine he let slip that Helen was to have the house in Notting Hill and Susie Musselbergh was to receive £250,000 and an option of permanent residence in Peloros, should she wish to take it.

Now I knew why Susie had already left Ithaca. Once she had found out who the new chatelaine was to be, she couldn't stay. (In fact, for a time, Susie went on to become Helen's full-time assistant and housekeeper in London – though seeing her beloved with a series of handsome actors couldn't have done much for her fragile self-esteem.) I wouldn't miss her chafing, irritable presence at Peloros, that was for sure.

But even as Demetrios sat back in his chair, shaking his head over the generosity of Ari's bequests, my mind was already turning away from legal matters, from Peloros and even from Ariadne herself. What now preoccupied me was that my long, unplanned stay in Greece was almost over. Within twenty-four hours, experiencing a strange mixture of anticipation and dread, I would be back in London, awaiting Francis's return.

Francis had followed Maggie Bruckmann's advice and taken the Haitian and the Timorese assignments. No one could tell me where he'd gone after that, and Maggie Bruckmann didn't return my calls. I knew that, wherever he was, there weren't going to be any touristy postcards arriving at Cage Street. Then, one morning in the *Guardian*, I saw his by-line on the front page under a picture of Kurdish refugees. Inside the paper there were more photographs, and I pored over them greedily, reading them like runes. They had a troubling poignancy, as if happiness had stripped away his immunity to suffering and left him raw and vulnerable. I stared into them and suddenly knew that these pictures had developed on his skin, etching their images into his flesh like tender tattooing ink.

I recognized them, because recently, for the first time, I, too, had felt guilty taking pictures of unhappiness.

The idea of 'Bereft' had come to me on the plane as I flew home from Ariadne's funeral, finally and definitively parentless. And while Francis had been travelling between war zones I'd been photographing orphans. Marco was pleased with the results. He especially liked the shot of a middle-aged man standing bewildered beside his parents' derelict Morris, plainly wondering when they would be returning from their long stay in the cemetery to make his tea. Predictably, I liked the spotty, pierced face of an adolescent girl who glared out of the window of a Place of Safety every bit as soulless as the one Helen and I had stayed in twenty years before. The only picture I wasn't sure of was one I'd taken at Battersea Dogs' Home: a huge Irish wolfhound, coiled in stupefied unhappiness in a corner of the kennel, having been found wandering on the hard shoulder of the M4. Suddenly incapable of deciding whether the shot was sentimental or not I'd closed my ears to its soft whining and got on with taking the picture.

I visited bereaved places, too. One rainy morning I stood outside the tiny house in Kilburn, then walked to the playground with its miniature swings and slide. Even when the sun came out and people arrived, mothers and fathers pushing buggies, old men sitting reading newspapers, there was a temporary quality to their presence. Soon they'd be gone and so would those who followed them. When Francis still didn't return I slipped back to Peloros for two days and took pictures of the empty terrace, the shuttered courtyard and its trees. I photographed the new white marble monstrosity in Vathi cemetery. Then I flew back to Cage Street and stood for hours watching the crowds flowing up and down the streets like rubbish floating helpless on the tide.

I'd been in London for six weeks when Francis finally came back. I was shocked at how haggard and withdrawn he looked. He stayed in Camden the first night, then, almost reluctantly, set up a camp bed in the attic at Cage Street. I thought I understood why and moved around him as considerately as I could, waiting.

Three days passed before I felt a light touch on my shoulder. 'I'm sorry,' he said. His eyes were still vague, his skin still dry and taut over his big crooked nose. 'Sometimes this comes back on the plane with me. Unwanted baggage.' He sat down beside me on the sofa and turned around slightly to look at the window. 'It's been bad before, but I've always seen it as part of the job, like jet lag. It's worse this time, that's all.'

He rubbed his eyes, his face, his neck. 'It's not hard to figure. I drop into some godforsaken country for a few days. I live alongside people, watch them fighting to survive. They ask me for bread and I give them chocolate. I watch some of them die. Sometimes my photographs of victims are on the front pages in London before the relatives even know they're dead. Then I'm there again taking pictures as they identify their children's bodies. And then, when the assignment's over, I drive to an airport lounge. Three, four, ten hours later I'm here with a pocketful of little black film cans, reading my junk mail and listening to the answerphone.'

'If it bothers you, why don't you stay on?'

I'd meant it to be generous, but the minute I'd said it I knew that he hadn't told me the whole truth. His work was troubling him, sure, but that wasn't what was making him suffer. No, what had defeated him was the fact that he'd abandoned Helen.

I kept my face immobile, and Francis looked sadly at me.

'Why don't I? Because I'm not a doctor or an engineer. I wouldn't even make a good a truck driver. No, logic tells you the best thing you can do is stay behind the camera and take the pictures. But, Jesus, there's just so much misery you can watch, you know?' He ran his hands back through his tangled hair. 'Just once, I'd like to feel I'd done something real, something honourable. Just once.'

I pointed to the pile of newspapers on the floor. 'You do. You produced that. Look.'

He kicked the papers listlessly, spreading the pages. 'Yesterday's news. The government'll send a couple of million and we'll all feel virtuous for a few minutes. We're overloaded with other people's suffering in the West. Nowadays we dip our fingers in it, cross ourselves and move on.'

'What did you do before when you felt like this?' I asked.

He smiled faintly. 'I hid in Ashmore.'

I looked enquiringly.

'In Dorset. A cottage so bloody isolated you have to climb three stiles to reach it. I stayed there till I was ready to go again.'

A lair for licking wounds. I understood that right enough.

'Perhaps you should go there now,' I said, feeling proud of my strength. *Helen* would never have been able to say that to him. *Helen* would have had him at her side at the film première this evening in Leicester Square, his big tuxedoed form shambling along between red silk ropes and competing flashlights like a dancing bear, while the photographers yelled at them to smile.

But I, the Big Bad Baby, the Beast, the ugly observer, made no such selfish demands on him. *I* understood. And I would keep him, even if it meant giving him more freedom than I had myself.

'Go on,' I said, 'it's allowed.'

Francis smiled gratefully. Then, after a short silence, he suddenly said, 'No', and took me firmly by the shoulders. I leant my forehead against his, feeling his breath on my cheek, the beat of his heart through his sweater, the warmth of his groin against my belly. This is tenderness, I thought, wondering what the Big Bad Baby would make of it. All of a sudden she seemed to have vanished.

I should have known she hadn't gone far.

9 November 1999, 10.37 a.m.

Though it doesn't tick or tock, the computer tells the time, and so that's the time it is, I guess. My watch is in the suitcase with my clothes. It kept slipping off over my wristbones, and so I rely on the laptop now. Without it I wouldn't know the hour, the day or even the year. Hickory dickory dock, no mice and now no clock.

Whooooa.

I lie here gathering my flickering strength into a single, hardened ball, so I can tell the end. (Even though it isn't quite over yet. After all, I am still here in the white room, pretending to drink tea, pretending I can see the sky, hear the bells: a living postscript to my own life.)

Perhaps the Fates have forgotten me. Perhaps I've been overlooked.

But no, they'll come. Soon. My body's already closing down. My hair is coming out in wiry grey-black tufts, my nails are dry and split, my legs are scaly yellow. With my knuckles I explore the dark, concave pits beneath each cheekbone and slide a fingertip into the puckered scar on my arm, where the bullet hole is stretched tight against the bone. Now when I try to remember the past the lens is stiff to turn and things swim blurrily in and out of vision, like the damaged memory of an accident.

In preparation, I have spoken to Dr Mike, who has promised to send news to Marco when the time comes. Apparently he is no stranger to e-mail and has been playing virtual chess with a Japanese gynaecologist in Osaka for a year now. Anyway, he will do it, so I can rest easy – no need for baggage now. I go on from here on foot.

So.

There are only two more things to tell: the Conclusion and the End of the Story.

Because it's more important, perhaps I should begin with the Conclusion.

Ahem. Quiet, please.

The Conclusion. I thank you.

Why didn't our lives go on, as so many others do, happily? Why weren't there thousands of long, pleasant days ahead, days full of everyday detail and closeness, which would carry us on their shoulders into shared and delightful old age? Was it too much to ask? Yes. Apparently.

After all, there is no one who (or Who) decides such things. There is no divine weighing out of joy, no rainbow's end in whose

Glockamorra glow we all bask for ever more. And even if there were, most of us know that our own natures wouldn't let us lie in eternal content: we secretly fear the atrophy of happiness. Even in the instant we are marvelling at the view from a high place or the sweep of a musical phrase or the amazement of love, our minds and bodies are already counting down to the moment when they can intervene and remind us how hungry, irritated, restless or jealous we are.

But that doesn't matter.

It's only human.

Francis and I experienced a few moments of flawless joy, of essential truth. There have been a handful of other such moments, good and bad. I can recall them still. They light what's left of my life. But I'm no Proust or Vermeer. I know I can't make you live them, too. At best, perhaps you'll compare my moments to your own, so that for a brief, brimming second of human understanding we two connect.

Which is all one can hope for, I believe.

And, surprisingly, almost enough.

So that's the Conclusion, you say. Now, tell us The End. How did it go for them? For that Francis and that Cassandra?

Oh, that's hard to say.

Come on, baby. You can do it. Become an extension of the machine.

Ha! Yes! Good idea.

Click on Search.

Subject?

Francis + Cassandra.

Aaah. There they are again. Enjoying their brief passage of sunshine.

Quickly now.

Francis and Cassandra travelled together for six months, as if knowing that their time together was too short for distance to intervene.

Then Francis died.

Too short. Unsatisfactory. Did she kill him? Or, rather, was she responsible for his death?

When I began the story I thought she had.

I thought I was.

And now?

No.

10 November 1999, 3.00 a.m.

Still here?

Still here. To tell the end.

I remember

We were in a village in Kosovo that summer. My idea to work together: Byrd's- and Hammond's-eye view. Make us a couple he could be proud of, happy with. And we were at first. We slept under canvas within the UN quarters or sometimes in the fields in more remote areas. For all his angst about his job Francis appeared at ease here, understanding the arcane language of military briefings, travelling fast over the disastrous roads to the latest scenes of carnage, methodically wiring his pictures home to meet the paper's deadlines, day after day after day.

It was only when he was alone with me that he became morose and silent again as he had been in London in the latter days. Things will be better when we're home, I thought, forgetting that I had thought they would be better here.

And then, one morning, we drove into that terrible village, what was its name? What *was* its name? Odd, I thought I would never forget it. Anyway, it was late summer, and the flames of the burning houses were pale in the sunshine, and the smoke was thin in the bright light. When the army told us that it was safe, we climbed down from the jeep and began to explore. I picked my way over piles of rubble and looked into the empty houses, the ruined rooms.

It must have been a quarter of an hour later that I saw Francis. He was standing looking at a woman who was kneeling by the roadside, hunched over what looked like a bundle of clothes. As I watched he spoke to the interpreter at his side, and the woman looked up at him. He spoke again and the woman shook her head. Unthinking, I lifted my camera and zoomed in on the scene, took a picture.

Francis was tugging at the bundle on the ground and speaking curtly to the interpreter, who seemed to hesitate before relaying whatever he had said to the weeping woman. Then, I saw Francis take something from his pocket and press it into the woman's hand. I took another photo. The woman stared down, then as if in a dream, folded her fingers over the thing he had given her. She began to pull at the heap of clothing, and I saw that it was the body of a young man. Francis and the interpreter helped her raise the body until it was draped across her knees. I took another picture. Then Francis raised his camera and something in the pose struck me: the angle of the woman's head, her headscarf, the sprawled body over her knees. Suddenly I saw and understood the image Francis was re-creating: the Pietà from Peloros. As he stared through the viewfinder the woman looked up at him, her son in her arms, and screamed. And Francis took the picture.

Mother Courage was the caption on the photograph that appeared across the world's media that night. *Mother Courage*.

I said nothing that afternoon when he wired the pictures home. I said nothing for days.

We were making our way back to the border and had arranged to spend our last night in the company of the UN peacekeepers. They treated us to drinks in their bar and promised to take us on a last sortie the following morning. We were relaxed now that the trip was nearly over. Even Francis appeared more cheerful – news had filtered back to him about the ecstatic reaction to his photograph.

'They're talking about a Pulitzer nomination,' said Gregor, his assistant, slapping him on the back. Francis blushed and smiled and downed his drink as the soldiers crowded around to congratulate him.

But by the time we went to bed his good humour had evaporated. He staggered against me as we went upstairs, and inside the room he sat down heavily on the bed, his head bent down over his chest.

'Cassandra,' he said, and I waited for the bad thing he was going to say.

'I can't go on like this.'

I didn't say a word.

'And *we* can't go on like this.'

I'd sidestepped this conversation so many times in the last six months and now it was here. Christ. He didn't even have to tell me. He was going back to her.

I let him struggle to find the words. I didn't help him at all. And when he'd said everything and asked me to forgive him, I even said I would. But in the morning I wired my pictures to Marco and told him what to do with them. Francis would be devastated, I knew, but then he should have known better.

Ah. Now, this is not just pain. This is

Oh, dear

Oh god oh god oh god odh goh oh o o

We left atttttt tenn. At midddddday on theroad we found a father and his young daughter nd they were scared and the father kept ppppointing to the woods and gregorsaid we must go and ffrancis said what is he saying and gregor said they will comeback when we leave and they will rape his daughter and kill him.

And I looked at the thin dark man and his daughter was plain and unlovely and clinging to her dadda's leather jacket and I said d 'Francis, we must take them with us'''' and he was still photographin them and didn't say anything. And the driver was revving the engine and Gregor was in the car and was holding the door open for us and shouting at us to getin and there were men coming out of the wood.

And the man screamed and pushed his daughter towards us and I pushed pas Francs andpicked her u p in my arms and she was heavy. And Francisssaid no nono Cass but I wouldn't stop and then F was there and lifting her from me saying here give her to me and he pushed me behind the door of the car and then he turned to the father and rose in the air with the girl in his arms like a bear. TTT-Then there was a bang and another and then he twisted like a dancerand fell on the road and then there were more bangs and the father was lying nearby with blackred on his face and francissss coat was full of blloodd and tears and I went to him crawling under the car door and there was dust on his face and red everrrwehe and the girl was painted red with it and her head was gone at the back and I saw grey grey wet and felt my arm kick in the air as I touched his cheek ;

His eyes were shut becas off mee Id kelled him my
gtsmvod
it was dark
sdark
now
aaaaaaaaaaaaaahhhhhhhhhhhhhhhhhhhhhhhhhhhhhhhhhhhhhh

ytidy ,r *
vsdddddsmft †

---

* Transcribed one space to the left on a computer keyboard, these two words read: 'trust me'. They are followed by a blank page.

† This is apparently the author's attempt to sign her work. Transcribed, it reads: 'cassssandr'.

AT THE REQUEST OF THE LATE AUTHOR'S SISTER, HELEN BYRD HAMMOND, A LETTER

My name is Helen Byrd Hammond.

Yesterday I buried my twin sister Cassandra in the place she had instructed, on a hillside in Ithaca. My sister had apparently requested a private ceremony, and I respected her wishes. There were only four of us at the graveside: my friend Susie Musselbergh, an American called Marco Bertone, a Greek lawyer Demetrios Gregoriou and myself. It was bitterly cold on the mountainside; below, the sea was iron grey, whipped to a froth of white horses, and the wind from the east sliced through our thick greatcoats and made my eyes water.

My husband, the photographer Francis Hammond, who was badly injured by sniper fire in Bosnia three years ago and subsequently suffered a complete breakdown, was unable to make the climb and waited for us in the car at the foot of the hill.

It was dark when we got back to Peloros, the house that once belonged to our family friend, the film star Ariadne Vassos. There we drank coffee and sipped brandy, sitting around a wood fire. After a while, Susie stood and walked over to what had been Ariadne's desk. She opened a small drawer and took out a slim white envelope and handed it to me. 'Cassandra's disk,' she said simply, 'When you have read it, you are to give it to Marco, the man you met this afternoon. He's expecting it.'

After dinner I came up to Cassandra's room, where Susie had placed the battered laptop my sister took everywhere with her. I inserted the disk and began to read. Francis knocked softly at the door some time after midnight to tell me he was going to bed. I kissed him, reassured him that I was comfortable and told him that I intended to read Cassandra's journal through the night. Which I have done. The light outside is pale grey now. In a moment I shall go next door and sleep.

Cassandra was right: there was a time when I found other people quite unreal, the idea of their having inner lives unconvincing. A surprising confession for an actress, you might say, but then the profound truths of human behaviour are often best simulated by the shallowest personalities, wouldn't you agree? I am one such myself, absolutely; I admit it: a personality with no draught or dagger-board. I flow into whatever shape I am obliged to adopt, metamorphosing cleverly and without undue angst.

Yet, oddly, my sister Cassandra wallowed in what she saw as the depths of her own character. As if she believed she had 'depth' enough for both of us – a double share, like mine of our joint store of calcium. And, for all her story's flaws, I acknowledge there is a certain profundity to her account, though very little accuracy. But then my sister always skipped like a stone across reality: one can only ever expect occasional, accidental touches of truth from her.

So why did she write it?

I think when she began she simply wanted revenge on certain people she believed had wronged her, doubtless including me on that list. Yet towards the end of the disk one detects a change of view, the softening of a character so extreme that at times it made normal social contact impossible and led her to do irreparable harm to others. Her Conclusion, if one can call it that, has a mellowness she never displayed in life.

But who can say what was really in her mind? And who, now, can ever know? No one.

Whatever her motives may have been, it falls to me, as she surely knew it would, to decide the fate of her disk. Of course I could simply destroy it. And often, as I read her words last night, I itched to do just that. Yet something tells me it is wiser to let her have her say. So, yes, I shall give my sister's disk to Mr Bertone as she asked, and as far as I am concerned he may publish its contents, subject only to two conditions, which I shall attach to these notes.

But before I finish may I pass on a piece of advice to its future readers? I think I am entitled to do that, don't you?

So, remember that, just as she warned you at the start of her account, there are many lies on Cassandra's disk. And not just those she owned up to, either. Many, many lies. It's fair to say that all through her life my sister distorted reality to justify her own conduct and present it in a better light. Occasionally she went to grotesque lengths to achieve her aims, deliberately coarsening her looks and her manners until she personified her *alter ego*, this infamous Big Bad Baby.

Of course, even knowing that, you may still prefer to believe her rather than me, since when this account is published it is her voice you will have listened to so far rather than mine. Perhaps even now, as you read this, you are thinking how right Cassandra was to dislike me. And, even if your view of me is scrupulously neutral, you may decide that my version of our past is just as partisan and unreliable as hers. But, though I am an actor, I am not a liar. I could tell you truths that would shock you, that would prove how you've been cheated and betrayed by the writer whose words you've just read. Yet if I did that, if I listed every lie of hers, small and large, there's a chance it might actually prejudice you against me even more.

And my husband and I know all too well how vindictive public opinion can be. So, instead, I shall simply lay a fact and a photograph in front of you. Make of the fact what you will, but photographs do not lie.

> I hereby consent to the publication of my sister's memoirs on sole condition that the notes below and the enclosed portrait are appended as postscripts.

Helen Byrd Hammond
Ithaca, 18 November 1999

Note 1

My sister Cassandra Byrd died of cancer on 13 November 1999 in a private room in the Aghios Georghios mental asylum in Vathi, on the Ionian island of Ithaca, where she had been a patient for the past three years. She was thirty-nine years old, childless and had never married.

Note 2

This previously unpublished photograph, *Twins*, was taken by Tom Pfeiffer in 1983. You will observe from the photograph that Cassandra and I were virtually identical.

CASSANDRA BYRD'S
LAST E-MAILS

Here are the texts of two e-mails with their attachments supplied to the publisher by Mr Marco Bertone

From: michaelides@infotron
To: marcobertone@nyphoto.com
Dated: 10.16 a.m. 11.11.99
Sent/Received 13.11.99

Marco, please do as we have agreed with this.
Love.
C.

Attachment: Cassandra's Disk. doc

From: michaelides@infotron
To: marcobertone@nyphoto.com
Dated: 11.00 a.m. 11.11.99
Sent/Received 13.11.99

Hey, Marco
Put this at my feet, yes?

Attachment: Ithaka.doc

ITHAKA

When you start your journey to Ithaka
make sure it's a long road, full of adventures, new
experiences. Make it your own
curiosity-collection of gathered knowledge, knowhow.
. . .
Keep Ithaka marked on your mind's map,
always. Arrival there is your final goal.
Don't hurry your journey in any way. Better
to last it for decades. As you age, anchor
at small islands with the wealth you've acquired
voyaging. Never expect Ithaka to give you anything.
Ithaka gave you the journey. Without her
you'd never have begun in the first place.
She has nothing else to give you.

If you find her wanting, Ithaka
has not cheated you. From the wisdom
you've gained, the knowledge you've absorbed,
the experience you've embodied
you'll understand by then
what these Ithakas mean.

C.P. Cavafy

Attachment: Lastword.doc
Ha!